I0679180

RICHARD O. SNELSON

Scrimshaw Foxes

A SARA RANDOLPH NOVEL #2

Scrimshaw Foxes, A Sara Randolph Novel #2
Copyright © 2023 Richard O. Snelson
All cover art copyright © 2023 Richard O. Snelson
All Rights Reserved

This is a work of fiction. Names, places, characters and incidents are either the product of the author's imagination or are used fictitiously, and any resemblance to any actual persons, living or dead, businesses, organizations, events or locales is entirely coincidental.

No part of this book may be reproduced or transmitted in any form or by any means, electronic or mechanical, including photocopying, recording, or by any information storage and retrieval system, without permission in writing from the author.

Edited by – Chelsea Cambeis
Proofread by – Leal Kennedy
Publishing Coordinator – Sharon Kizziah-Holmes

Rogers, Arkansas

ISBN -13: 978-1-959548-20-1

DEDICATION

Dedication: To the Wildlife Training Officers of The Arkansas Game and Fish Commission for their assistance and insights from my visits to the R.C. 'Red Morris' Training Center in Mayflower, Arkansas.

ACKNOWLEDGMENTS

Scrimshaw artist Bob Hergert
Story Editing by Chelsea Cambeis
Text Editing by L. Kennedy
Dr. Ekkehard Othmer MD, PhD. For his help in supplying background studies on the treatments for PTSD.
For her help and support on this series of novels,
Sharon Kizziah-Holmes,
Publishing Coordinator for Paperback Press.

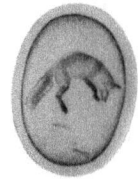

ONE

THE BIRD'S SONG RANG OUT again, a lonesome sound of calling for a mate or friend. Sara Randolph knew right where it sat at this moment. This wasn't the first night she had stood outside her dorm room and echoed the whip-poor-will's call. She knew this bird's voice and felt it knew hers. Its long voicing always quivered near the end, unlike any other she had heard before. She whistled her whip-poor-will call in answer. The bird, sitting just a short way up the road, replied with its song.

This bird, like so many other animals of Arkansas, held special places in her heart. Protecting them had become her dream job. The trees along the road in front of her formed an archway over the street into the R.C. 'Red' Morris Training center. A place where only a few of the best were selected to study and strive to become Arkansas Wildlife Officers.

It was late, so Sara echoed the bird's call only once tonight. She went back into the dorm before checking her cellphone. The time blinked and two o'clock in the morning lit the screen. Wanting badly to hear Luke's reassuring voice tonight, she almost called him. Instead, she clicked the email program on her laptop and then his address. She began to write.

Sweetheart! Let me see if I remember you. You're the guy that asked me to marry him, right? It's been so long I've got to be sure. Please take me away from here for a weekend soon.

She paused her typing. Her night had been filled with study

time and finding answers to questions she needed to know before tomorrow's exam on criminal law. Luke had been through these same classes. She needed his help. The thought only lasted seconds. Luke's place in her life during her seventeen weeks studying to be an Arkansas wildlife agent needed to be as her fiancé, not as an easy way through the testing she had to pass. Her study time would have to do. She finished the message.

I love you so very much.

She hit send and the screen cleared. It took her only a couple minutes to fold her study outline and file it with the criminal law materials. The laptop clicked with an inbound message.

Hello, I've found you. I thought you had fallen in the lake there at the training center. It's a deal on the weekend. I'll check with the commission tomorrow for my upcoming days off. I'm thinking it will not be this weekend but the next. Planning on taking you to a castle in the clouds. Love, Luke.

She wanted badly to take the phone outside and talk to her lover. Instead, a quick note.

I'll hold you to that promise. My eyes are so heavy I can barely see the screen. I'll call you tomorrow after class. Love you.

There were so many things she wanted to tell him about her day, about the ache and empty feelings that not having him close brought her. She traded her thoughts of talking to him for those of what the morning and scheduled testing would bring for her. Only two weeks remained until she would complete the training to earn the position of an Arkansas wildlife agent. She realized it would be a lifetime achievement when the commission pinned the gold badge on her chest.

The day after graduation, she would put on the badge and strap a holster with a Glock 9mm pistol to her side and join the dozens of other Arkansas wildlife agents protecting the animals and hunters of their state. The test in the morning would be a big tell on her making the grade. She had to sleep now. Turning off the computer and desk lamp, she dropped on the bed, hoping her roommate would shake her awake at reveille. She would find the morning, somehow, between the moments of deep sleep and those of panic and waking, to realize her Humvee crew had been blown apart once again in her nightmares. Months ago, she had stopped taking the drug the VA had prescribed to avoid nightmares. The drug dulled her edge in the daytime, and no way would she live in a cocoon of stupor. Instead, when the terror of war overcame her, for even an instant, the techniques other doctors had suggested were to press her thoughts of fishing the White River forward in her thinking. Touching the tattoo of a little minnow on her wrist would remind her of their cabin on the river. It seemed to help her more. A night's sleep would rarely come without having to use this technique.

***

The folded test booklet sat on Sara's classroom chair, waiting for the testing to start. She finished her second cup of coffee and placed her cup into her backpack under the chair. She needed the coffee. Not getting enough sleep had become routine, but she was still damn ready for this test.

When the signal to start came, she opened the test and skimmed the first question, getting a feel for what would always be a tough one. Earlier, at Morris, she had learned candidates would stall at the first question and then not have enough time to finish the test. She read it and then skipped ahead. Digging deeply into her study time from the night before, she finished the rest of the pages of questions. Now equipped with knowledge of the heart of the criminal law test, she went back and read the first question again. Her answer fell out onto the page. She knew the material cold. She wrote the answer and then shut the test book, finished and satisfied she had aced it.

Sara sat, waiting. Training protocol required the class to remain in place until the scheduled time for the test expired. It would be all right. She ran the rest of the training week through her mind. Working with the camp's Labradors this afternoon would make her miss Tank, her German shepherd. Tank would be having a lazy afternoon on the porch of her dad's cabin, or maybe riding in the bow of his jon boat while he fished on the White River. Thinking about it all made her homesick.

This same dog had been riding in the back of her Humvee in Iraq when the incoming fire came. She had realized that in an instant they were all going to die. Her driver and both men on the machine gun were shredded by the missiles and machine gun fire. She was hit and barely alert when her first sergeant dragged her out of the passenger seat of the burning vehicle. He later told her the wounded German shepherd struggled and followed her into the ambulance she had been placed in. Only the determination of her commander and first sergeant got the dog out of Iraq and smuggled into the U.S. on a military flight. Later her commander arranged for her dog to be brought home to her in Arkansas.

Her thoughts were wrapped around the commander, Captain Bartlett. Maybe sending the dog to her in Arkansas had been his way of saying he was sorry for the times he had abused her in Iraq. He had advanced her rank too quickly in those war-torn days. Only later did she realize it had been a reward to keep her quiet about his sexual abuse as her commander. It would be a lot better for the captain if she never saw him again. There were still cuss words she had stored away to use if they ever met again.

The test period ended. Relieved, she stood and stretched the war wound scar in her side. Bartlett and the things he did to make her hate him would be there in her mind on another day. Bringing Tank to her in Arkansas never overshadowed his past actions. Not today, or tomorrow. She dropped her test booklet on the class officer's desk and gave him a little wave that meant, *it went well.* He would know soon enough. Fellow class member Patrick Reid joined her as she left the classroom. He was shaking his head.

"Oh boy. I don't know about that test," he said.

She and Reid were the only two candidates in the training class without college educations. He came to Morris from law enforcement and had been friends with Luke Matthews for a few years. Reid's shaved head, tan look, and muscular physique hinted at his past life of being outdoors.

"It's a good thing we get graded on our abilities in the field as well as the tough college-level classes like this one," she said.

"Luke had told me when I applied to the academy to prepare for a lot of hard work to get through the class," Reid replied.

"He told us both."

"I've got water rescue training this afternoon. You?" Reid asked.

"I'm going to be following one of the Labradors on a tracking mission. Suits me fine. I miss my dog," she said. "And my man."

"Tell Luke hi for me when you get a chance."

"I will. Want to join me for lunch?"

"You noticed I was starting to walk a little faster?"

"See if you can catch me," she sprinted ahead toward the dining hall. It caught Reid by surprise, and he fell well behind her. She slowed at the door and turned to wait. The weeks of physical training at Morris had brought her to a new level of physical fitness and endurance.

"After you, old man," she taunted as she opened the door for Reid.

"Show off," he said.

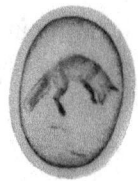

Two

FRIDAY MORNING BEGAN LIKE ALL other weekday mornings at the Morris center. Doors to the dorm hallway would be thrown open and the academy's officers would storm through with loud calls to wake and shake up the cadets. Rarely did the morning start without a call to fall out for early-morning calisthenics and dismounted drill. Finally, with breakfast call over, a few minutes could be stolen from the day.

Reading a morning text from Luke still made her shudder when he hinted at the lovemaking he wanted and planned during his promised get away. His words of their moments together, naked in body and bare emotionally, in each other's arms, struck a deep chord echoing and ringing in her mind and body. She needed to stop reading and go to him now.

Darn, it was still a week or more away. His promise of taking her to a castle on a hilltop for the weekend still remained a mystery. She liked the suspense of not knowing where this could be, but it didn't help her focus on today's weapons training and the final weeks at Morris.

Her two tours of duty at the prison camp in Iraq had conditioned her to always welcome the feel of a Glock pistol strapped to her side. Rarely did it need to be drawn in Iraq. Still, drawing it had saved her twice from being cut or killed by a clever Iraqi prisoner trying to escape. She had held back and hadn't shot either prisoner. Coming close to shooting someone only an arm's length away left an imprint on her. The thought of firing at men trying to kill her on the battlefield didn't bother her. Her AR-15 could get hot as hell firing at men advancing on them. She needed and wanted to see the men trying to kill them fall.

She pushed the memories of Iraq aside and strapped the pistol belt on. With the pistol's magazine empty as hell, it felt strange and lacking to her. Soon, graduation would allow it to be loaded. She rushed out of the barracks just in time to catch the bus heading for the shooting range. She slid into a seat by the window. Another cadet took the seat beside her.

"Good morning, Randolph," he said.

She nodded to at least acknowledge his words. Her run-in with the man had happened weeks ago. She remembered well what it was about. Just because he sat by her was not a reason to speak to him. She wanted to remain quiet for the next ten miles to the pistol range.

"We need to clear up something, don't we?" cadet Edgar asked.

Her head twisted and both eyes trained on him. Putting him on her bucket list to hurt had happened weeks ago. Why the hell did he wait weeks to talk about it now? She had avoided him for the past fifteen.

"You know it was hard for me to live down getting my head pushed into the sand by a woman in Parker's pit," Edgar said very softly.

Oh yes, Parker's pit. The twenty-by-twenty sand pit where doing something off kelter got you sent to do pushups in the foot-deep sand. She had been sent to the pit with this guy on her second morning at Morris. At the time, his under-the-breath chauvinist comment about her female roommate having trouble finishing her series of pushups had gotten her temper up. Her comment back at him got them both sent to the pit for pushups. The pit punishment had ended in a brief fight this man had lost.

"Our weeks of training have taught me both of you ladies have more endurance and perseverance than most of us men do. I'm sorry for what I smarted off with on our second day of training."

"It took you a long time getting around to saying this, didn't it?"

"I was embarrassed. Morris's training has changed me."

Sara eased off on her bucket list item of wanting to push this man's face into the sand a few more times. "You're right about the changes it has made. It has helped me control my snap temper, but I'm still a work in progress."

They both laughed. She offered a handshake and made sure it came across as her firmest ever. The rest of the ride to the pistol range was spent with small talk about the past fifteen weeks of training.

With the bus unloaded at the range, the cadets were issued a pistol magazine loaded with six shots. All the weapons training at Morris had been second nature for Sara. Her background in the military police unit made her welcome the chance to improve her accuracy firing and handling a pistol again. At the weapons officer's command she loaded the magazine and chambered a round.

"Cadets, this will be a rapid-fire exercise. Your target will advance toward you rapidly as you fire. Do your best to group your six shots in the target's center ring. I'll give the ready command for you to fire when the target moves. Take your stance. Ready."

She assumed a side view stance and extended the Glock with both hands. With only an instant for a glance at her little minnow tattoo on her wrist the target came toward her.

Sara's last shot cleared the pistol and the action opened ready for another loading. The targets stopped close by the cadets for them to check firing accuracy.

"No one advance yet. Is your weapon's action open? Is the pistol's chamber empty for each of you?"

One of the cadets stood with his left hand high above his head. His right hand held the pistol pointed at the ground.

"Sorry, sir. I think I have a jammed action," the cadet yelled. He kept his position for the instructor to reach him and take the pistol.

"Give me a minute. I'll clear this weapon," the instructor said. He removed the magazine and opened the pistol's action to clear the chambered cartridge. "Cadets, holster and then check your firing score on the targets."

Sara ran her finger around the six holes in the targets. Two of the holes were out of the center ring by only a fraction of an inch. Her score would be passing but it wouldn't be to her own standards. It had been too long, and she still needed more slow fire practice to get her grip and trigger pull improved.

After four more rounds of full magazine firing the exercise ended. Sara took the last paper target down and folded it to put in her pocket. Her dad and his adopted son, Jimmy, would be proud of her improved range practice. Her old marine father put a lot of stock in what a tight circle of holes in a target meant when his daughter had fired the rounds. At least he always told her it did.

The issued class notes for today included a short, cryptic sentence. 'Rapid reaction to attacks.' It didn't mean a lot until the two instructors walked over to her.

"Randolph, because of your service with the military police, we would like your help with this."

A little bit of not volunteering for anything had stuck with her from the military. However, finding a way out of this exercise didn't seem probable or possible. "How can I help, sirs?"

The men positioned her outside the passenger door of a commission pickup. One of the men stood in front of her. She had lost track of the second officer.

The man in front spoke, "Go ahead. Question me. You found me on the way back to this truck, carrying a rifle, and the head of a poached trophy deer. Start now."

The situation set up for the class surprised her and she knew darn well how things like this could go in the woods. Unholstering her weapon would not be an option. Doing so would only escalate the situation. Having the strap off the pistol's handle would have already happened.

"Put down your rifle and deer kill, sir," she demanded. She stood, facing the man, with her hand draped over her Glock. "Now, sir. Put them down." The man pretended he had dropped the deer head but still held the rifle.

"I ain't done nothing, lady." He lifted the barrel of the rifle slightly as Sara sensed someone behind her. The man grabbed her arm and pistol.

She exploded! The Iraqi prisoner had shoved past her. Her pistol flew out of his hand as she went for him, and she nearly broke the arm of the man holding it. The twist of her body forced the man around in front of her and onto his knees. She pushed his robe aside and seized him around the throat, causing a gurgling sound instead of the Arabic words he tried to get out. Not stopping, she went to the ground with her death grip on the prisoner attacking her.

"Stop, now. Stop—."

The other officer yelled out for the trapped man, "Randolph, let off!" He pulled at her arms, finally breaking her grip on the man's neck. She turned, ready to fight him, and then slumped down on the ground beside the other man.

It took her a moment to come to the reality that the takedown hadn't happened in Iraq. The way she had gone after the agent shocked her. The adrenaline rush could have been enough to push her to kill him. She stood and turned to pick up her Glock from the ground. She needed to learn more control for her lingering PTSD. She heard the muted conservation between the two officers. She heard something like, *whatever we do, never pull this stunt on an ex-military policewoman.* The class stood gathered around them. Several offered a handshake to her; others were still giving a hand over their mouth chuckle to the scene.

"All right, cadets, we'll call it a day now." The officer she had taken to the ground stood, brushing the streaks of dirt from his uniform.

With the bus loaded, a cadet she didn't know well started to sit beside her. He got a polite shove away when Patrick Reid sat down beside her.

"Wow, some takedown. You learned it in Iraq, right?"

"I just don't like someone sneaking up behind me. At all."

"I saw a lot more from your reaction."

"Shut up, Reid. After dinner, let's take a walk down to the lake. We can talk," she said, giving him a light squeeze on his arm. "I'm still breathing hard from him coming up behind me, is all."

***

She shared the dinner table in the training center's dining room with Reid, her roommate, and two other cadets. Being the only two females in this training cycle, Sara and Audrey often spoke up for each other when one of the males pushed their luck teasing either of them. Her talks with Audrey proved to both of them they fit the man's world of being a wildlife agent just fine.

Her companions at the dinner table scarfed the meal of spaghetti and meatballs down quickly. She ate more slowly; certain the others were rushing to finish eating and ask her questions about her explosion in today's training. It surprised her when two of the cadets finished and got up, taking their dishes to the washing tables. Reid looked at her and smiled.

"Why the smile?" she asked after sucking in and swallowing the last bite of the long spaghetti noodle.

"I think both of those boys who left are afraid as hell of you," Reid said, wiping his lips with his paper napkin and putting it down to smile again.

"Am I really so mean?"

Her roommate finished and looked up from her empty plate. "No one thinks you're mean. I think the way you reacted and took down the man just surprised everyone," Audrey said. "They're jealous it wasn't them doing it."

The five-foot-six redhead had just spoken out for her. Sara smiled. She knew Reid had been spending more than a few meals making sure he got to sit at a table with the redheaded soon-to-be wildlife agent.

"I think you're right, Audrey," Reid said.

"I'm going to leave you two to talk. I've still got a dozen pages to study before tomorrow," Audrey said, standing with her tray and walking away.

"She lives by the word 'study'," Sara said, "Did you know her grades are top of our class on book study?"

"I guessed it. Do you two talk a lot at night?" Reid asked.

"We don't. She's either nose down in her books or texting with her friend. It's all right. Gives me more time to talk to Luke and get in some study time afterwards. Is it just the red hair you like?" She had slipped it in at the end of what she had to say.

"Well, now," Reid got out. He decided to change the subject. "Let's go for a walk."

Having Luke's friend Reid around when she had questions about their training helped because of his prior law enforcement experience. She went to him on questions she didn't understand. His background helped with solutions to many of the problems.

"Down by the lake?" Her over-reaction in the training exercise had embarrassed her, and she liked for Reid to be a sounding board for what happened. She walked alongside Luke's friend toward the wooden bench seat set back a dozen feet from the lake's shoreline.

The fellow cadet who had been sitting there passed them.

"Have a beautiful evening guys."

"Thanks," Sara said. She paused, listening to the water's soft whisper as the shallow waves kissed the rocks along the bank. For a moment, it made her long for the river, her dad's 'Little Minnow' jon boat, and her family. Reid took a seat on the bench.

"You still with me, Sara? Come and sit."

Wishing some of her Iraqi prison memories would go away only made them fresher after how she reacted today.

"Reid, I don't want to ruin an evening of study with talk about today." She knelt and slumped down to sit on the ground with her back against the bench.

"Well, don't then." He gently patted her on the shoulder. "You need to relax. You're still wound up tight."

"I know. I just need to talk about why it happened."

"If it's for your own sanity, I'll listen."

"I've never talked about it."

"Iraq?"

"Yes. A prisoner grabbed me from behind with his legs."

"His legs?"

"Hang on, I'll tell you. I expect I deserved his attack. I had been forced by a CIA agent to torture this prisoner. Everything we did to the man was against the rules of war. The fact a woman inflicted the torture only made it worse to him. Aziz, a bombmaker and extremely high-level Iraq prisoner and terrorist, possibly could give us information on the next bomb attack. The CIA wanted the info badly. They used me to try and get it. They pushed me to dress to intimidate the Iraqi. I wore a tight army green t-shirt with nothing under it. I would often be wet with my sweat.

"Aziz would try to turn his head and not look at the heathen in front of him. He wanted me dead. The concrete bunker where he had been held shut out all sounds and air movement. It didn't matter. The man rarely uttered even a whisper, only gurgles of spit from his mouth and nose at the worst of what the CIA did to him with electric shock. I got careless. The man's back was against a fence of iron rods. His hands tied up above his shoulders. The CIA had him there with his feet inches above the floor. Electrodes were tied to each of his hands. He knew what was coming.

"I got too close and dropped something on the floor from my

belt. I turned and before I could bend to reach it. His legs trapped me. Both of them over my shoulders pulling me close, with his feet locked in front around my neck. I screamed. His twist of the legs came and pressure against my neck forced me down on my knees. He never let up. The choke hold he had on me had me close to blacking out. I was certain the camera in the upper corner had been turned off by the CIA when Aziz had been brought in, so no help would be coming. I had no weapon to fight him with. Another dead U.S. soldier on this man's hit list would mean nothing to him. Suddenly Aziz released his grip on me. I dropped to the floor and crawled away out of his reach. Then he spoke to me. Not in Arabic. Fluent English. *'Remember this day when I let you go. I'm saving my torture for you for another day. I will find you someday and tie you to a fence with your breasts bare and your entrails hanging from the cavity of your belly. No one will believe I spoke this to you now, but you will remember.'*

"He never spoke to me again while the CIA tried to break him. The man's arms around my neck today caused it all to come back. Aziz was right. I will always remember."

"My God, Sara. I had no idea. Luke has never said anything about your service in Iraq, except telling me about the attack on your convoy."

"What I did to torture the Iraqi prisoner was a war crime. I'm embarrassed and torn for letting anyone order me to do the things I did to Aziz in the bunker cell. He had good reason to try to kill me. Even hearing his name sends a tight cramp across the back of my neck. I was pushed hard to keep my mouth shut about what went on. Bartlett, my company commander, had groomed me to the point where whatever he wanted, he got. I kept getting unearned promotions for doing their shit. Oh, man. Some hard lessons learned. Right?"

"Does Luke know about what happened to you?"

"No. I'm not sure how he will react to me being a war criminal. I've told him pieces of what happened but laying it all out is just too damn grim for me right now."

"Luke has told me you have PTSD attacks. He didn't go beyond saying anymore."

"He doesn't know about this. I've promised myself not to marry him until he knows it all. This stuff isn't just baggage I'm carrying, it's a horrible past I'm more than ashamed of."

Sara was ready for the conversation to end. She had already told a man she had only known for a few months things her life partner-to-be didn't know. Reid had been there today and saw what happened. He and others hadn't realized it had been a total breakdown in her self-control, a key needed element in being a wildlife agent. Would the effects of her war ever end? She would have to will it to happen.

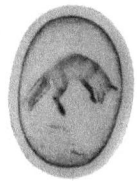

THREE

SARA STARTED PACING THE ROOM an hour before Luke promised he would be there for her. She opened the backpack again and sorted through the clothes she had packed. Three outfits would have to do; it was all she had. Then the thought entered her mind maybe they wouldn't even leave the motel room. Her face warmed as a small flush spread across her cheeks. It had been a while since they had time alone. The one-piece bathing suit she used for swim class was stuffed in the backpack's side pocket. She would do all she could to get him to a shop in Eureka Springs so she could get a raunchy-looking bikini to wear for him. She knew the scar on her side from the surgery to take out the shell fragments would show; at this point she was beyond caring who would see it. She closed the bag. Her roommate had been sitting quietly, paging through a journal of class notes.

"Audrey, maybe you and I can get away soon on a weekend. Too much study makes Audrey a dull gir—."

"No kidding. One of the fellows hinted about a Saturday getaway," she said, "I'm not sure he's going to get up the nerve to ask me. I'm sure ready if he does."

"You just ask him, then," Sara said, carrying her backpack and opening the door. "See you sometime Sunday."

"Yes. I'll be here." Audrey gave a little laugh.

She stopped under the front canopy of the doorway and checked her blue jean outfit. One of the pant legs of her jeans stuck down in the top of the western boots she wore. She reached to pull it out.

"I don't mind if you wear it in the boot." Luke's voice surprised her.

"You're here early?"

"A little," he said, walking to her and hugging her. "I came in a commission's truck. Would it be all right if we take yours?"

"Of course. It might need some gas, but I can handle getting it."

"Nope. This is my date. I'm buying." He let up only a little on the hug.

"Let me go and I'll try to remember where I parked it," she said, tossing her backpack over her shoulder and taking his hand. "Over here I think, by the labs' kennels."

Two of the dogs in the kennel began barking as they approached the parked truck. Luke took her hand and gave her a little tug. "Come over here a minute. You need to meet these fellows."

She didn't say anything until they stood by the kennel fence. "You mean Kylie and Hank? Everybody gets to meet these labs their first week. They're award winners and can be real buddies. I love walking them."

"I got to work some trials with them back a few years ago," he said, holding his hand against the fence so Hank could smell it. "Do you think he remembers me?"

"Who could forget Luke Matthews?" she jabbed. She held her hand against the fence. Both dogs whined to get out of the kennel. "Later. I promise a walk on Monday."

"Ready? Give me the truck keys. We'll stop close and get gas."

The two-hour drive to Eureka Springs went quickly. Both were anxious to get there, and Luke drove fast. She didn't mind at all.

The winding streets of Eureka Springs slowed him way down. Traffic seemed backed up for blocks.

"The town is packed. Do you have reservations, sir?" she asked. Watching the dozens of motels pass by all with their 'no vacancy' signs on, Luke kept driving up the ever-climbing streets.

"Not to worry. I think you'll like this place. It's a little old, however."

"How old, mister?" she asked, pinching his arm.

"How about 1886?"

"Do they have straw beds and the like?"

"Aye, madam, and a rack for those misbehavin' while there."

"Planning on the rack, then. My back needs a good stretching."

Luke turned off the mountain road and into the drive leading to what she thought had to be a castle. "It's beautiful. This is our hotel?"

"The Crescent," he said, pulling up to the huge wooden door entrance. "Built in the eighteen hundreds, as I said."

An older man wearing a smartly fitted bellman's suit stepped up and opened the door for Sara.

"Welcome to the Crescent Hotel and Spa."

"Thank you, sir," she said, getting out of the truck and reaching to grab her backpack from behind the seat. Luke joined her, carrying his. Sara leaned back, looking up at the five stories of ancient rock building in front of them.

"You weren't kidding about 1886, were you, Mr. Matthews?"

Luke smiled and shook his head no.

"Could I carry those for you?" the bellman asked. "The valet will park your vehicle."

"We're fine. Thanks anyway," Luke said, heading for the check-in desk. She followed and stood at his side in front of the desk.

"Welcome to Eureka Springs and the Crescent Hotel," the woman said with a far Eastern accent Sara recognized.

"May I have your names, please?" the woman asked.

"Mr. and Mrs. Luke Matthews," Luke said, taking out a pen to sign the check-in form. Sara smiled at what he had said and squeezed his arm.

It took the woman a few moments to sort through a dozen or more three by five cards. Then, "Mr. Matthews, we have you and your wife staying on our third floor. Your room has a fireplace and a lovely balcony facing to the west." She had marked the form for Luke to sign. "Mrs. Matthews, have you been to Eureka Springs before?"

"I haven't. It's my first time here. Your accent is so familiar."

"I'm from Iraq. My husband and I came from there four years ago."

"I was there for two tours of duty with the military police. I'm

17

Sara, it's nice to meet you." She looked closely at the woman's name tag. "Calla."

"You also, Sara. I hope your time in Iraq has better memories for you than it did for my family."

"There are some bad memories and nightmares I still have about it," Sara said, wishing to leave the counter and sorry she had brought Iraq up.

The clerk laid two keys with large antique key markers on the counter for them. Each had 1886 engraved on them.

"I bet you lose a lot of these keys for souvenirs and keepsakes," Luke said.

"Really, we don't. Our souvenir gift shop offers an old key and the fob for just a small price."

Sara looked at Luke and gave him a nod of '*yes, please*'.

"The elevator is just over to the right," Calla said.

Luke led the way and pushed the button for the elevator. The door opened slowly, and they stepped in. Sara was certain a kiss would be coming as soon as the elevator door closed. She watched the doors slowly start coming together, wishing they would hurry.

A man's hand blocked the doors, and they crept open again. A man well past middle-age stepped onto the elevator with a much younger woman, then turned and stopped to stand in front of them. The woman stood close to the man and wiggled her butt against his hand.

Sara was amused and lowered her arm and hand behind Luke. He didn't see it coming—the butt grab and hard pinch. His reaction took him forward just enough to bump the wiggling butt of the young woman.

"I'm sorry," he said. "My leg went to sleep and almost made me fall."

Sara had her hand over her mouth and came close to choking on her laugh. Luke stepped back behind her. The man turned and looked Sara over from top to bottom. "Why don't you two join us for dinner? We can have drinks later, I'm sure," he said, and smiled.

Sara knew she had caused the dilemma and had to get them out of it.

"I'm taking this fellow up to our room to celebrate our honeymoon. We won't need any company, but thanks anyway."

She swore she heard the woman say, "Honey, you know I'm all you'll ever need."

The elevator stopped at two and the couple got off. Again, the doors of the elevator slowly closed. Luke didn't wait, he turned her into his arms. The kiss lasted through the hard bump of the elevator stopping and the slow groan of the doors opening.

"I'm going to pay you back a dozen times for the butt pinch, lady."

"Please, do. It'll be like our foreplay, right?"

They walked down the ancient hallway to nearly the end. Luke put his key in the door of room 324, and the lock turned, giving a long squeak as it finally unlocked.

"Boy, things really move slowly here, don't they?" Luke said, opening the door for her to go in. He followed, shutting it and setting the chain lock. She walked across the room and tossed the heavy curtains open on a wooden door with an ornate glass inlay. She opened it and stepped out.

She called, "Luke, you've got to see this view of the mountains. We've got to move down here."

He walked out on the balcony beside her, sliding his arms around her and leaning his chin over her shoulder.

"This view will be even more beautiful at sunset," he said.

She reached and rubbed the pressure he brought against her butt. Then she spun away and brazenly ran for the ornate bed. She tossed the top covers back.

"Aren't you going to join me for our honeymoon?" she pleaded, waiting for him to get into bed. Luke's shirt fell to the floor even before he got to her. She started on the rest of his clothes, opening his belt buckle. She didn't pause when he kissed her, his top button and the zipper opened before the kiss finished. Her bra slid off. She wanted this to be about her, and she pulled his head down to her breast. She held him against her flesh, wanting the hard suckle of her breast and then his bite to come with it.

She reached down, down past the zipper, and found what she wanted. Luke didn't need any encouragement. She fell backward on the bed, her last element of clothing pulled down and sorted around her ankles and feet. She reached for her deepest breath as he came toward her. Her breathing suddenly became sharp, quickly syncing to the rhythm of their lovemaking. She matched his with her own, not pausing when she knew he had finished but pushing on for her high to sweep across her pelvis in a surging shutter. It came upon her as if in a dream, but it wasn't a dream, it was real.

She savored each little flinch and shake of her body's reaction. It told her they belonged together. He paused, lying against her, and then he kissed her. His sharp bite on her lip sparked a reaction she didn't expect. She pulled him against her and begged for more of his lovemaking. Luke pleaded for a few minutes rest and promised, later. Finally, exhausted, with little discussion they both agreed to call out for dinner to be brought in. They ordered for two nearly starved people.

When the knock on the door came, both of them realized they were naked and neither one of them had a bathrobe. She rushed to the bathroom to get a bath towel. Doing a turn and a half around her middle with the towel, she went to the door and opened it. A tablecloth covered cart rolled through, pushed by a young man in a bellman uniform. Luke sat up in bed, keeping the covers over his bottom half.

"If you're ready, I'll take the lids off the plates. Management sent along a bottle of champagne for your honeymoon."

"Thank them for us," she said, reaching for Luke's pants and billfold. She gave the bellman a twenty-dollar tip and thanked him again.

"You're very welcome, Mrs. Matthews. By the way, there are fresh bathrobes for you in the hall closet."

She didn't say anything, only went and chained the door when he left. She went to the closet and took out two of the four bathrobes, put one on, and tossed the other on the bed for Luke.

"Please put it on. I won't be able to eat with you sitting there naked and tempting me."

Luke slipped the robe on and came to her and the food, doing a little strip tease, opening and closing his robe.

"Really? How's this?" She had already started giving him a quick flash of what she knew to be her best side. Luke dropped his robe and it fell to the floor beside the one she had been wearing. Dinner would have to wait.

Ten o'clock in the morning found her tugging at Luke to hurry. They stopped at the desk to ask Calla if there was a bus downtown.

Calla pointed out the door. "Hurry, it's about to leave. You can just catch it."

She beat Luke onto the open-air trolley and took a seat near the rear. He joined her and took her hand.

"I thought you would never quit last night," he said.

"You ungrateful boy," she said, "You never wanted to stop, either."

"You do know I'm talking about your snoring when you finally went to sleep."

"Really? After the big bottle of champagne, you could still hear?"

After the trolley made a hair-raising trip down the mountain, it turned into a narrow street lined with artist shops and markets. She pulled him up from his seat.

"We're getting off here." She led him through a dozen art shops featuring paintings of views of the Crescent Hotel and other nooks and crannies of Eureka Springs' parks. A store window filled with wildlife art stopped them to look and talk about a painting she liked of an elk, and another of a beaver. Luke admired the work of the Arkansas artist pictured in the window.

She loved the fact they both had the outdoors and Arkansas wildlife as their common interest. They started again up the steep sidewalk, past the many other shops. Luke pulled her back and led her into a doorway. The store's windows were filled with beautiful handmade bracelets and gold chained necklaces with ornaments of pearls and scrimshaw carvings of eagles.

"Come on, we're going in," Luke said, pulling her after him through the door. "I want to see the scrimshaw necklaces on you."

After a quick introduction they learned the woman who owned the shop was also the scrimshaw artist. She went to the front window and got her scrimshaw collection and brought it to a glass top cabinet with a mirror. She lifted the necklace with the eagle.

"Can we see how this looks on you? I think this young woman could soar like an eagle. Don't you, sir?"

Sara saw the hundred plus dollar price tag dangling from the necklace. She quickly pointed to the fox necklace. But still, the price?

"Could I try the fox instead?" she asked, reaching and picking out one of the two fox necklaces. "This one is beautiful." She ran her finger over the fox's back. The animal floated in the air with its body arched, head down, poised to drop on its prey. The beauty of the spontaneous jump of the fox raised her pulse. It would be going home with her. She fastened the necklace around her neck and moved the fox to the center of her chest. The chain was long.

"I can shorten it if you would like." The artist said, reaching to take it off.

"No. I'll take it just as it is," she said, opening her blouse just a bit to show the fox just about to enter the pathway between her breasts. "I love it." She reached for her billfold to get a credit card and Luke stopped her.

"Wait. I'm buying yours." He reached for the second fox scrimshaw and put it around his own neck. "Would you like to buy mine?"

She loved his idea. It made her feel like it brought them closer together. They had been separated over miles of Arkansas mountains in the last weeks and she had missed seeing and talking with her Luke. He always used his gentle voice when he was with her. Still, he could be harsh and commanding when it was needed, with so much of his life in law enforcement. She lifted the fox for another view and touch before letting it drop to her bosom.

With a ten percent discount for buying the two items, they both settled and left. She noticed his hand rubbing the edges of his scrimshaw fox piece as they sat down on the trolley for the ride back to the Crescent.

"Rubbing it for good luck tonight?"

"No. I'm rubbing it for good luck for you and me in the days ahead."

She kissed him and sat with his arm around her back for the rest of the ride. Jumping off the trolley at the hotel, she led the way to a marked pathway at the side of the hotel.

"Come on. This will give us a chance to walk and talk. There hasn't been a lot of talk so far on our visit to Eureka Springs."

"All right. Want me to start?"

"I'd love it if you did," she said. Drawing their future plans out of the man had been difficult, so any chance to get him to talk would be a welcome moment.

"My dad called me this week. He and Mom had a lawyer draw up the papers to give us both the Calico Rock cabin along with the forty acres of their bluff land."

She pulled him close. "Giving us the cabin? They were planning on giving it to you."

"Dad hasn't been well, and he had said they might never get to build their dream house up on the bluff. I had told them how much we love it up there. They want us both to have it. We can build us the dream house they never got to have."

"Do you still want to marry me, Luke Matthews?"

"We could do it here today," he said, taking her hand in his. "You are saying yes? Right?"

"So soon?" she asked, "The answer is yes, but could we wait only a couple weeks until I'm through my training?"

"Still being practical, aren't you?"

"Only if you promise we'll be living together soon," she said, lifting her necklace and holding the fox out to touch the one on his chest. Luke held the two symbols of their love together for a moment and then kissed hers as he let the scrimshaw fox pendant slip away to her hand and then in between her breasts.

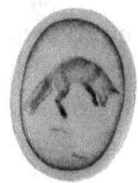

FOUR

WITH THE FINAL DAY OF classes drawing to a finish and their camp issued gear turned in, Sara and Audrey both sat on their bare mattresses, waiting for the day's end signal. Now it all came down to next weekend's graduation ceremony at the Antioch Baptist Church in Conway, Arkansas. Sara, her dad, and Jimmy were planning to show up midafternoon to show them around the Morris Training Center before the ceremony. With only minutes left in her final training day Sara got up, swung her duffle over her shoulder, and headed out the door.

She turned to her roommate. "I'll be back in five." She got a nod in return.

Reid and another cadet were leaning over their trunks and tossing bags in. Reid saw her coming and waved.

"Hard to believe it's over," he said and then shut the tailgate on his pickup.

"I guess we'll see each other Saturday. Do you have any ideas about our assignments?"

"None. Did Luke tell you what he thought for you? You know, based on your living in Cotter." He opened the door of the truck for her.

"Thanks. No, he hasn't." she said, tossing her bag into the truck's backseat. "I'm headed back in to check my room again."

"I'll follow and—."

The camp's loudspeaker clicked, "Cadets Reid and Randolph

report to the office."

They looked at each other. She couldn't come up with a reason. They both headed for the office, walking a little faster than normal.

Captain Gentry stood just inside the door, waiting. Sara pulled up at attention and offered a salute. Reid followed her lead.

"Relax. There is a ride for you both, about to leave for the Arkansas Game and Fish Commission headquarters in Little Rock. It's unusual. The call came right from the top of the department a few minutes ago. You both have been selected for something. I don't have any idea what. I'm in the dark here. You don't have to go. It's strictly on a volunteer basis."

The captain's volunteer basis statement again tripped Sara's old Army axiom of not volunteering for anything she hadn't thought about and studied the consequences of. This time she kept her mouth shut.

Reid leaned over and whispered, "Did you know anything about this?"

"No, I guess we will have to go and find out."

"I thought you would speak up and ask questions," Reid said, turning to follow Sara and the officer.

They were being escorted out the door of the office. A late model Ford SUV idled, and the driver held the backdoor open for them. She looked and studied the man for a couple seconds before following Reid into the back seat. She wanted to whisper to Reid. Based on the tan slacks and sweater the man wore, this guy was either CIA or DEA. They were being escorted by a man carrying an issued sidearm for certain. The man offered a hello and little more on the drive into Little Rock. She tried several times to dig in with small questions.

"Do you work at the commission headquarters?"

"Sorry. The commission's staff wants to brief both of you before you get questions answered."

His statement was enough to shut her up for the rest of the drive. There had been some talk early in their training about drug enforcement and work with other government agencies. She realized this rooster may have come into her life to roost. Reid looked at her with what she knew were a lot of questions he wanted to ask. She shook her head in a profound *no* before he asked.

When the driver drove up and stopped in front of the main offices of the Arkansas Game Commission, he didn't get out. A young lady dressed in the agent's field garb opened the backdoor of the SUV and gave them a smile. Sara was glad the drive was over. It had been way too stuffy between them and the driver. They both exited the vehicle.

"Would you both come with me? I'm sure you would like an explanation as to why we asked you here so late in the day."

Sara wanted to say something smartass about the time of day. It probably didn't have a lot to do with the escort and secrecy. They both followed the woman into the building and then an elevator. The elevator offered another quiet, stuffy ride, taking them to the top floor of the building. The agent led them down the hall and into a conference room with a long oval table. Six chairs were set, and they were motioned to two on an empty table side. The one chair at the head of the table didn't need questioning. It would be for someone in command. The three other chairs were spaced a foot apart on the other side of the table. The question of why the meeting bounced in her head. Still not sure about the chair at the front, the door opened and an old fishing buddy of hers came in. Brad Johnson, the head of the Arkansas Game Commission approached her and offered a hug.

"Sorry, Cadet Reid. This lady and I went through hell on the White River to save my family."

Sara wished Reid hadn't been there to witness Brad's welcome for her. She was way past the point of wanting favoritism from those over her. A hard lesson from Iraq.

"Hello, sir," she offered, trying to tamp his welcome down a bit. He turned and offered a handshake to Reid.

"I've read everything I could find about you, sir. You've been an outstanding cadet at Morris and your past record as a law enforcement officer was just as outstanding. Both of you, have a seat. We'll start when the rest of the team arrives. They're on the way up." He settled in at the head of the conference table. A young aid came in and set down glasses of water and a large plate of cookies. His question of did anyone want coffee got mostly ignored and he left. Two men and a woman joined them taking seats at the table without introductions.

"Before we start, would you, Sara Randolph and Patrick Reid, both stand and take the Game Commission's oath of affirmation?"

Reid looked at Sara with a question of, *what the hell? showing on his face.*

"Affirmation?" Sara asked.

"Repeat after me: I 'your name,' do solemnly swear (or affirm) that I will support the constitution of the United States and the constitution of the state of Arkansas, and I will faithfully discharge the duties of Wildlife Enforcement Officer, the office of which I am now about to enter."

Both Sara and Reid quoted the oath as Brad had read it to them. He extended his hand and shook both of their hands. "This completes your training at RC 'Red' Morris, and now you are both sworn agents of the Arkansas Game Commission. Congratulations to you both."

The three people across the table got up and came around the table to shake hands. They didn't offer their names. Brad handed out gold badges to Sara and Reid.

Sara sat down first. She realized what had just happened, and it made her too happy to ask questions. With the group seated, Brad explained.

"You both are here because of your police backgrounds, Randolph's extensive military police training and Reid's training in law enforcement. We wanted you because we are sure you can hit the ground running in our new program with the DEA for drug enforcement throughout the south-central United States. This enforcement program includes Arkansas, Texas, and beyond into Mexico. We moved your oath of office swearing in here because we want to keep your names under wraps if you decide to be a part of this program. If you have an interest in our undercover operations or not, it's time to say what you think."

"It sounds like a long step from being in the woods or on the river acting as a game warden," Sara said.

"It will be quite different from an Arkansas Game Warden's job. I know neither of you are inspired by money—however, the pay here will be triple the warden's pay. You will be on your own except for information and leads from a contact with our DEA, AGC group." He pushed a button on his phone and said, "Please send in the waiting group member."

Reid spoke first, "I'll be damn."

Sara only smiled at the contact coming into the room. Luke went to Brad and shook hands before sitting down alongside Sara and Reid.

"Our three folks from the DEA would like to get to know the two of you. Our cafeteria has dinner set up for the six of us. So, if you'll join us, please, we can head down."

Sara and Luke lagged back a bit as the others left the room.

"How long have you known about this, mister?" she asked Luke.

"It's a totally new program. I was drafted just this week. The powers at the top knew about you two and wanted to take the chance you would join the drug interdiction efforts they are starting. You both are perfect for undercover since you're becoming agents without a fanfare."

"I don't know about this. All of our training was about chasing poachers and not about being drug agents. It sounds like I'm about to enter another war zone."

"I think they are planning some extensive training for both of you. Including the DEA in Washington. It would be a career jump for both of you. You are correct, it is a war zone."

Sara nodded her head in agreement.

"Meet the agents on the program before you decide."

She followed as he led the way to the elevator and the path to the cafeteria.

Two hours later, she and Reid had signed a non-disclosure agreement and were both part of the combined drug task force. A two-week leave with no strings attached would fit in well for her to get to know her family again before hell would start on a job she still had some doubts about. Thinking of the time away from her dad and Jimmy sunk in hard. The challenge they presented had been huge and it struck home in her 'I can do this' mind. One thing she knew for sure, the gold badge Brad had presented would rest close to her heart.

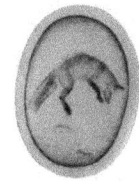

FIVE

SARA LAY PARTLY AWAKE, WAITING for the siren and bullhorn to pound her eardrums and cause her to lunge out of bed and beat her roommate into the bathroom. The soft knock at her door surprised her. She sat up in bed.

A voice asked, "Aunt Sara, you awake yet?"

It had been her last weekend home when she had promised Jimmy, she would take him back to where his home had been blown up by his dad's meth cooking and his mother and father had died. Jimmy had been playing across the road when the meth fueled explosion took the top off his family's house trailer. He watched both his mother and father come out of what was left of the trailer screaming and covered with fire. They both perished in front of his eyes. From the burns she had found on Jimmy's hands, Sara knew he had tried to help them. She had resisted taking him back to the hillside where this horror had happened. Her visit to the site, with Luke, had turned into a standoff when two men confronted them about why they were there. She was certain from what she saw of them they had been meth dealers working with Jimmy's parents. Luke had shut down the back-and-forth argument with the two men.

Jimmy's persistence in going back to his home won out when he told her it would be the last time he would go, and he needed to look for something his mother had given him. Jimmy had a stubborn streak. She finally gave up on getting a full answer on why he wanted to go back. Taking him now would put an end to him insisting on going.

"Oh, Jimmy. Let me get dressed and we can stop in town for breakfast on our way."

She picked out a pair of blue jeans from the dresser drawer and a blue denim western shirt from the closet and dressed quickly. She took down her two pistols from the shelf in the closet, loaded them, and strapped on the Glock. She slid the small black widow pistol into her boot's holster. She needed to be ready if the locals showed up this time at the burned trailer site. After a quick trip to the sink to wash her face, she walked into the kitchen. Jimmy sat on a stool with Tank sitting at his side. He slid off the stool and gave her a sloping arm salute.

"We are ready, Officer Randolph."

"Yes, Jimmy. Give me a second." She snapped her heels together and returned his salute with her best.

"Stand at ease, troops," she said, and then looked around the kitchen for a thermos jug to take some coffee.

"I think dad has the jug. He left early to go fishin'." Jimmy went to the cupboard and got her a tall coffee cup with a lid.

"Will this do okay?" he asked, handing it to her.

"Sure. You're ready? Teeth brushed, hair combed, and clean clothes?" She paused for a moment, wondering why she had asked this. The young, snake-bitten boy she first met in a mountain cave now showed signs of a boy much older for his age. War and trauma, like they had both been through, can do a lot to age a person.

"Mostly, I am," he said, and turned to disappear into the bathroom, giving her a look that said, 'why are you asking me this?'. Tank still sat in the same spot, looking at her.

"Come here, boy. Darn, I missed you guys so much." She knelt beside the dog and held his collar while she took one finger and scratched the underside of his jaw. She knew just how much the dog loved her touch in his sweet spot. Jimmy came out of the bathroom and paused.

"I've got to get something." He headed out the door, letting it slam in his rush. She heard him open the shed alongside the house. Tank followed her as she went out to the truck.

"You coming?" she yelled. She could hear him rummaging

through the tools in the shed.

"I'm coming. I just had to get something, is all," he said, carrying a long handle shovel over his shoulder.

"What's the shovel for?"

"It's to do something the doctors made me remember."

Neither Jimmy nor Sara's dad had told her much about Jimmy's visits to the psychologist in Springfield. She knew from her own holding back on telling Luke about what happened in the Iraq prison, Jimmy's mind could be tormented with unexpected, repressed memories. Breakfast would be a good time to learn more about what he had remembered.

"But you can't dig around the trailer, Jimmy."

"I'll show you what it's for when we get there," he said, dropping the shovel over the edge of the pickup's bed.

With Tank loaded in the back seat and Jimmy in front beside her, she headed out to find a place to eat.

At breakfast, she poured her second cup of not-so-warm coffee as Jimmy finished the last of his four bacon strips and toast. With her index finger through the cup handle, she lifted it slightly and wiped the edge with a napkin. A nervous gesture to hold back from the questions she wanted to ask the boy. She would broach the subject slowly.

"I need to hit the bathroom," Jimmy said, wiping his hands on a paper napkin and standing.

Oh well, so much for slowing him down for her talk. The boy headed down the hall and out of sight.

To herself, she thought, *"It didn't go well, did it, Sara?"*

The closeby waitress asked, "Did you need something?"

"I smell fresh donuts. Right?"

"Yes. We just got some out of the fryer."

"Two chocolate ones for us. Please." This would at least slow Jimmy down for a few minutes. The donuts and Jimmy got to the table at nearly the same time.

"One is for you," Sara said, pushing the dish to Jimmy's side of the table.

"Man, I'm so full."

He gave in when he saw her bite into the one with the sprinkles on it. She swallowed the bite. "Your doctor in Springfield, do you remember his name?"

His second bite of the donut had just landed in his mouth. With a little sputtering, he said, "I just call him doctor or sir."

"Is remembering living with your mom and dad hard for you?"

"Things I did together with my mother keep coming back to me. She kept me away from my dad. She said he sucked up too much of the stuff he was making."

"Did she drive and take you places away from him?"

"She did, but then he took the keys away from her. After that it was him always going to town and getting groceries and stuff. Can we go now?"

He had finished the last bite of the donut and put down the napkin after wiping his hands. Jimmy was more than ready to get on with their morning's journey. She still didn't know why he had brought the shovel and what he had remembered. She would let it play out with the morning.

She headed west toward Boxley Valley and a nightmare burned-out trailer site. She thought it wouldn't help Jimmy to have to witness it again. She may have given in to the trip too quickly.

The morning was cool, and she opened both windows of her truck to enjoy the wind rushing through, carrying the scents of the pine trees along the road. She rolled the windows up fast when they passed the stink of a pig ranch along the way. Nothing seemed to bother the boy. He sat on the edge of his seat and often reached behind to pet the sleeping dog on the head.

"Poor old boy. He just sat there in the yard with the saddest look on his face," she said, "I had to bring him along."

"He follows me and Blue everywhere we go. Even when I go over to Miss Marty's place to work."

"How is she? Does she take you horseback riding?" She checked the gas gauge and realized they would need a stop soon. "Watch for a gas station. I'm getting low."

"She's okay. I ride the horses almost every time I'm there. Once she took me up the hill across from the barn."

"Did you ride Dusty? The big white horse?"

"Nope. She got a new horse for me to ride."

"Maybe she'll let me go riding with you some time."

"The sign just said two miles to a gas place to stop," he said.

Mad at herself for letting the truck get so low on gas, she pulled into the single gas pump at a small wooden-sided building with a faded red Marathon sign. The front garage door was open, and a pickup had been lifted on the oil change rack. A man came out of the garage door and took the gas pump's nozzle from its rest.

"We only got regular, ma'am." He already had the tank cover open. She watched the man with his grease-stained blue shirt put the nozzle in the gas tank's opening and start to pump gas. She had a picture of this man stored in her mind from sometime before, and now it came together. He had been holding a rifle and standing across the road from her and Luke at Jimmy's parents' burned-out trailer. The man taunted them about being there, but he backed down before the other man with him did. Luke had pushed hard at both of them. She had watched, standing behind her truck with her pistol in her hand, ready. Lucky for the men, Luke had won out, flashing a badge and a sidearm at them both. The men had left, shouting threats at them.

"I need to go to the bathroom," Jimmy said, starting to get out of the truck.

"Stay here, we're leaving now," she said, getting two twenties out of her billfold.

"Hey, stop it at forty, I'm in kind of a hurry." She heard the pump shake as he stopped it.

"There. Just got it stopped in time," the man said, hanging up the pump handle and coming to her window. She handed him the two twenties and started the engine, shifted into gear, and started to roll.

"Youn' from around here?" he asked with his hand on the windowsill, walking alongside the slowly rolling truck. "I thought I'd seen this here boy before. Ain't your name Jimmy?"

He didn't answer the man. The smell of his breath flooded through the window and choked her. She made a guess the smell of his meth rotted teeth was nearly covered by the aroma of the pot he had been smoking. Jimmy looked up and touched her arm but didn't say anything. Tank alerted in the back seat, trying to get his head out the side of the front window by Sara. His deep growl could not be mistaken as he pushed at the back of the seat to gain more of the window space toward the man. The dog barked the attack warning he had been taught in training.

"Down, Tank. Nope, we're not from here." She hit the gas

pedal hard and came close to running over the man's foot with her squalling back tires. She looked back and scanned the half dozen trailers in a semicircle with a large dirt yard in front of them as she pulled away. She was hoping like hell the man didn't remember her and the time they had met in front of the burned-out trailer on the Boston Mountain top. Jimmy had changed with age and the man knowing his name may have been only a guess. No way did she want to deal with him and his outlaw friend again. She had been ready back then when Luke had faced them to shoot if they crossed the road toward them. She pushed the truck hard to get away from the man and the compound.

"Did you know the man, Jimmy?"

"I don't know his name. He came to see my dad all the time. I never liked him none," Jimmy said. He had leaned over the seat with his hand on Tank's collar.

For the next two miles, she looked in the truck's mirrors every few seconds to be sure no one followed them. Turning the truck around and heading back to the cabin could be an option.

"I really need to take a piss now."

"Hang on, I'll stop for you in a couple of minutes."

After a quick stop for him to bless the side of the road, she started looking for the rough road leading up the mountain to the burned-out trailer. Her memory of the conflict they had with the two men hadn't gone away. Her sixth sense of wanting to turn around and go home spoke to her.

Then, a look at the boy convinced her this trip needed to be made for his sake. He sat forward, tight against his seatbelt, almost scooted to the edge of his seat in anticipation of his trip home. Jimmy looked more like the driver of the truck than she did. He leaned with his body against his hands, pressing on the dash at every curve.

Certain she had the right place, she turned in on the gravel and drove toward the rocky-ledged climb the road made.

"My first dad always hated this road," he said, now sitting back in his seat and tightening his seatbelt.

"I don't like it much, either," she said, slowing and turning the truck's four-wheel drive on. "This will help with the climb."

The truck pulled ahead slowly. She steered to straddle the parts of the road with the smallest rock ledges. She let the front wheels grip the edge of a ledge before she called for more power from the engine. Limbs from the brush along the climb reached for them and brushed the truck's side panels.

"No one is taking care of this road. It's getting so damn grown up along here," she said, trying to steer away from the limbs.

"We're just about at the top," Jimmy said, getting up on the edge of his seat to look forward.

In another mile she slowed and pulled off the road just across from where she and Luke had found the burned-out trailer. Only a few black hulks of trees still stood at the back of the site. The trailer and the demolished car and yard junk had been cleaned up and were gone. A hand written wooden sign and post stood where the car had been parked. It warned to keep out, without any mention of the still present danger of chemical contamination in the area. It didn't surprise her the county commission wanted to keep the knowledge of meth manufacturing under wraps. Jimmy sat up on the edge of his seat, looking at the trailer site.

"I used to hunt all back in those woods," he said.

"I'm sorry we can't go back in there," she said, wanting badly to get away from the site.

"My mother almost made it across the road to me," he said. "I couldn't help her. Her clothes and skin were all on fire."

She knew the thought would have had her in tears just coming close to her home's site. Sara wanted to hold and comfort the boy, but Jimmy showed no emotion about what he had told her. Did he really have this hard of an edge?

"When are you going to tell me why we brought the shovel?"

"I'll try and show you if you'll drive back the way we come."

Sara made the turn back down the road in one try. She had been way more than ready to leave the burned-out trailer's site. She expected Jimmy to be looking out the back of the truck at his old homesite. He wasn't. Instead, he looked ahead, watching the woods on their left.

Less than thirty yards back down the road, Jimmy pointed to an open gap in the brush line.

"Turn in here," he told her. There was excitement in his voice.

"Is it a road?"

"Nope. Just a place we can go in the woods. My mom went there often when dad wasn't around."

He pointed at a broken gate and a dirt trail leading along the edge of some heavier timber on the upside of the hill. Pausing on the road before turning in, she checked her rearview mirror and again a look ahead. The man at the gas station knowing Jimmy wasn't good. She and Luke had been harassed for just stopping on the road across from the burned-out trailer. Were they being watched? Pulling through the gate, she stopped.

"Is this where we're going?"

"No. More down through here out of sight of the road, my mother always said."

Sara drove ahead along the path. She liked having the heavy woods now on both sides of the truck. Around a bend, the path stopped at a place she could tell had been a turn around. She pulled up.

"This must be it, isn't it?" she asked, looking at Jimmy already half out of the truck's door.

"Yep. The spring where we got water is just over there." He went to the side of the truck and tried to reach the shovel in the bed.

"Hang on. I'll get it for you." She stepped out again, checked the Glock, and slid it just around her back. She leaned over and adjusted the small Spider pistol holstered inside the top of her boot. Now she was ready if they had been followed. Her fingertips just reached the shovel, she stretched and pulled it to the side of the bed before lifting it out and giving it to Jimmy.

"Okay, you're the man. What's on your mind?"

"Come on." He led the way to the spring and stopped to lift a cup off a post. "Want a cold drink?" he asked, starting to dip the cup into the clear spring water. Tank had already started drinking.

"Jimmy, stop, and stop Tank. The trailer fire may have washed some bad stuff down the hill into the watershed."

"I always drank it before," he said, pouring the water back into the spring's runoff, which was bubbling down the hill.

"We better get it tested before you drink it again." She looked around, hoping to see a clue to where Jimmy was leading her. He put down the cup and walked to the uphill side of the spring's wall and started taking long steps up the hill.

"One, two, three." His steps reached twenty-five before he stopped and started pushing brush and weeds aside. "I think this is where my mom buried it."

"Buried what?" she asked, standing a few feet away and not seeing any sign of where something could be buried.

"She snuck away money my dad was making for his meth cooking. He was so crazy he didn't even know."

"She hid his money?"

"It's here somewhere. She told me to get it if anything happened to her." He had started ramming the shovel blade into the soft ground.

"Here, let me help," she said, reaching for the shovel.

"No. I know what it sounds like when I find it. It's a big metal box." He moved back down toward the spring and stopped when they both heard the thud and ring of the top of the box. He started to dig out the top of the box.

"Let me help you out." He handed her the shovel. She dug an impression all around the box's top and then scraped away the dirt on top of the lid. It surprised her the box was more than three feet long by two feet wide.

"It ain't locked or nothin'. Just pry it up." He crawled up to the lid on his knees and dug along the edge with his hand. Tank couldn't stand the digging any longer. He pushed alongside Jimmy and dug in with his front paws. With the dirt cleared away, they managed to get the rusted box lid open. As it came open, she saw the mason jars inside. The glass of the jars were green with what looked like money. As the lid plopped fully open, she dropped back on her butt in disbelief to look at what Jimmy had brought her to see.

"This is a lot of money," she said, "How long had your mother been hiding it?"

"I don't know. I started paying attention when I was still little. I just saw her take most of it and hide it after the men came to get stuff."

Sara had reached one of the rare places in her life where she didn't know what to do next. She knew sitting below their feet lay a lot of money. Yes, it was drug money, but in her mind, it belonged to the boy by her side.

"Can you get the jars out for me?"

Before she finished asking, he had two sitting in the dirt by her side.

"How many are there?"

"Lots more," he said, setting three more by her side. She started taking the lids off the jars and stacking the money in piles. She tried to sort out the hundreds, but then found most of the bills were hundreds. Her pile grew.

"There, you got it all," Jimmy said, sitting back and watching her stack the bills.

Without counting it, she realized there was a hell of a lot of money in the pile. She stared in disbelief at what they had dug up. Then she started stuffing the bills in her backpack.

"Help me, Jimmy." Both pairs of hands stuffed money through the zipper opening.

"What are we going to do with Mom's money?"

"First, we've got to get it home. Then we can sock it away in a trust for you."

"What's a trust?" he asked, finishing stuffing, and then closing the zipper.

"It's like a bank. So, the money will be there when you need it. Let's get this to the truck." Jimmy dropped the shovel back into the truck bed while she stowed her backpack behind the seat.

"Let's go, Jimmy," she said, sliding into the driver's seat and starting the engine. Jimmy jumped in the truck beside her and Tank and put on his seatbelt. Backing the truck against the brush, she turned the wheels hard and got turned around and headed back toward the road.

The hell she had worried about stood side by side in front of her. She slammed on the truck brakes. Two heavily armed men stood, blocking the open gate. The grease-stained blue shirt man from the gas stop stood with his fingers on the trigger of a shotgun. The barrel pointed up alongside his chest, ready to drop and fire. She concentrated on the other man with him. The danger of the AR-15 hanging across his chest frightened her. His gray t-shirt hung like it covered a thin piece of cardboard. His dirty camouflage pants ended in tatters surrounding his invisible feet. She knew they were the same men she and Luke had faced before, only now this one looked like meth had gotten the best of him. She watched him swing the war weapon up and point it toward the truck. She eased the truck into reverse and jammed the accelerator to the floor. The truck lunged backward into the turnaround just below the spring. She skidded to a stop. The rush back had given her a moment to think. Trying to call for help fell about last on her list with the thousands of dollars in her back seat. Certain seventeen weeks of training, plus her combat experience would equip her to handle this. She sat for a moment to psych herself up.

"Jimmy, get down on the floor, now! Keep Tank in here with you." She had thoughts of trying to run over both of them, but the AR made her think again. Her truck would be no match for the bullets from it. She slid her Glock to her side so it would be in plain sight and got out of the truck to walk three steps away from the side of the truck and toward the two men walking toward them. She had to take this fight away from the truck and Jimmy. She gripped the Glock, and it came out of the holster in the automatic way it had so many times before in Iraq. She turned her side toward the advancing men and aimed the pistol double-handed at the guy holding the AR.

"Get out of here. We only came so the boy could see his old home."

"Shit, bitch. We knowed his old mother had been hiding money for years. You found it, didn't you?"

"Didn't find anything. Just some cold spring water. You might get a shot into me, but before I'm dead you're going to have a .44 slug right between your eyes, mister."

"Ain't going to shoot you first, just going to blast your truck to hell and kill the kid, so drop the pistol."

She paused, knowing what the AR would do to the boy huddled below the dash. She paused to see if the man would do it. She heard a click, and the AR was being pointed at the truck.

"Wait!" She dropped the Glock at her feet. The next move would not be hers. Both came at her at the same time.

"Now we're gonna see just how sweet you are, you scarred up bitch," the meth head said, hitting her in the side of the face with the stock of the rifle. The blow glanced off and knocked her to her knees. She fell face down on the ground. She stared at the blurred gravel and dirt in front of her face, then someone took her arm and pulled her around onto her back. She blindly reached for her weapon. She got only a handful of dirt. She shook her head, trying to get her sight back. Someone had pulled her pants down and off her feet. The shock of the cold ground pressing against her bare ass restored her full consciousness. Her boot with her .22 caliber Spider Pistol lay off to her side, too far to reach. She wanted the Glock to blow the men to hell and beyond. The man at her feet pulled at his belt buckle. His pants slid down over his knees and around his shoes.

"Hey, George, ride her down. Hurry up, I'm next." The man yelling held her hands and arms to the ground. It had to be now to stop their rape attack. She yanked one hand out from the man's grip. A drawn and cocked foot struck straight out. She felt the crunch of his filthy privates from her strike. The man doubled over, reaching with both hands to cover the pain she had laid on him as he fell back onto the ground.

She heard the truck door swing full open and sat up to see what was coming. Tank charged the man still trying to gain control of her free hand. The German shepherd's rush knocked the man over and her hands were free. She saw the crushing bite the dog gained on the man's arm. Jimmy ran toward her just behind the dog. His 22-rifle was pointed at the man at her feet. Jimmy stumbled as he pulled the trigger and his shot hit the dirt alongside the man's leg.

It offered her a chance. She scooted across the ground and grabbed the Glock. In a second, she fired two shots. Her ears pounded and tried to rebound from the loud blasts from her pistol. She yelled at the man, but barely heard her own voice.

"The next shot and you'll be dead, Ass Head." She had placed her shots, one on each side of the man at her feet. Shooting to warn someone had been no part of the army's or the Game Commission's training. She kicked the stunned man in the gut and pushed him flat on his back.

"I'm shot, Oscar. Kill this bitch."

She didn't tell the man different, thinking he was shot would be fine. She had to get Jimmy back in the truck.

"Jimmy, run and get in the truck. I've got this." She could tell the boy was reluctant to leave the fight. "Go, Jimmy."

She staggered, holding the Glock in one hand and trying to get her pants on with the other. She didn't like the dance it took to finally pull the pants up and button them.

Tank still shook the man's arm, slinging dripping blood. The man yelled at her to get the thing off his arm. She knew Tank was trying his damn best to tear the man's arm off.

"Stand still and I'll call him off you." She had both hands holding the Glock pointed at his chest. Tank still held on to the man's arm. The dog's deep guttural growl surrounded them all.

"Tank, back off."

The dog released the arm and went to a halfway down stance, ready to attack again. The growl and show of teeth make the man lift his arms over his head. She turned toward the other man.

The Glock was aimed at his head. His breathing came in snorts as he ran his hands over his belly, looking for the bullet wounds. They didn't exist. She didn't like her weakness for not shooting to kill the man. So much of her key training had just been wasted. The man had been a threat ready to rape and kill. Her reaction had been too soft for a military police person or game warden. She pushed the feeling back, there was no time for it to continue right now.

"You're not going to die. Get out of here," she demanded.

He pulled up his pants with his only free hand. "I'm going to find you and your dog. I'm going to cut his throat and then yours for shooting at me. Then I'm going to—."

Her regrets got even stronger. "Enough. Get out of here or I'm gonna' finish the job of killing you." She hoped the bluff would work, only down deep it wasn't a bluff. She wanted the man who had attacked her dead.

He gestured for the other man. "You gonna have to help me walk, Oscar."

She watched him stagger off, still thinking he was shot. Jimmy had come to her side.

"I wanted to kill both them sons of bitches," he said, checking his rifle and injecting another cartridge into the firing chamber.

She broke the double barrel shotgun the man had dropped open and tossed the pieces in two different directions. She looked at the AR thinking of doing the same. This fight wasn't over, and the two men would be back for the money. She lifted the rifle off the ground and checked to be sure it was ready to fire. She would end this fight at the gate if the men waited there.

Her mind spawned a dozen random thoughts of what the charge of assault would bring. None of which offered a good outcome when it came to Jimmy's money. What the hell had happened? The men could have killed them. She had to shield

Jimmy if they tried again for the money.

She looked at Jimmy, "Are you okay?" She realized what had just happened would age the boy, just like his having to watch his mother and father burn to death from the meth-fueled explosion and fire at their trailer. Jimmy had been more than willing to kill to save her. What they had been through hit her hard. She realized what could have happened if she had killed the man and they were caught with the money. She slumped to her knees and wiped her forehead with the back of her hand. Tank and Jimmy came to her side. Tank licked her face.

"I tried to shoot the man," Jimmy said, still holding the rifle in his hand. "I wanted to kill him."

She reached for the boy with both her arms to hug him. Then realizing he still held a loaded, ready to fire weapon, she eased it from his hands.

"It's over. I'm going to clear your weapon and be sure it's safe." She ejected the cartridge in the chamber and removed the loaded magazine from the rifle. She handed the rifle with the magazine out back to the boy.

"Just keep the cartridges and magazine in your pocket for now."

"Are those men going to come back for us? We need to be ready."

"I don't think so. They know we'll be ready next time. It's all right. Your shot scared him and saved me. It gave me time to grab my pistol."

Her life as an Undercover Drug Agent may have just been shot into high gear. Shooting a local man in the county where he lived would have gone badly for her. She was way out of the commission's idea for their agent's jobs. She needed to be strong for Jimmy. She got up and went to the truck.

"Tank, load." The dog jumped through the open door and settled on the back seat beside the boy.

"It's over out here," she said, standing and rubbing her cheek where the man had hit her. Thinking, "*This isn't nearly over with those two. Is it?*"

She laid the AR across the passenger seat with its safety on and the chamber loaded to fire.

"Stay in the truck, Jimmy. I need a little cleanup." She went to the running water at the spring and didn't feel the cold as she poured it over the top of her head. She glanced back at her truck and the flat ground where the men had her pinned down. Jimmy stood on her truck's nerf bars, still holding his rifle and watching in the direction the men had gone. The boy had a toughness bred into him from his hardass old man. Without his attack, things could have gone way differently today. She knew dad would be very proud of his adopted son.

Back in the truck, she got Jimmy and Tank settled and pulled out toward the road. She saw the old truck with the man named Oscar driving and the other man leaning out the open window and yelling at her. He shook his fist at her and spit a chew of tobacco. She knew they both would have a lot of bragging to do when they got to the trailer compound. They would have the whole place out looking for her in the next few days. She needed to be hours away when that happened. She turned out behind the truck and followed until it turned off on the highway, headed toward what she was sure would be the compound. Not sure how she would explain it all to Luke, she headed home.

"Sorry, Jimmy. We'll have to see your grandmother another time."

"We had better be sure they aren't following us," he said, rubbing Tank's head.

Between the dog's deep breaths and his pants, Tank licked the boy's face.

"We will," Sara said over a long slow breath.

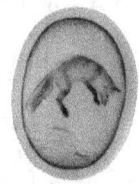

Six

DRIVING AND THINKING OF A backpack behind the seat filled with thousands of dollars frazzled Sara's thinking. Finding the money began the steamroller fight, it nearly got her raped—or worse, if the men had overcome her. Jimmy's safety flashed in her mind. The men probably would have not let either of them live if they had gotten the money. Regrets came at her fast as she drove for Cotter and the cabin. Going back to Jimmy's family's home area without taking Luke had been a mistake.

She was certain the fight at the spring, finding the drug money and keeping it could end her just-started life as an Arkansas wildlife agent. She turned off the main highway several miles before coming to the filling station with the trailer compound behind it. Passing the compound after what had happened could be a death wish. She drove north for fifteen miles before finally turning back east toward home.

"Jimmy, thanks for shooting at the man and letting Tank out to help me," she said, reaching and petting Tank on the head and then giving Jimmy a rub on the shoulder.

"Tank went crazy trying to get out to help you. I opened the door and we both came to help." He rubbed both his eyes with the side of his arm. "They were hurting you."

"It was so brave of both of you. I was in some bad trouble out there."

"What made Tank go after the man holding you down?"

"Some of the reason is German shepherds are natural protectors of their masters. The other is he had weeks of training from the military police to protect me. Tank is a trained soldier."

"He knocked the man down and grabbed his arm. His growls sounded like he wanted to kill the man."

"Maybe not kill him but hold onto him until I told him to let go."

What she told the boy seemed to satisfy him.

They both got quiet for the next two hours of the drive. She knew she had to talk to Jimmy about the backpack full of money but didn't know where to start.

Then Jimmy spoke up, "We gonna hide the money, ain't we?"

She thought for a minute and then, "We need to keep it a secret and not tell anyone except John. He'll know what to do." She looked at her watch and nearly missed the turn onto the highway to Cotter.

"Ain't you gonna tell Mr. Luke?"

"Shit," she thought, *"What should I do about telling Luke?"*

She didn't like being boxed in by what had happened. He had to be told about the two men. They damn well would be hunting her and the money.

"I'm going to tell him."

She pulled into the cabin driveway and stopped. She leaned forward, putting her forehead on the top of the truck's steering wheel, trying to think what to do next.

"Hey, in there. You driving asleep?" her dad, John, called from the yard as he walked toward the truck.

Sara sat up and took a deep breath. Now it starts. How would she explain what just happened?

"Dad. I've got some things we need to talk about right now."

"Get out, then. No need to talk through an open truck window, is there?"

She opened the door and let Tank slide past her legs into the yard. Jimmy went out the other door and ran to greet his hound, Blue. Leaving the backpack in the truck for now, she took her dad's arm and headed around the cabin to the faded white metal chairs on the deck. She knew her mother had used the place and chairs often for talks with John. She hoped the old chairs would serve her just as well today.

"Sit down, Dad." She dropped into a chair and patted the seat of the other with her hand. "Here."

She knew John was curious and wouldn't wait long for her take on what had happened.

She started. "First, I've got a backpack in the truck stuffed with thousands of dollars." She paused to get John's reaction.

It came quickly. "You got what?" He sat forward in his chair looking at her.

"You heard me. Thousands."

"Thousands?"

"Jimmy knew right where his mother had hidden it over the years, and he took me right to it. She had buried the money in a metal case."

"What the hell do we do with it now? It's got to be drug money, but both his folks are dead."

"Yeah, Dad, drug money. Now it's Jimmy's. All of it came rightfully from his mother."

"Us putting a lot of money away for him ain't gonna' be easy. Banks will want to know where it came from. Is it less than ten thousand?"

"More. A lot more."

"Are you gonna talk to Luke about what to do?"

She hesitated before answering, "A lot more happened right after we found the money." She needed to tell someone right now. "Jimmy shot at a man who had ripped my clothes off." John didn't need to know more than this.

"Your clothes? Did he kill him?"

"Two armed men had me flat on my back and coming for me. I wanted to kill them."

A pause before the explosion she knew would be coming, and then John jumped up from the chair. She remembered the expression on his face months ago when the man in the bar had hit him hard in the gut. He came up off the floor with his eyes gaping open and his teeth clenched, ready to kill the son of a bitch.

"What?"

A part of the Marine in him she knew would still be there came out. She could see the blood rushing to his face and the pulse of his heart in the clenches his fingers were making in the air.

"I'm going to find the bastards and cut their fucking balls off."

She knew it would be exactly what her dad would do if he found the men.

"We had just dug the money up. The men must have known about the money being hid and cornered us in a valley. Tank attacked the man holding me on the ground. He tore his arm up bad."

"Who are those sons of bitches?" He stood, looking at his daughter. What she had told him had triggered an old Marine who would still go to war against her foes.

"Months ago, Luke and I ran into them when we went to see the burned-out trailer where Jimmy had lived. They threatened us then, but Luke stood them down. I'm sure they were dealing meth with Jimmy's dad before he got killed in the fire."

"God, I hope they don't know where you're from." He sat back down hard in the metal chair.

"The way I fought them, they'll know I found the money. They'll probably find us."

"Let them come. I'll be ready. It's Jimmy's money from his mother," John said, hitting his hand down hard on the old chair's arm.

"We need to get it somewhere safe."

"I've got a lawyer friend. He'll know how to get the money in banks, so it will be there for the boy."

"There's more, Dad. I'll be right back," she said, leaving and heading for the truck.

She returned carrying the backpack and the AR-15 rifle and its cartridge magazine.

"I took this from the guy who tried to rape me. I figured we might need it for protection if they ever find us."

"You took them down when they were armed with this?"

"Me, Tank, and Jimmy," she said, handing the rifle and magazine to her dad.

John checked the rifle's chamber and then pushed the loaded magazine into the weapon. He didn't chamber a round. He laid the rifle on the deck next to the side of his chair.

"The money is in here?" he asked and reached pulling the backpack to him.

"Don't open it. We need rubber gloves to handle the bills. They could be contaminated with meth."

"My lawyer has had meth cases to defend. He probably got paid with some of the same hot bills. He'll know what has to be done." He pushed the backpack away on the deck.

"Don't do anything until I talk to Luke. Jimmy knows not to talk or tell anyone about the money."

"Again? Are you going to tell Luke about all this?"

"Yes, I am. I'm afraid this is going to end up hurting us all." Asking Luke to keep the whole incident secret galled her. She would need him to face a situation he had been trained to expose. This is something she didn't want to put on the man she loved, but she had to tell him what happened.

She got up from the faded white metal chair and stood for a moment, looking at the rapidly surging waters streaming down below. Now she was afraid her life had been moving at the same pace as the sometimes out of control and flooding river. She had to find Luke.

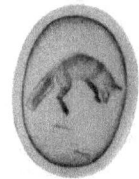

SEVEN

LUKE MUST HAVE HEARD THE concern in her voice on the phone. He had come off the river in Cotter to meet her at the park near the trout dock. She drove down the steep hill to the park where she saw him waiting. It was so much like the man she knew. He sat on top of a picnic table, his feet resting on the board seat. His green uniform stood out with the button over bulletproof vest with lined pockets for work materials covering his chest. There on his left side was his gold badge. She carried hers against her chest. She realized Luke needed the full truth from her.

She rushed to him. He would know for certain something bad had happened when her tears came and her grip around his waist got even tighter. He held her honestly without asking prying questions. Minutes went by before she loosened her grip on one of the most stable things in her life. Finally, she let go and they both turned and sat down on the table's bench seat. The table tilted, like the rest of the day. Of course, it would. They both stood and then sat on the table's top. She leaned forward with her face covered by her hands.

"I took Jimmy back to the trailer site where he had lived, and we were followed."

"Followed by who?"

"I stopped for gas at the station with the trailers behind it. The man you and I confronted at the burned-out trailer months ago pumped our gas. He recognized Jimmy and must have followed us with the second man we had seen." Telling Luke what happened got harder with each statement. She explained getting caught in the spring hollow by the two men. Luke got up from his table seat and turned his back.

As he spoke, he turned back to face her quickly. "Why in the hell did you go there without me? The whole area is just a stomping ground for getting drugs. Crap!"

The thought of not going on and telling him more echoed in her mind. Luke had already gone up in flames like a stray spark in a kindling box would cause. She didn't answer his question.

"Please sit down, Luke." She wanted the comfort and understanding she knew Luke would be capable of being right next to her before she told him more about what went on. Luke sat back down, only this time he sat close to her. His arm gently resting along her shoulders.

"I'm sorry. You're trained as well as I am. What I said was stupid."

"Maybe not so stupid." He had just given her the opening she needed to continue with her horrors.

"The armed men came at our truck. I got out and took a stance to fire at them. Their AR-15 was pointed at the truck with Jimmy in it. I dropped my pistol. It was a fucking mistake. I should have fired on him and killed the bastard before he had a chance to shoot at the truck.

"I don't think so," Luke said, pulling her closer.

"I'm not finished, Luke. The one with the AR came at me and knocked me off my feet with the rifle's butt. It knocked me out for a few seconds, and I must have fallen on my back. Next thing I knew my pants were stripped off. The other man was behind my head and had my hands pinned to the ground."

"Those bastards are going to die slowly for this," Luke said, he had just put both of his hands over his face. She knew he ached for her and what had happened.

"Jimmy jumped out of the truck and fired a shot at them, and I broke loose before they could rape me."

He didn't say anything and wrapped both his arms around her and pulled her tight. Some hardness in her psyche from the military and Iraq prevented her from a total breakdown there in the safety of Luke's arms. She needed and wanted to go on telling him what had happened.

"Have you called the sheriff?"

She needed to finish telling him. Not telling him about the money would not be an option.

"The men were after money Jimmy's mother had buried on the hill by a spring. A hell of a lot of money, Luke. We dug it up, and now John has it at the cabin."

"I'm not sure where to even start with this. Again, did you call the local sheriff?"

She shook her head no. "Jimmy had shot at the man at my feet."

"He didn't hit him, did he? I would have shot the bastard too."

"No, he didn't hit him. Tank attacked the other man holding me and tore up his arm pretty bad. By this time, I had my Glock back and was ready to fire. They backed off quickly." She didn't tell him about firing the warning shots at the man. It had been a weak moment she didn't want to own up to.

"There have been no reports of anything happening." He checked his phone for messages. "Nothing."

"What should I do?" She looked at Luke, certain she knew what the engrained lawman he had become would say. She wouldn't argue with him when he said the money would have to be turned over to law enforcement.

"You want Jimmy to have his mother's money, right?" Luke asked.

This wasn't the argument she expected at all. "Isn't it drug money?"

"It's not drug money because it wasn't seized in a raid or arrest. Likely, Jimmy can keep it."

"Oh, God," Sara said. She was back in his arms. "I want what happened to just go away."

"This was awful for you and Jimmy. I'm so sorry. We'll both need to talk to him to be sure he's okay."

"Can you radio for the sheriff? Wait! I can't explain why I didn't call from the burned-out cabin."

"Were you afraid the men would be following you?"

"Yes, or someone else from the compound behind the filling station where we had stopped earlier for gas." Looking in the rearview mirrors of the truck for the drive home had been enough to convince her for now she hadn't been followed.

"Should I call?" Luke asked.

"Call. I need to go back to the cabin and tell dad and Jimmy about this." She stood, looking at the man she loved and trusted for advice.

"Do you want me to drive you?" Luke asked.

"Just make the call. Tell them I'll be at the cabin."

What Luke had said still hadn't convinced her the money would be Jimmy's to keep.

***

Sara arrived at the cabin just as the sheriff pulled in. She put her head down on the steering wheel for a second to rally the strength to get out. The sheriff opened her truck door.

"Are you hurt, Sara?" This wasn't the first time she had met the man. He had helped in the search for someone taking pot shots at her on the White River during her dispute with the male guides. The men had been mad at her for taking a lot of their guide business. Her quiet seconds before she got out of the truck gave her a moment to prepare for what she would say to the sheriff.

"If getting hit in the head with the butt of an AR-15 and being held on the ground counts, I'm hurt," she said. Leaning over to show him the bump that had risen on the side of her head. She left out the part about Jimmy trying to shoot the man with his 22-caliber rifle.

"Come on, let's sit in my car and I'll get some photos and take some notes."

After she told the sheriff about the attempted rape, he photographed her head and the torn zipper and ripped buttonholes on her pants. She left out a lot of the details of the attack, including Jimmy's shooting and her firing warning shots at the man at her feet. Not a lot had been mentioned about the money she and Jimmy had dug up. Sara told the sheriff Jimmy's mother had hidden all the money his dad had made working. She couldn't be sure where he was going with his questions about the money. Finally, the sheriff passed it off as the money belonged to the boy since his parents were both dead.

"When they are caught, the men are going to have a lot of questions to answer. It's a different county, so I'll get this information to the sheriff there," he said. "We never get a lot of cooperation from over that way."

As the sheriff pulled out of the cabin driveway. John, Jimmy, and Sara stood in the yard watching him drive off.

"What happens now?" John asked, walking to her truck and opening the tailgate to sit down. She slid up beside him. Jimmy tossed a ball for Tank, but he had to go get it himself. Tank didn't move from under the tailgate. She knew the old dog had a tough workout hanging on to the man's arm. The dog would lay stretched out on his side in the open wire cage in her bedroom without making a sound tonight. She remembered her dad had asked a question.

"I guess we will have to wait and see."

She slipped off the truck tailgate. "I need to call Luke, dad."

She went around the cabin where she could hear the sounds of the rushing river and carried a rusty white chair off the porch and put it down in a spot in the yard where she could see the clear rushing river waters. Luke answered her call on the second ring.

"Hey, Lawman. What do I do now?"

"I talked to the sheriff after he left your place. He's passing the information over to the sheriff in Newton County. I don't think there's enough to arrest the men for the assault unless Jimmy testifies."

"I don't want what happened brought up in any court."

"You're right. It would only raise questions about Jimmy's money."

"Can you come hold me?"

"Do you hear the boat coming down river? In a couple minutes, my love."

EIGHT

WITH STILL A WEEK OFF before she had to report for her DEA training, Sara made it a point to get to know the boy her dad called his son. Jimmy lived on the river in her dad's boat when John didn't need it. She knew Jimmy needed to talk when he invited her to join him on a short river trip.

Jimmy sat at the helm, with her sitting on the front board seat of her dad's jon boat. The Little Minnow name her dad had given the boat was still there, carved into the top of the board seat. The letters had been worn thin from the dozens of anglers who had walked across them, getting into the boat to fish with either John or her. The million splashes of the White River's waters across the seat had faded, the blue paint filling the letters. Now the letters were all gray.

The rising and falling of the river never ceased, as the Corp of Engineers adjusted the water flow to maintain the lakes upstream from the dams. The river could still mimic her emotions, often overflowing to flood all those daring to live and work on the lower banks. And yet there would be days when all the valleys would be met with an even tide of flow. In the banks, the clear water flowed, kissing the edges of the cut channel where man had wanted it to remain. Sara did her best to stay in her own banks of life. More than anything, she wanted to know the boy sitting at the helm of the jon boat and piloting it upriver.

To be honest, Jimmy now knew the river better than she ever did. Her dad had spent many river trips teaching him where trophy fish hid and to take his losses when a line broke or the fish jumped high in the air and shed the bait. More than fishing, she saw coming from the boy, a young man she and her dad could feel proud of. His willingness to storm out of the truck, shooting to protect her, showed a bravery she wanted to talk with him about.

Jimmy slowed the jon boat and turned into a creek flowing into the river from the west. It surprised her she had never investigated this creek entering the White River before.

White-barked sycamore and maple trees lined the banks. Some leaned out and created a tunnel over the water. Each budding tree showed the signs of the warm day and the coming springtime. Going into the small creek changed the rushing tumbling wide world of the big river they had just left. She hoped Jimmy would pull up. The low bank areas to their right would be a prime place to find her favorite type of mushrooms.

"Where are we headed, Captain Jimmy?"

"Just a little further." He shut the engine down and tilted its prop out of the water to let the jon boat coast.

"It's getting shallow now, and the beaver dam is just ahead. Dad doesn't like it when I ding a prop on the rocky bottom," Jimmy said, reaching for a paddle and handing one to Sara. "We need to bank her over there."

He had pointed to a small, sandy beach and dipped the paddle, giving the boat a pull in the right direction. Sara joined him in the fun work until the front of the boat slid up on the sand.

"I found this little cave just up the bank, in the cliff. It's a place I like to go to get away from the other boats on the river out there. Besides, if we're quiet, we might get to see the beavers building on their dam."

It pleased her Jimmy had a quiet spot. Often, she had wanted a spot like this, to be off by herself. "I'm glad you're going to share your getaway place with me," she said.

The beaver dam he talked about lay just ahead. In spite of being on many Arkansas streams she had never seen a dam so large. The beavers had built their very own Hoover Dam across the creek. She could see the dam held back a good-sized pond. It reached out of sight in the trees on up the stream.

"Jimmy, that's the biggest beaver dam I've ever seen. How did you know it was here?"

"John told me about it. He said the beavers have been building dams in this stream for years. The trappers caught them all out a few years back. Somehow, they've come back now."

A loud splash just across the dam, in the pond, sent a shower of water into the air.

"That beaver is upset we're here," he said.

"That was one big fellow. I saw his tail and back just before he took that dive. They're fun to watch."

When both of them got out of the boat, Jimmy led the way up the steep path to the front of a cave entrance. She leaned over and took a couple steps under the cave's front. It surprised her there wasn't a lot of graffiti splashed along the cave's side walls.

"This cave is really hidden back in these woods," she said. She picked out a place to sit on the rock floor at the front of the cave. Jimmy found a place just across from her.

"Coming by boat up this creek is the only way to get here. The land all around is covered with 'no trespassing' signs," he said.

"Are you sure it's all right for us to be here?"

"John takes the landowner fishing for free. They're friends. The man gave us permission to come watch the beaver and see his cave any time we want."

Both of them sat quietly for more than a few minutes. Another beaver swam across the pond, carrying a freshly cut branch. When it got near the three-foot-tall mound of woven limbs, it pushed the stick under and dove following it.

"I'd bet she's got babies in that hut," Jimmy said.

"I don't know. It's still a little early in the year for them to have kits."

Getting to know Jimmy came hard for her. For her really to get to the heart of what a young boy thought about didn't come from any of her life experiences. Still, she stepped up to what she did know. Bringing her here to this place had to mean something was bothering him.

"Are you worried about something, Jimmy? Is that why you brought me to your secret hideaway?"

"It's about Dad. He has changed so much. He sits in his chair, just looking out the window. It's like he doesn't feel good. I have to beg him to go with me fishing."

"I've been away so much. I didn't know," Sara said.

"Look, there's the big beaver we saw dive. He's dragging half a tree."

He had been so quick to change the subject. It could mean he's very worried about John and doesn't want to talk anymore about it. She needed to find out if there was more to John's health issues she didn't know.

"Has my dad been sick?"

"He tells me he's going to visit a friend, but I think he goes to see a doctor."

"I promise I'll try to be around more. I'll have more talks with him."

Being around more may not fit with her new life as a wildlife and drug agent. She regretted making the promise.

"Can I go to work with you sometime?"

"Not for a while. I'll be working with other people, and I wouldn't be able to take you."

She knew Jimmy was dancing around a subject he really wanted to get out. She needed to help him with it.

"What happened to us after we found your mother's money was terrible."

"Shooting at those men hurting you made me feel good. I wanted to kill them."

"I'm glad you didn't kill them, Jimmy. Killing the man would have left memories that a person, you, can't forget, ever. I wouldn't want that hanging on your shoulders. I'm glad you missed hitting him. In spite of missing, though, you saved me from those two men."

"I'm not stupid. I know what the men were trying to do to you. Weren't you afraid of them? Why didn't you kill them after getting your pistol?"

"I was scared as hell and helpless until I got loose. I put a .44 caliber pistol shot on each side of that man at my feet. The fear in his eyes and on his face was my punishment for him."

"They know about the money. I heard them say it. They ain't stopping till they get it. My mom knew both them, and she said they were bad men."

"I'll have to face them when that happens. I would have shot him if he still had a weapon. Maybe I let him off too easy."

"I would have killed the bastard," Jimmy said, brushing his hair back off his forehead in a defiant gesture. "I'm afraid they'll come back."

"They could come back, you're right. The sheriff and his men will watch for them, and Dad is no pushover when it comes to a fight." She hoped what she had just said about John would be true and provide safety for both her dad and Jimmy. The men had others that could help them find where her dad's cabin was, and then they would come armed and fighting for the money and revenge on her. It would come sooner rather than later.

"My dreams about our burning trailer come back. I see my mother running toward me. She always has fire burning her clothes. Why does that have to happen to me?"

"I don't know for sure. I feel things we try hardest to get out of our memories somehow have a way of pushing their way back in."

He stood staring at the beaver dam and kicking at some of the loose rock on the front of the cave. He didn't say anything more about the fire. It wasn't hard to tell he had reached his limit on talking about his own PTSD. He turned away and started down the hill toward the boat. Sara made a mental note Jimmy may still need to speak to a professional.

"You comin'? I'm getting hungry."

The boat ride back to the cabin went quickly. Jimmy ran the motor at full speed and did a couple tight turns tilting the old jon boat to its limit. When the boat came around, the bow would splash into the cold river water, sending it into the air and into her eyes and mouth. She knew he did the turns on purpose to cheer her up, and it worked. It got her laughing.

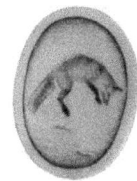

NINE

SHE HAD GIVEN THE FARM store's clothing section a complete search for a pair of jeans that would fit her. With two pairs wrapped and paid for, she started out the door to her truck. The screen on her phone suddenly turned white, and a flashing button with her father's name appeared. It surprised her he would call. She had told him she was on the way to the cabin.

"Hello, Dad," she said, letting a little bit of *'why are you calling?'* stray into her voice.

She heard his hard breathing first. "Dad, are you all right?"

"Just listen. I'm out of breath. Jimmy's gone and the cabin is wrecked."

"What?" She started for her truck, holding the phone to her ear. "Go on. What's happened?" Slamming the truck's door, she started the engine and spun a half loop in the gravel parking lot.

"I was at Marty's, helping her with a bad stall door, when I got terrible news. His grandmother was murdered."

"Murdered?"

Her foot got even heavier on the accelerator of the truck. The dark shape of something in her lane got bigger in front of her. She braked to thirty in time to see the wagon of hay bales taller than a semi-truck in her way. The yellow line on her side of the road pissed her off and she buried her foot into the floor. The truck surged toward the left side of the hay wagon. The front of her truck was over the yellow 'no passing' marking and out in the other lane when she had to brake, and brake hard. A dark colored car took the side of the road with its driver cussing at her.

"Shit!" she yelled into the phone. She moved in behind the wagon again. The wagon had almost slowed to a stop and traveled slow as hell.

"Are you listening to what I just said?" John asked.

"You said Jimmy is gone?"

"Yes, and his grandmother has been murdered."

"Murdered?" She accelerated around the tractor and wagon, yelling, "Get the hell over!"

"Fuck—" She didn't hear the rest from the kid on the tractor. Her mind raced like the engine of her truck. An old woman, murdered. Why? Then she knew. Jimmy's grandmother knew where the boy and the money might be. "Crap, Dad. Has Jimmy been kidnapped?"

"The jon boat is gone, and the shepherd. Something else, the AR-15 is gone. I had it behind the fridge with the money in the hidden closet. The other guns and the money are still in there."

"Anything else? Come on, damn you. Faster!" she screamed at the truck.

"What?"

"Anything else?"

"Most everything in the cabin is tossed around. They must have looked everywhere. Except behind the old fridge. Jimmy must have seen them coming and got the rifle. He dumped the money in the closet and took the empty money bag."

"We've got to find Jimmy. He's trying to lure them away."

The speedometer swung past eighty like she didn't even see it. The big V-8 engine took the challenge of passing one hundred miles per hour as something it had always wanted to do. The turnoff to the cabin was just ahead. Time to lift her foot. She sat forward, vowing to keep the pickup centered on the narrow lane of the back roads she was now on. Braking, she turned into the cabin's driveway.

"Get in the yard. I'm here." She slid to a stop and jumped from the cab, letting the door swing.

John came out of the house wearing her Glock on his side.

"No, Dad. This one is on me. I brought it down on us, letting Jimmy dig up the thirty grand. These fools after the money are a bunch of meth heads. If they killed his grandmother, they'll kill us for the money. Give me the pistol. I lived with a pistol on my side for years, and I've killed with it. Give it to me." She took the belt and holster from her dad and put it on, then yanked the cabin door open to go in. "I've got to think."

"I'm calling the sheriff," he said, starting to punch in the number.

"Wait. Don't bring up the money. Tell them the cabin was ransacked and the boy is missing. Have them watch for a 2000 or older black pickup truck that will have a couple meth heads in it."

"The men you told me about?"

"Tell him they came after us for revenge."

She listened as John followed her instructions and passed along the information; she wanted the sheriff to know.

"We need another boat. Why would he take the AR? He doesn't know how to shoot it. Why?"

"Because I taught him how."

"You what? A fucking assault rifle in a kid's hands?" Wanting to kick her father's ass had never been a thing with Sara. Right now, it came close.

"We did some target practice. I wanted him to be able to handle a rifle."

"An AR-15? He has a twenty-two rifle, like the one Mom got me."

"I kind of wanted to get the feel of the thing again myself," he said, backing away from her temper.

She stepped back from her dad and flicked her cellphone open. Without thinking, she punched the single button to call Luke. He answered quickly. The whole money thing had gone to hell around them, and regrets were not going to stop what had now happened with Jimmy's grandmother. Finding the boy and ending this with the Oxfords needed to happen and soon.

"Luke, I'm in trouble and need help. Where are you?"

"In Cotter. What's wrong?"

"We need a boat and a couple rifles at the cabin. On the water. Jimmy is gone with the AR in the jon boat. I think there are some people we know about chasing him."

"Can you give me thirty minutes?"

"Just you, Luke. Not your partner or friend. I'm serious."

"Just me, then." He hung up.

She called him back. "Could you get Reid for later? Have him wait for us at the Cotter dock. Tell him to be armed. We can use his help." They both hung up.

She was certain Jimmy would run to someplace he knew. The cave on the mountainside where she had found him, snake bit, was her first place to look. She packed a box of nine mm cartridges, unsure just what the boat ride would bring. She wanted to be ready. At his thirty-minute mark, she heard the boat round the steep bend in the river and glide the last few yards into an empty dock slip.

Luke caught the side of the slip. "I didn't bring the commission's boat. It sounded more like this unmarked boat I've been using might be just the thing." He carried a sidearm, and three ARs were stashed alongside the boat's rail. There was no sign of any of his commission gear anywhere; he was dressed in hunter's camouflage.

"You have just what we need," she said. Then she turned to her dad.

"When the sheriff comes, tell them no more than we talked about."

"All right."

"Ready?" Luke asked, his hand on the reverse for the engine.

She jumped in the boat and went to him. "Thank you for this." She gave him a tight squeeze on his arm.

"You need to tell me what's going on."

"Shove off and head for the Buffalo River. We're going about five miles upstream on it. I'll tell you on the way."

With the boat running at its full speed Luke asked again.

"I'm sure the men that cornered me when we dug up the money found out where we lived. They came to kidnap Jimmy and try to find the money."

"They kidnapped Jimmy?"

"I don't think so. He ran in the jon boat, armed with our AR-15, while they were breaking into the cabin."

"He's one brave ass kid."

"It's sad, Luke. I think they killed Jimmy's grandmother when she wouldn't tell them where to find Jimmy."

"They must be desperate to get the money. Chasing a kid! Damn. Are you sure about Jimmy's grandmother?"

"On the news, Dad heard she had been killed."

"God. I wish I would have been with you when you took Jimmy back to the trailer site. We have been having eyes on the meth operations and those two Oxford brothers are a part of it."

"I didn't know you were directly working meth."

"Yes, I've been helping the DEA with it." He slipped one of the rifles out of its mount and handed it to Sara.

"Jimmy is out there. I think he ran on the river. If they saw him, he's being chased. He knows how to shoot the rifle, so I think he'll hole up back where I found him on the side of the mountain. He could keep them from climbing up to the cave."

"Jimmy shooting an AR to hold them off?"

"What else is new in today's world? I just hope he doesn't kill anyone. I don't want him to ever suffer from doing that, like I had to do." She turned away from looking at him. The wind from the rushing boat ride brushed her face and flushed away the tears she didn't want Luke to see.

"Jesus, Sara. Iraq?"

She didn't answer quickly. The rifle like she had carried in Iraq was back in her hands again. "Yes. I shot a man we surprised while he was planting a bomb on a roadway. I still see him grab his chest and fall." She touched the memory on the side of her face. Touching the scar helped her to realize the Iraqi she had killed needed to die.

"That would be a hell of a terrible memory."

Slowing the boat, Luke made the turn into the Buffalo River channel.

"Listen. I heard a *pop, pop*. It's the AR firing single shots," Luke said.

She pushed the safety on her rifle off. Rounding a long curve in the river, Luke slowed the boat and cut the engine. He dropped an electric motor's shaft into the water and turned it on full. The boat lunged ahead, making little or no sound.

"We use these motors in night approaches."

She didn't ask about the approaches. She was too busy watching the shoreline. There, a hundred yards away, she saw a metal V-bottom boat beached with no one around. Luke had a pair of high-power binoculars scanning the side of the mountain.

"There's a cave about three-quarters of the way up there.

That's where I found him snake bit."

Again, and louder, she heard the pop of the AR and then a short burst.

"I see him. He's on the top edge, just above the cave. He's firing into the woods down below him."

"Where are the men?"

"I think the kid's got them pinned down about halfway up to the cave," he said, putting down the field glasses and lifting one of the ARs. "Those men will have us like sitting ducks out here when we start shooting."

"We need to get upstream from them. They're so busy they might not notice us go by if we look like we're fishing. We can flush them out then and run them back toward Cotter."

Luke steered the boat away from the bank and put the trolling motor on full.

"Start the engine. We'll put on a show going by. Sit down." He lifted the trolling motor and started the engine. She dropped a hood over her head and opened her jacket to go lean against Luke with an arm around him. He eased the engine into full as they passed the V-bottom boat, and her jon boat pulled up on the bank. They went out of sight around the bend before killing the engine and started drifting back toward the jon boat.

"We must have fooled them." He dropped down the trolling motor again and turned it on full.

"Maybe. Using meth screws with their thinking."

"Ready?" he said, chambering a round in one of the rifles.

"Yes. Shoot to run them out," she said, working the familiar action of the rifle and lifting the scope to her eye, "Just a little closer." A bullet smashed into the water next to their boat.

"Close enough?" Luke asked, raking the side of the mountain above the men. She followed his lead and emptied her magazine. Luke tossed another to her. Another shot whistled between them.

"That was close. Lucky for us they're using pistols, not ARs," he said.

"Look, they're running. Let them get in the boat and we'll light up the water around them. I just hope Jimmy doesn't kill one of them."

Three men, two of them she thought she recognized, jumped into the boat, and hit the floor.

"He's the one I shot at. The thin one," she said, looking through the scope at the fleeing boat. "Here you go, asshole," she said, filling the water on both sides of the boat with ricocheting lead.

Luke had his rifle up to fire. "It would be so easy right now to end this, Sara."

"Do you want to have to explain killing them? I damn sure don't, Luke Matthews. Let's find our boy."

She saw him first. He scaled the rockfall halfway down and slid on past the turnoff to the cave. She worried about the way he carried the war weapon and was uncertain if John had taught him to put it on safety. He stopped and stood with the rifle over his head to shout, "We ran them bastards off, didn't we?"

She took a deep breath and Iraq came again. The U.S. soldier she saw stood in the sod doorway with his rifle raised over his head. The powder smell floating in the air burnt her nose, and she raised her rifle to protect the man's approach. The man's head tore open, and his face was gone. She had made a mistake and missed seeing the Iraqi sniper on the top of the building. She took aim to shoot and kill the sniper but now saw only the woods and the mountainside behind Jimmy. She shook in horror.

"Sara! It's the boy. Lower your rifle, Sara," Luke said. His voice showed his uncertainness about what just happened.

"Come on, Jimmy," he shouted, "it's all right now. We're going to find those bastards again." He had pulled to the bank to pick up the boy. "Jimmy, is the rifle on safe?"

"Yes. John taught me good," he said, handing the rifle to Luke with the barrel pointed at the floor. "You can check." Luke looked and then lowered the rifle into a holder in the boat. He kept his rifle slung on his side. "Tie the jon boat on back, Jimmy. We need to head back to the cabin."

"If they stop, there's going to be hell to pay," she said, dropping to the front seat of the boat and holding on to her weapon. "Come here, Jimmy. I really need one of your big hugs."

He came to her side. "Me too, Aunt Sara."

Sara concentrated on the river in front of Luke's boat. She knew of a couple branch streams where the men they were chasing could enter and ambush them as they passed. She pointed each out to Luke and both of them kept AR-15s pointed as they passed the streams. Nearing the cabin, she knew the men had fled and would leave the stream somewhere ahead. When Luke pulled into the cabin's dock, they found John headed down the steps from the cabin.

"They passed going like hell up the river," he said, stopping at the front of the slip to grab the boat. Sara noticed the revolver stuck in his belt.

"Did you get that old pistol fixed?"

"Hell no. Your mom filed that firing pin off. It'll stay that way long as I have it. Good thing she did, isn't it?"

"In more ways than one," she said. Her mom's actions had saved both of their lives.

John slapped the side of his pistol. "This is a new one."

She hugged Jimmy again. He had enough and pulled away. She had something to tell him. Jimmy would have to be told about his grandmother's death. She needed to talk with John about how to tell the boy the last of his family was gone.

She went to Luke and lingered a long moment in his arms. Drawing the man, she loved into the fight over the money frightened her. It needed to be only her fight. She had dug up the damn money, after all. The kiss he had started didn't last long. His radio boomed with a call for him to come join a meeting.

"You will want to be with us if what I'm being called about goes off tonight."

Sara didn't need to ask. She had suspected a raid would be coming on the trailer compound.

"Come armed when I call," Luke said, kissing her again and getting into the boat to leave.

She stood watching him until the boat was out of sight around a bend.

Back up the riverbank at the cabin, she called for Jimmy and her dad to join her in the rusty white metal chairs on the cabin's deck. Jimmy and his blue tick hound came running around the cabin's side. Her dad and her war-ravaged German shepherd came out of the cabin much more slowly. Sara and Jimmy both were quick to rise from the chairs, offering John a place to sit.

"No, stay there, you two," he said, and took a place to sit on the edge of the deck. Tank laid down alongside Sara's chair.

"I ain't done nothing wrong, have I?" Jimmy asked.

"No son, you haven't," John said, "Come and sit by me here." He patted the deck for the boy.

Sara took the hint too and sat down next to Jimmy. She could tell Jimmy knew something must be coming. He kept standing and reaching for a stick he tossed for Blue to fetch. She was ready to tell Jimmy the news about his grandmother, but John beat her to it.

"Jimmy, I'm sorry we haven't been better about taking you to see your grandmother."

What he said didn't do much to stop Jimmy from getting up and playing with Blue.

"I have some bad news about her," John said, "Can you sit down, please?"

"Has my grandmother gotten sicker?"

Sara put her arm over the boy's shoulder before she spoke. "I'm so sorry, Jimmy. Your grandmother has passed away."

Jimmy slipped out from under her arm and stood. "Can I go now?" He left them with his hound following at his heels.

Sara wasn't sure how the boy would share his grief, or even if he would have any to share.

 Losing his mother and father in the horrible way they died cut a path through the need to grieve. It had happened to her after losing her Humvee crew and friends. Finding her way back to grief wasn't easy. She hoped it hadn't built a callousness in Jimmy that would be impenetrable by another family loss. Telling the boy what had really happened to his grandmother would have to come years later. Damn the Oxford brothers.

"Is he going to be all right, dad?"

"He's going down to the boat to sit with his dog. It's his way of grieving, I think. He's done that after coming back from therapy. He just sits there for hours. I hear him talking to Blue sometimes."

"Should I go sit with him?" she asked.

"I don't think so. He'll handle this in his own way, Sara."

She could feel the boy's loneliness and wanted to be able to comfort him. Deep down, though, she knew her dad was right in letting Jimmy handle his grief for now. She needed to change the subject and prepare.

"Where's the AR-15, Dad?"

"In the kitchen."

It took her only minutes to field strip the rifle and lay out all the parts across the kitchen counter. She used a rag with only a tiny bit of oil to wipe each part down and check it carefully. Satisfied, she assembled the weapon and worked the empty action twice. It pleased her, and she placed it and two loaded magazines in her bedroom under the edge of the bed, ready now for Luke's call.

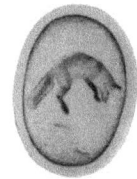

TEN

WITHOUT SO MUCH AS A hint to her dad about where she was going, Sara carried the rifle slung over her shoulder as she walked across the yard to her truck. She slid it off and chambered a cartridge and carefully lowered it onto the backseat with the safety on. After tightening her gun belt, she unstrapped the Glock, lifted the pistol slightly, then dropped it back into the holster. Convinced she was ready, she slid into the driver's seat. She would join the hunt Luke had called about earlier to find the men that had tried to kidnap Jimmy and had murdered his grandmother. She knew she could shoot them dead in their tracks and feel good about it. She sped through Cotter and turned into the parking lot of the farm store where Luke would be waiting.

She pulled up next to the green truck with the black commission letters on the side. Reid sat in the passenger seat.

"I thought we were going to keep this off-book," she said, leaning out of her truck window and pointing at the commission letters.

"I've got two warrants to go in and search the compound. So, it must be done this way," Luke said, holding the large envelope up for her to see. "We have the sheriffs and deputies from two counties joining in this take down."

"All right, but there's no way those men are going to slide out of this because of only a damn search warrant." Her hand tightened against the butt of the Glock and her finger brushed the trigger

69

guard. She had gotten hard about getting the Oxfords, and she knew it.

"Park and come on."

Sara recognized his sharp snap to command as a call to battle. She didn't move the truck from where it had stopped, only reached into the back and grabbed the rifle before getting out and slamming the door. She pointed the AR at the ground and checked to be certain the safety was on. Carrying the rifle, she opened the door and stepped up into the back seat of the commission's truck.

"I didn't expect to be getting into a commission vehicle carrying a weapon for a fight this soon."

"It's all part of our life now, Sara," Reid said.

Her personal battle with the men they now hunted had started when she and Jimmy had dug up the money. She was damn glad to be part of the fight to end the battle.

"Hello, Reid. This going to be old school for you two guys, working together?"

"Taking this bunch down without somebody getting killed is gonna be tough," Reid said.

She checked her watch as Luke sat and didn't start the truck. In only a few minutes, she asked, "Are we waiting for the sheriff's men?" She moved her rifle around, opening the chamber and closing it with her nervous energy.

"We are. It has to be a coordinated attack with both departments."

They had been sitting for more than an hour and her nerves were getting hard to contain.

She sat the rifle on the seat and got out. She used walking to her truck and opening the cab as her excuse to not tell them she had gone way over her edge for the fight ahead. She tried to slow her rapid breathing and the nervous energy shoving her toward what was ahead. She came back and stood outside Luke's truck, listening for his command to get in.

Luke turned on the cab light and checked his watch. "It's a little after midnight, so we're rolling," he said, starting the truck and pausing for her to get in. He pulled out of the lot and started the hour-long drive. Neither of the men spoke to her, and she remembered it had been the way her soldiers had acted when getting ready for a battle.

"The filling station and the compound is just ahead," Luke said, not slowing and driving on past.

Reid turned in his seat to look back at the trailers on the hillside. "They keep the area in front of the trailers well-lit."

"You've checked, now let's get back there," she said, checking the action on the AR-15. Luke pulled into a field turnoff and stopped.

"What's the time?" he asked.

"One-thirty. Come on, Luke. What the hell?"

She heard the wind whip off the cars with gold letters on them as they drove by with their lights off. Two ambulances were following and had pulled over and stopped well back from the compound.

"That's eight cop cars. We've got a damn army."

"We couldn't do this by ourselves, Sara. This is a hell of a mean bunch."

He backed out and followed where the sheriff's cars had turned into the compound. He pulled up alongside the row of cars.

"The sheriff's coming over," he said, rolling the window full down.

"Luke, we won't be needing your warrants. We have an arrest warrant for the two men for murder. You're welcome to join in. I'm sure this is going dirty on us. We already have two men stationed up on the hill behind the compound, so I think the men in the trailers are boxed in."

"Glad to help, sir," Luke said, reaching and shaking hands with the sheriff before he walked away. With the sheriff gone, he added, "Sara, you don't have to wade into this fight. Someone needs to watch our backs."

Sara pounded the back of Luke's seat. "No. Damn it. That son of a bitch in there tried to rape me."

"Yes, and you already had one chance to kill him," Luke said.

"You think I should have killed him instead!" It had just slipped out.

"I don't," Luke said.

The conversation ended too soon for her. The men left the truck carrying AR-15 rifles. She got out and joined them, standing with a group of deputies. The sheriff addressed them and his deputies.

"Those men and women in the trailers are about to get a hell of a wakeup call. Our main objective is to get the Oxfords, but just to be clear, shutting down this whole bunch will help end the meth distribution in several counties."

It seemed like minutes, but only seconds later, eight cars all turned on their flashing lights. Then she heard the bullhorn. "Attention in the trailers. This is the Crawford County Sheriff's Department, and we have a warrant for the arrest of George and Oscar Oxford for murder. Send them out and this will be over."

She knew what the sheriff said was a lie. They may get the two men for murder, but the deputies would never stop before searching all the trailers for meth trafficking evidence.

She couldn't keep standing still. She saw a front window in the compound shatter and saw flashes from rifles and pistols stuck over the windowsills pouring bullets into the wall of sheriff's cars. She rushed behind Luke, running around the back of the last trailer.

Bullets shattered the trees over their heads. She wanted to slump and cover her ears. Not this time. She had asked for this battle. She was aware her PTSD could kick in. She raised her rifle. Her burst of fire shattered a window. Luke stood beside her, firing at the trailers and the men running out the backs of them, trying to escape to the hills. Most fell within a few yards of the trailers. She heard women screaming for the shooting to stop.

"We got kids in here, you bastards!"

The pleading women's screams didn't matter. The firing from both sides got more intense. A white flag of surrender stuck through a half open door fell to the ground after a half dozen rounds cut the handle in half.

She heard men scream on the hill when they were hit. Screams like she had heard before in battle. Men cried for their mother, cried for a loved one, cried to a God they thought had let them down; she had heard it all. The shooting stopped and it got quiet for a few seconds. Then the crying out became moans of the wounded and dying. She frantically looked at the men around her, searching for Luke. He had just been standing and firing with them.

"Where are you? Luke!" she yelled.

Someone answered. "He's here!"

Two officers were leaning over him. She rushed to the officers and pushed them aside. "Give me room to see where he's hit," she yelled, falling on her hands and knees.

Her adrenaline-fueled mind saw the Iraqi desert sand push around her fingers as she leaned forward to help the soldier bleeding from the sniper's shot. It took her only a moment to see the circle of blood surrounding the back of his head in the grass now turned to sand. Small gushes still pulsed from the side of the soldier's neck. She shook her head, trying to shake away the thoughts of Iraq. Another soldier had fallen, and she had caused it. It was too late for the soldier, and for her.

Someone's hands pulled her back. She heard them say, "We're medics, Corporal. Let us have this."

She didn't shout, only gave a guttural, "It's an order, you save him."

One of the two medics pressed his hand against the bleeding wound in the soldier's neck. She shook in horror. The soldier on the ground was bleeding to death. The devastating realization of knowing the soldier hit her as the medics tried to stem the bleeding. It was Luke, and Sara knew he was gone before they stopped and turned toward her.

"We're sorry. There isn't anything—."

Her scream shattered the night and silenced the cries of men just learning of their own wounds from her ears. Struggling to her feet, she stood, looking down at the soldier lying just past her bloody hands. Pushing the medics aside, she dropped to Luke's side and started CPR, pushing in the rhythm she remembered from Iraq. Four arms grabbed her and pulled her back from his body.

"He's gone, miss."

She stood with her clothes covered in his blood. She wiped her hand across her mouth to clear her own slobber. His blood taste blistered her lips and shook her far past PTSD and Iraq. For a moment, she didn't realize she was insane. Insane with horror and guilt. She ran.

Reid stood beside the driver's door of Luke's truck. She ran up to him and shoved him hard.

"Get out of the way." Vaulting into the driver's seat, she slammed and locked the door.

"What the hell? Where is Luke?" Reid yelled against the

rolled-up window. He had his hand on the door handle, trying to open it and get to her. The still idling engine raced as she dropped the truck into reverse. The truck's engine screamed, and the wheels blasted gravel and dust into the air around the man trying to stop her.

He ran again to the truck and slammed his fist against the window. Holding the door handle, the truck drug him backward.

"Stop, Sara."

The truck moved forward. Gravel pelted him and then the truck thundered off the line of sheriff vehicles. She gained the blacktop and floored it. She didn't see the serene cattle pastures along the road, only adobe walls with open slots with RPGs and rifles ready to fire at her Humvee. She sped on into her darkness. The bullet hole in the front window whistled.

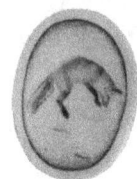

ELEVEN

THE FIRST HINT OF DAYLIGHT lit the sky in front of her as she blindly turned into the farm store parking lot and slumped out of the Commission's truck. She reached over the back of the seat and took her rifle. A search of the truck's compartments gave her the stockpile of ammunition and survival gear she wanted. With her arms full of all she could carry, she staggered through the fog of what had happened to find her own truck. There it sat, across the parking lot on the other side of the driveway, where she had left it. She crossed the drive and didn't stop for a truck pulling in and nearly hitting her. The truck waited for her and pulled up slowing alongside her. Her ears still echoed from the gunshots at the compound and the Iraqi battle going on in her mind.

She didn't hear the "Hello, are you all, right?" from the fishing guide she knew. Without even a nod, she went past him to her own truck. She dumped all her protection in the backseat.

She let the deaths of her Humvee crew in Iraq and now Luke flood her mind with guilt she couldn't handle. Running away had become the only way she could stop people around her from getting killed.

Not sure where she would go, she stopped in Cotter at an ATM and got all the money her credit card would give her for the day, then headed away.

She pulled into the parking area of a service station and pushed her dad's quick dial number into her phone. She heard it ring several times and then go to voicemail.

"Don't try and find me. Death has followed me. I love you both very much." She turned off the cellphone and tossed it into the truck's side pocket. In her mind, she could only reason Luke had been at the compound because of her. Her regret for going back to Jimmy's burned-out trailer and finding the buried money made Luke's death even more cutting to her now depleted self-esteem. She had caused too many to die.

Driving south had become an almost automatic thing since starting training at Morris. The realization the town of Mayflower was only ten miles ahead surprised her. She needed a last look. She made the short drive to the Morris Training Center. Turning off the blacktop, she stopped under the red metal semi-circle over the driveway. Since starting her training here, never had the idea of not working as an Arkansas game warden entered her mind. Now, losing Luke left no room in her mind for anything but running away from the officer's commission she had earned.

With her head pressed against the steering wheel, she wanted to cry. Somehow the battle hardening in Iraq had slowed her tears. Backing her truck out of the Morris gateway, she again turned south to just escape from the hell of it all. Even from herself.

South of Little Rock, she turned off the interstate onto state route 67. It slowed her pace and gave her a look at the small towns along the route. Three more hours of driving, and she knew a stop would have to happen and soon. A road sign told her Hope, Arkansas, was just ahead. A local family diner caught her bleary eyes, and she turned in. When she slid down out of the truck's seat to the blacktop driveway, both of her legs slumped, and she went down hard on her knees. She grabbed the door handle and pulled herself back up to standing. Facing the side of the truck, she leaned to rub both of knees. She straightened and then stretched her legs and back. She hadn't realized her stiffness from sitting so long. She pushed her head hard against the truck's bed and then gave her forehead two hard hits. It hurt; she wanted it too. Then a wipe of her hand across her forehead, checking for the wetness of blood. When she found none, she needed to go into the place quickly.

She went into the diner and followed the bathroom signs. The door wouldn't open, it was locked. She pounded twice.

"In a goddamn minute, bitch." The man's voice coming from a

women's john surprised her. She didn't wait, only tried the men's, and went in, locking the door behind her. She checked the pistol she carried and moved its holster around her waist, out of sight. Finished; the mirror in the bathroom captured the picture of a sad face torn by the loss of the man she loved. She staggered against the sink, then turned and started for the door.

A pounding on the door. "You're in our bathroom now, bitch."

It pushed her over an edge she had been on for hours now. She had fallen to the bottom level of her sanity. She pulled her holster around to her front and drew the pistol. Throwing open the door, she went into a double arm pistol aim straight at the man's face.

"This had better end now, mister, or one of us is going to be damn sorry."

The bearded middle-aged man backed away like he was about to be bit by a rattlesnake. She slammed the door, locking it and going to the mirror.

Staring into it, "Stop this now. You are not this crazy bitch." With both hands under the faucet, she lifted the water and flooded her face. She didn't realize her hands and face had still been covered with Luke's blood. A part of her knew she had let loose her crazed self in her grief for Luke. She had fallen over the edge. She had struggled to keep away from her PTSD, but it was now sweeping her sanity away.

Leaving the restroom, she didn't bother to check for the man. Caring if he was still there became the last thing on her spinning mind. She found a booth off to herself and pushed the menu away.

"Coffee, miss?" a waitress standing at the side of her table asked. Sara nodded yes. The waitress turned the cup on the table over and filled it with steaming black coffee.

"There. I bet that might get you out of the bad mood we all heard a minute ago. That trucker left without stopping to pay his bill."

"It's been one hell of a long night and day," Sara said, "Give his bill to me." She tested the cup with her fingers before lifting it to drink. The coffee had no smell. The gunpowder smell of nitroglycerin on her clothes from the trailer battle had burnt her nose too badly.

"Can I fix you right up with bacon and a couple eggs? It's on special for four ninety-five and comes with hash browns. Some protein will make you feel better."

She didn't say anything, only nodded a yes.

The window by her booth gave her a good view of the parking outside. The thought someone might be following her crept in. She tried to remember what the VA doctors had taught her about dealing with the onset of her PTSD. She couldn't put thoughts together. Only glimpses and flashes of their training came back. Her mind resisted taking her to the river and her dad's jon boat. Going there mentally had worked so many times before, but not now.

A pickup pulled in beside her truck and two men in their twenties got out. They got her close attention when they stopped briefly beside her truck. Certain that one of the men had looked in her truck's window, she started to get up to go outside. They left her truck and came into the diner to take a booth just behind her. She wrapped her arms around her waist and tightened them against the shakes she had coming on. The men were danger and she needed to fight them or leave this table. Leaving her coffee cup, she slid to the edge of her seat and started to get up. The waitress was at the men's table and pouring coffee. She must have needed to tell someone the damn news.

"Hell of a shootout up north. The TV had it on this morning."

What she heard caused her to stay put and pay attention.

"You boys heard about that mess? Officers were killed, I heard," the waitress went on, sitting the coffee pot on the men's table. "The sheriff's department went into a bunch of trailers after a couple meth dealers wanted for murder, and it all went to hell on them."

Sara blindly took a twenty from her billfold and dropped it on the table. Without a word, she staggered past the waitress and the men's table, leaving the diner and then going behind her truck. Hearing about it going to hell had brought back the moments of the real hell she had experienced going through it all. Leaning over, she held on to the top of the truck's tailgate with one hand and threw up what she had left in her gut. She twisted away and spun, slamming her fist hard against the truck. The pain meant nothing to her right now. After staring over into the truck's bed for more than a few minutes she looked back up the highway from where she had just come. She fought with herself not to go back. Still standing, she turned to the south, and a nearby sign on a rundown motel called Ruby's caught her eye. She needed the darkness of a room. The day and the horror of the night had stripped her of any physical or mental reserves she still had.

With a key to a room in her pocket, she left her truck parked where it had stopped alongside the office and went into room 115 with the AR-15 draped openly across her shoulder. The stink of stale smoke almost choked her. She didn't care. The stains on the top cover of the bed weren't even there. She dropped the rifle on the floor and fell facedown across the bed.

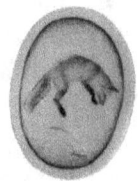

TWELVE

THE POUNDING ON THE DOOR dragged her out of nightmares and into a dark, stinking room with a light from the parking lot blazing bright under the half-drawn window shade. Sitting up in bed, still dressed in boots and all, she rubbed her eyes and tried to cut out the noise of someone yelling for her from outside the motel room's door.

"What is it you wa—?" she tried to get out, now standing. "I just got to sleep in here. Goddamn it." She slid her pistol into her side holster and slipped the AR-15 under the bed covers. Staggering, she went to stand at the edge of the door. She didn't open it.

"What is it?"

"Nobody saw you today. You need to pay for another day."

"What?" She tried to make sense of what the woman's voice had just said.

"You came in yesterday. Tonight costs more. Second day for you."

No way what she had just heard could be true.

"Isn't this Tuesday still?" Sara mumbled to the closed door.

"No. Wednesday night now."

It all sunk in but only a little. She needed to get rid of the woman at the door. She opened the door and handed the woman a hundred-dollar bill from her billfold.

"I'm sorry. Put this on my account. I'll come up later and settle with you."

The woman took the bill and didn't say anything. She shuffled off.

Sara stood in the open doorway looking in both directions. The lights were still on at the diner, and she felt weak and way beyond hunger. With a jacket on over her nine mm, she got into the truck and drove past the diner and a Mexican restaurant to stop at a small dive called The Hornet's Nest Bar and Grill. Not sure what she wanted more, a Jack Daniels or a cheeseburger, she took a seat at the bar. She started with the J.D. and ended up asking for a fourth when the bartender cut her off.

"Are you sure you wouldn't want some coffee or maybe a burger before leaving?" he asked.

"Just another drink," she said, and laid three twenties on the bar. The closeness of someone sliding onto a bar stool next to her didn't bother her. She hardly realized he was there. She didn't look up.

"Why don't you put those bills away, miss? This one will be on me," the middle-aged man said. He pushed the bills toward her. "Give her another of whatever she's having, and another Miller for me."

She smiled, looking down at the bar. "See, it's all right for me to have another."

"Mister, this lady is way past me serving her anything but coffee. She's got car keys sitting there and in no shape to drive."

"I'll see she gets safely home, Ted," the man said, tapping the bar with his hand.

"Will that be with the help of your wife, Nathan?"

She looked up at the man. "Ted, maybe you should do what the bartender said."

The man slid off the barstool and with a grumble under his voice walked away.

"He's Nathan. I'm Ted, your ever-watching bartender."

"Okay then. I've got to get ba—."

"To Ruby's? I saw the room key lying there."

"Oh, that's what the place is called?" she reached for the two keys on the bar. Ted grabbed them first.

"Jose, come out here. I want you to drive the lady home."

"Yes, sir. Where is home?" Jose asked, leaning out of the

kitchen area off to the side of the bar.

"Just down the street. She's going to have a coffee, and I want you to fix up two cheeseburgers for her to take with her."

"I'm on it, sir."

The side of Sara's head was on the bar. She slurred, "Coffeeee. Those burgers will never stay down."

"Jose, skip the burgers. Make a pot of new coffee. She's going to need it."

"Why are you being nice to me?"

"It's maybe because you sat there going through all those drinks without saying a word to me. Your problems must be deep. Most people drinking never shut up to me."

"I talked a lot to myself."

"I know. I heard a lot of what you were mumbling about. It wasn't pretty."

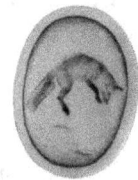

THIRTEEN

AFTER SHE PUT THE SIM card back into her phone, the screen filled with text messages from the commission about Luke's funeral. Her dad's last text message said she was wanted for taking Luke's truck and stealing some of the commission's property. Text messages were stacked deep on her cellphone. She only read a few of the other text messages from her dad. One from today got her attention.

Sara, I'm sure you want to know. Luke is being buried tomorrow at the Calico Rock property. Love you. Please, please contact us. Dad.

***

Sara drove through the open gate leading to Luke's family's land at the top of the Calico Rock bluff. She was certain arriving before dawn at the grounds where Luke would be buried today would give her time to hide away in the heavily wooded thicket to the west. She drove through thick brush on a rise and stopped with her truck hidden and facing the small cabin she and Luke had known so well. A blue open tent with chairs along the side sat out in front of it. She opened the case of a pair of high-power binoculars she had taken from Luke's Commission truck and used them to scan the tent area. Her scan stopped when she saw the ridge of fresh clay lying just under the tent. The meaning of it struck hard at her core. It was ready to cover him. Luke. Could he really be dead?

She reached under the truck's seat for one of the fifths of cheap whiskey she had brought. The short time he had been gone seemed like a jumble of sleep and a lot of whiskey at the bar. Drinking seemed to be all she could do to survive what had happened. She took a stiff drink from the bottle. It didn't gag or choke her. She had been getting too much whiskey practice for that. This bottle and then another would be empty shortly. Nothing phased her now, not even the whiskey, and lots of it. The binoculars slipped from her hand and slid to her waist. There would be time before Luke arrived.

***

Her head pressed against the side window. She awoke at the short blast of her truck's horn from her resting arm. Surrounded by darkness she rubbed her eyes, trying to make contact with the reality of what had just happened. Her watch clearly displayed ten-thirty p.m. Lifting Luke's binoculars, she slipped on the night vision and looked again at the cabin and tent. The tent and chairs were gone. Only a large hump of clay remained, stacked with flowers, in a nine-foot-long profile of the man she loved.

Staggering from the truck, she reached back under the seat for another whiskey bottle. After opening it and taking a long drink, she carried the bottle draped from her hand as she pushed through the brush. She gave little notice to the cuts and scratches the thicket of blackberry vines left on her bare arms and hands. Clear of the brush, she staggered across the pasture toward the grave.

The clay hump ahead frightened her. She passed it and then walked around it, measuring it with her eyes and thoughts. A thousand thoughts filled her mind, calling out *"No, he can't be gone!"* Yet for moments she felt him close, even there standing beside her—but then far, far away.

It troubled her no one had left a cross to mark his burial. She laid in two more deep drinks before turning and heading back to the truck. She didn't feel the recoil of the truck's door hitting her when she threw it wide open. Reaching into the truck, she took the AR-15 out of the hiding place under the seat and swung it sling over her shoulder. Going back through the brush and across the pasture, she stopped at the grave at what would be the head position of Luke's body. She stuck the barrel of the AR-15 deep into the loose clay to mark her hero's grave. This was not the first time she had left a memorial to honor the dead. She had helped to leave boots and a weapon graced on top by a steel helmet to honor her fellow servicemembers in Iraq.

The bodies of her Humvee crew were not buried there in the foreign soil. Far away from Iraq, they were taken off large airships at Dover airbase in the states. She paused, realizing she had never honored any of their graves with a visit. The thought deepened her grief.

Staggering alongside the clay ridge over his grave, she brushed the flowers off into the grass. She knew Luke would hate them. Pausing, she took off the scrimshaw fox necklace he had bought her. With no place to leave it safe, she went to the middle of the clay pile and dug with her hands. Deeper and deeper she went. Finally, kissing the fox for her lost love, she dropped it into the hole over him and covered it, pressing the clay tight against one of the treasures she knew they both had loved.

With her back leaning against the grave's clay bank, She tilted the liquor bottle high, sucking out the last drops of the mind-numbing liquid she needed so badly at this moment. The bottle fell from her hands.

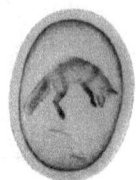

FOURTEEN

THE ROUGH CLAY BANK AND a long sleep left a deep impression on the side of Sara's shoulder. She sat up to rub it and wake up her numb arm and hand. A stiff wind blew in from the Calico Rock bottom lands and caused her to shiver from the chill. The cabin and the escape she and Luke had experienced there came flooding back. She could only look at the cabin, even though it seemed to cry out for her to go inside. She couldn't, not ever again. Their dream of building a home together near the cabin on the forty acres lay buried at her feet.

She stood and wrapped her arms tightly around her body, standing in the morning light watching the sun break above the trees to the east. Her pause was short; she forced herself to leave and head for the truck. Her walking took her closer and closer to the edge of the deep bluff rising from the White River. Stopping and standing on the brink of the rock ledge, she tried to see what would lie below in the path of someone going over. She moved an inch closer. Nothing, only blackness, lay below. Blackness and darkness came close to her only desire. She backed off the bluff's edge and headed for the truck at a stiff pace.

Starting the engine, she drove, shoving the brush cover down. She headed straight toward the cliff. As if certain of the next seconds, she floored the gas pedal and drove forward down the bank toward her end. Suddenly, in the morning's light, a bald eagle rose from the bluff trees in front of her.

Luke's voice came with it loud and clear. *"Stop, Sara! Stop!"*

The voice of her lost love startled her and took her breath away. She plunged her foot against the brake pedal. The truck slid to a stop. She sat with her head pressed against the steering wheel and her ears covered with her hands. Opening the door, she got out and stood, looking around for the man she knew she had heard. The tall grasses of the pasture whispered the sounds of, *"he's not here."* The clay pile on his grave glowed an eerie blue in the morning light. She knew Luke had saved her.

Leaving him alone, buried in the field in front of the cabin, came hard. She drove slowly and deliberately by the grave, past the cabin and through the property gate. Stopping just outside the fence, she got out and swung the gate closed. An open padlock and chain hung on the gate. She pulled the chain around the post and gate and closed the lock on all the memories she and Luke had on the bluff retreat. Leaning against the gate, she finally sobbed and cried a last goodbye to Luke.

The only place she knew to go lay miles south. She made the drive without any stops. Driving down the small strip of a downtown street, the two signs in the window of a dimly lit building caught the attention of her tired eyes. The larger of the signs hung at a slant in the window. The small 'open' sign got her to park the truck. The smell of the inks rushed around her as she went in the door of the tattoo parlor. It took her more than an hour to find just the right art for her left wrist. She fell asleep in the chair after selecting the artwork.

"I hated to wake you, sis. I'm finished."

It took her a few minutes to get her bearings. Then she didn't want to leave the comfort of the woman's tattoo parlor chair.

"You seemed so sad when you selected the fox tattoo for me to do, and then you fell asleep under my needle. Honey, I can tell you have had a lot on your mind, and it smells like you're trying to drink it all away. Let me fix us a pot of coffee before you climb back into the truck." The tattoo artist reached and picked something up off the floor. "This fell out of your jacket pocket while you were asleep."

Sara grabbed the gold badge from there in the artist's hand and rushed it into her pocket.

"You weren't supposed to see that. No one but me can see my

so-called badge of honor now."

"I have a feeling you earned the badge and what comes with it. You cried out in your sleep about burying the fox on top of the man you loved. Was it only a nightmare dream?"

Sara didn't feel ready for this talk with a stranger she didn't know. But then, why not?

"Were you serious about having some coffee?"

"Yes."

The coffee came, and Sara struggled to sit up in the lounge tattoo chair. The whirl of the electric motor pushing the chair back upright surprised her. Leaning back against it, she took the steaming cup of coffee from the artist. The exchange of names seemed inevitable. Sara liked knowing she had met Rebecca Conta.

Rebecca's tattoos seemed to be never-ending. They started at her fingertips and wound their way to her shoulder and on; far beyond where civil manners would allow seeing them. Sara glanced at each of her own wrists. There on the right wrist the little minnow and now the fox striking at its prey on her left. Maybe she was missing out for not having a lot more.

Rebecca must have picked up on Sara's thinking. After taking a short sip of her own coffee, she offered some to Sarah.

"You might not want to go there, honey. Each of these tattoos came with a lesson I didn't want to forget. Ain't none of them came free," Rebecca said, running her hand up her left arm and stopping after each climax of a scene depicted there. "I only see two gracing your arms, and it seems what they mean to you goes really damn deep in your soul. I'm not sure you have room in there for any more art."

What Rebecca said went way deeper than Sara could take. She broke into tears.

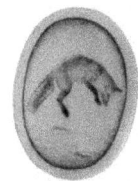

FIFTEEN

FOGGY, CLOUDY DAYS OF DRINKING turned into weeks. Her stool in front of Ted the bartender would soon be known as belonging to Sara. Offers of drugs from men drifting into the bar came often. Ted always seemed to be near when the offers came. On her worse days, she could fool Ted and take the men up on their offer. She gave little thought to the gold badge she now kept hidden under the mattress with the AR-15 in the motel room. Only a small memory of the meeting when the drug enforcement opportunity had been laid out remained with her.

Watching Ted take a lot of notes when the men offering drugs left seemed strange to Sara in her fog. Even curious. Too many days of staring at liquor bottles lined up on three shelves let her in on another curiosity. Clearly a camera lens sat mounted between the bottles. Just a little reflection off the lens glass gave it away. She wanted to ask him what she had gotten in the middle of. It could wait. Ted hadn't pried into her past, but he seemed to know more about her than she could understand. He spent more time offering her coffee than liquor. More time talking to her, trying to get to the heart of what had hurt her so badly.

"Why are you bothering to care about me?" she asked.

"I'm sure there are folks somewhere around that care a lot for you."

She didn't answer, only tapped the bar again for another drink. Ted dug into the glasses needing washing.

"You're trying to wean me, aren't you?"

"Just looks like you're sliding down a slope where there is no end in sight. Losing Luke has taken its toll on you, lady."

What he said about no end in sight got through. She held the remainder of her drink in her shaky hand looking at it wobbling. She had become a woman so unlike the self she tried to remember. She fought the feeling of, *'Oh, go ahead finish it. It's only one more drink'* and then she shoved it away, hard. The glass hit the raised edge of the bar and sailed past the man she knew was trying to save her.

"Fuck you and the goddamn drink, Ted."

She pushed back her stool—the one with her name stapled across the back on cardboard—and dropped her bare feet to the floor. It took her longer than a moment to slip the three-inch heels she had been wearing onto her feet. She bumped a man leaning to make a pool shot.

"You needing some company, lady?"

She only held up her middle finger and went on out the door. It was almost closing time for the bar, and she needed quiet and sleep.

She couldn't let what Ted had said about losing Luke rest. Running it around in the stupor of her mind didn't bring any answers as to how he knew about Luke. She hadn't talked to anyone about him, only a tattoo artist in her moment of completely letting go. She sat up in bed. There was still time before Ted left after cleaning up the bar. She didn't need to dress as usual, she only rarely got undressed to go to bed. Something from deep inside her pushed her to find out more about what Ted knew.

When she knocked on the bar's front door, it brought no one to let her in. She saw a shadow cross the window, but still Ted didn't come. Pulling her arms into the sweater she had on, she went around the building and stood just in the shadows, waiting for Ted to take the empty cans to the dumpster.

He came out, making a large rattle with two plastic bags filled with empty cans and bottles. She waited until he tossed them before saying anything.

"We need to talk about Luke," she said, stepping out under the single light bulb over the doorway's entrance.

"Jesus! Where the heck did you come from?"

She went aggressively to stand close, looking down at the man's face. Maybe a little too close.

"Back off, Sara. I'm not your enemy."

"I've never told you about Luke Matthews."

He didn't answer right away. She knew he had been caught off guard.

"Did you know him?"

"Yes. I knew him," he said.

"Why did it take a slip of your tongue for me to find this out?"

"Luke would come to the bar on occasion if he was working this area of the county."

"Did you work with Luke and the DEA?"

"What are you saying? Luke just came by for a drink now and then."

It was bullshit she heard coming from Ted. The high horse she came around the building riding had left her tired, worn out, and having a lot of trouble putting together where this was going. The hidden camera behind the bar and Ted always taking notes didn't add up to Luke just coming by for a drink. The other self she had lost would have gotten to the bottom of Ted's involvement with Luke. This one just needed another drink before she could get to sleep.

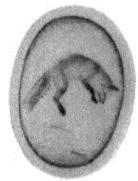

SIXTEEN

PUSHING THE BLANKET OFF HER head, she blinked at the dirty window curtains of the motel to see if the darkness she longed for had arrived. The days and nights had become upside down for Sara. Sleeping the day away in a drunken stupor from the night before became her norm. The dim sky of another day diminishing offered her the relief darkness would be there soon. Covering her eyes, she would wait for it. Spinning thoughts came at her, but rarely did she follow any of them. Just letting them in meant they would be followed by another that would hurt her even worse.

An hour later, she sat up on the edge of the bed. She lifted her arm, checking to see if she needed to force herself to get into the rust-stained tub for a shower. Likely the water would still be cold from a small tank somewhere that had been emptied of the hot water by other motel rooms. Her armpit smell repulsed her, and she turned her head away. She blindly pulled at the strands of armpit hair, trying to comb them down and keep them from showing if she went with a tank top.

She had slipped into the aloneness she preferred. Going out and looking for a male companion didn't fit any part of wanting to be alone. However, most days the liquor suppressed the urges Luke's love making had awakened in her. After Iraq, her sexuality had slept until Luke came into her life. Being a slave to an army commander had taken away her desire for sex. Coming so close to being raped made her wonder about her own sexuality ever becoming normal.

Nevertheless, she went to the motel room chair and picked up the black tank top. She held it in front of her to get a feel for what it would be like to go out wearing it. Buying it two days before in a Goodwill store had been on a whim. Wearing the sexy tank top would be her test to returning to a part of her life she had started to miss.

Her armpit smell had overpowered her dislike of the bathtub and shower. She stripped off the green commission-issued underwear and bra and went into the bathroom. Turning on the cold water became an awakening experience for the still-tipsy Sara. The motel's dirty water flow was followed by a surge and a belch, shaking the shower head and wall behind it. She waited a minute before checking the water. Finally, a warm feeling started around the fingers she held in the water. Then it got cold again. It had been her temper rising in her fingertips she had felt.

Taking a deep breath, she stepped into the cold-water shower. After a rub with a bar of soap in the places that counted, she tried to grab the soap as it slipped from her hand. Bending over for it in the cold water would not be an option, so she let the soap lay between her freezing feet. She turned in the shower twice to rinse the soap off, then stepped out, reaching for the towel. Her foot slipped on the wet linoleum floor, and she went down spread eagle on the edge of the bathtub. Grabbing for the rust-colored plastic shower curtain didn't help. Now the torn away curtain covered her shoulders. Her once dry hair was now getting a full bath from the still running shower as she sat, crumpled while half in the tub, half out. But, by God, for once in the last week she was really clean and awake.

***

The black tank top tucked her in tightly. The physical exercise of her past training program had left Sara a fit figure. It took the tank top to cause her to realize her waist looked more like an eighteen-year-old cheerleader's than a slumping drunken woman she had tried to be only yesterday. She patted her stomach and lifted her breasts to rest a little higher in the revealing top she had on. Maybe it had been the workouts with weights or sit ups that had brought out the chest on her. Going out in this top was going to get her in trouble. The kind of one night stand trouble she really needed tonight. Pulling on her only pair of blue jean shorts, she finished with her always present boots. After a quick brushing of her long black hair, she parted it and left half on each side of her face. She was ready to get out of her stinking rat's nest of a room for good. It took only one trip to her truck to clear out her clothes. She pulled out the box of food she kept under the bed. Often, she would eat something from the box to avoid going out in the daytime. Two mice jumped over the edge of the box when she picked it up. She dropped the box and shoved it back under the bed.

Still, she had no plan of where the day would take her. The first stop had to be at the bar to tell her bartender friend she was leaving. Her trip to the bar would be quick. She pulled up in front and went in. She had barely made it across the room before the hoots and whistles started. Only slightly embarrassed, she slid onto the bar stool still with her name papered across the back. She found Ted in front of her very quickly.

"That top is sure as hell going to attract some attention," he said.

"You like it? Yes?" Then it clicked. What Ted had said wasn't a compliment.

"I wanted you to know I'm leaving. Turned in my room key. So, I guess it's goodbye." She turned off the barstool and smiled at him.

"Wait. What the heck? We need to finish our talk."

"Why? Our talking wouldn't make a damn bit of difference to help me right now," she said, and immediately knew what she had said to him had been from a smart-ass side of her she didn't like. Still, she went on to leave the bar counter. She made it to her truck door before Ted caught up to her.

"I can tell by the outfit you're not going home to John and Jimmy, are you?"

"No. Just away from here. It's time. I've been in a hell of a deep hole, and I've got to start to climb out of it, Ted." She settled in the driver's seat and shut the door. Ted got close to the window she opened for him.

"Sara. Can we talk?"

She had other things in mind, like getting away from the

nearby dark, stinking motel room where she knew for sure her emotional bottom had been reached.

"You've been a friend," she said, giving his arm a tight grasp. "Goodbye." She pulled out of the driveway and left him with a final wave.

Her head seemed clear, yet the things she was thinking wouldn't quite make sense to a sane person. She wanted to find a quiet bar away from anyone she knew. Certainly, there would be someone to talk to in whispers and get promises of making love. She headed for Little Rock. Thirty minutes north of Hope, Arkansas, she slowed from her eighty-mile-an-hour driving when she passed a sheriff's car sitting in front of a deserted gas station.

She got only a hundred feet past when the sheriff's red lights flashed in her truck's mirror.

"Fuck, fuck, fuck." She pounded the truck's steering wheel rim and then turned to get off the highway. She bit off a good bit of the highway's grass side strip before skidding to a stop. The deputy sheriff pulled in tight behind her.

She leaned across the cab of the truck, opened the glove box, and got her license and registration papers out. She waited with them in her hand, ready for the officer to ask for them. Confused, she watched a state patrol car pull off the road and park directly in front of her. The trooper's car sat a few inches in front of her truck. She watched the officer lift a microphone.

"Randolph, step out of the truck."

"All this for a little over the speed limit?" she shouted out the window. She opened the door of the truck and stepped down. The sheriff's deputy had her hands before she knew she was even close. Spun against the side of the truck bed, she heard the click and then the pressure of handcuffs. They were way too tight and pinched her wrists. The stop had been a setup. Who?

Sitting in the deputies' car, she watched the two officers tossing the inside of her truck. The deputy returned, carrying the binoculars that had been issued to Luke. They took nothing else from her truck except the keys after they locked the doors and marked it for towing. The sheriff's deputy stashed the binoculars in the front seat of her car and offered her the whole back seat to herself. They had left her badge and about everything she owned remaining in her truck on the side of the damn highway.

The deputy got into the front seat and gave a wave off to the state trooper. Then she turned toward Sara and tossed her a jacket from her truck.

"I'll help you slip that over your shoulders if it gets cold back there. I run my air conditioning at full blast. The radios make it hot up here in the front. Something else I got for you." She tossed Sara's gold badge onto the back seat next to her.

"You might want to hold on to this as a souvenir, Randolph."

Sara watched her pick up the microphone and select another channel on the radio.

"This is Hempstead County Deputy Stagger. I have your subject on board. What now?"

The address coming back didn't mean anything to Sara. She only knew it was somewhere in Little Rock, and this deputy was going to take her there.

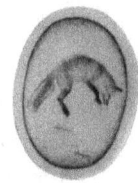

SEVENTEEN

THE BACKSEAT OF THE POLICE car smelled like the last place Sara would want her hands to be handcuffed and laying on. Memories of being told by Luke's friend Reid about what had gone on in his sheriff's car would have been enough to have her sit and try to arch her handcuffed arms away from the seat.

Being handcuffed behind her back became her first priority to change during what she knew would be a nearly two-hour drive to Little Rock. Fairly sure begging the deputy would be the last thing that would work, she resisted getting her arms down to slide them under her butt. It didn't matter, her butt stung like it had been stuck to the seat of the sheriff's cruiser for days. She didn't want to give up on getting some relief for her hands and arms. Maybe some psychology of need would work on the woman deputy.

"Officer Stagger, I really need a bathroom stop. Please?" Sara tried to lean forward to get some sympathy from the officer.

"You do know if we stop, I'm going into that bathroom with you, lady," Officer Stagger said.

"You tossed my badge back here. You do know I'm a sworn officer of the law, not a common criminal to be handcuffed behind my back for a two-hour ride?"

"For a sworn officer, there's a lot of people wanting you hauled in, lady."

She tried again for the bathroom ruse.

"Just ahead is a truck stop. You can take me in. I'm not going to run away," Sara said. She eased back into the seat, trying to keep the pressure down on her handcuffed arms.

The deputy turned into the truck stop and pulled up to park at the side of the double doors.

"All right, let's make this quick." She got out, opened the back door, and lent a hand getting Sara from sitting to standing.

"Turn around."

Unlocking the cuffs, she pulled Sara's arms in front and put them back on. She grabbed the jacket from the backseat and slipped it over Sara's shoulders.

"We're ready now." She motioned toward the doors.

Sara led the way past the hotdog carousel but didn't pause. She knew she could eat at least three of the overcooked ones.

In the large multi-stall bathroom, the deputy unlocked the cuffs and stood back against the line of sinks. Sara shut the stall door and stood for a second, rubbing her bruised wrists. Finished in the stall, she opened the door to go to the sink. The click of a cuff on her wrist happened before she got fully out the door. She didn't like being a prisoner, but there it was.

The deputy carried two drinks and two hotdogs. Sara didn't say a word to try to get one. It must have been a normal stop for the deputy. Several clerks knew her.

Settled back in the car, this time with her hands cuffed in front of her to drink and eat a hotdog. Then the conversation got personal.

"You lost the man you loved in the meth trailer raid."

Sara didn't answer. She was sorry it had been brought up.

"Honey, I've been there too. My husband got killed while he was serving in Iraq. But you probably don't know much about that kind of service."

"You mean the kind of service with RPGs coming at you from the walls on both sides of the street? Killing the soldiers in my command? I do know. I've lived it."

Only a few seconds ticked by before Sara realized she had been brutal to a dead soldier's wife. Her own Humvee crew were all dead, and their wives, children, and family members torn because she had sat in command of a vehicle and ordered it to stop. It was then the attack came down on them like hell's fire and fury. It had been her place to tell the wives, so much like the woman in the car with her at this moment, their husbands, their fathers, their sons, were all dead. She clenched her jaw from her harshness with this woman. She cried out in her silence to the dead soldiers.

And then Sara said, "I'm sorry. We have both lost someone we loved." She needed to shut up before breaking down.

The steady stream of businesses lining both sides of the street gave way at the southside of Little Rock. The offices for Pulaski County filled the windshield as the deputy turned into the parking lot for the buildings. The detention sign on the building they stopped in front of didn't register until the deputy offered.

"I think they have a room for you here. I'm sure they will have a change of clothes for you, also."

The double doors on the detention center swung open as two uniformed deputies approached the car. Deputy Stagger got out and shook hands with them and carried on a conversation Sara couldn't hear. One of the deputies took possession of the binoculars from the front seat of Stagger's car.

The door next to Sara opened and she was invited out. The surprise came when the deputy unlocked one of the handcuffs on her hands. The surprise didn't last very long. He pulled her arm around her back and cuffed her in the back again.

"Sorry, miss. It's protocol here. Hands in the back."

Inside the detention center, the deputies turned her over to a female detention deputy. Things for Sara went downhill from there. After logging her billfold and her gold badge came the strip search. Having someone stare at your ass while holding your cheeks open did it for the new inmate. The raging desire to never, never have this shit happen again struck home. After putting on her new outfit flooded with orange, she let loose.

"All right, who's putting me through this crap?"

"I would say her name is Sara Randolph, girl."

The room Deputy Stagger had promised turned out to be a hard metal bunk with a toilet and sink wedged into the narrow concrete space. As the deputy started to shut the heavy steel door to her cell, Sara tried the only out she could think of.

"How about my call to my lawyer?"

"Honey, you ain't even arrested yet. So, trust me, somebody is doing you a favor. I would keep my mouth shut and get some sleep. You look like shit."

Sara sat down on the bunk. It represented the only alternative to sleeping curled up on the floor. With the feel of the steel bunk hurting her butt, she opted for a corner of the cell on the floor. The cell lights never went out, but she didn't know it.

A clink of keys woke her. A drop-down shelf in the door opened and a food tray appeared.

"Take the tray. I'm going to pull it back out at a count of four."

She staggered toward the door and took the tray. The only thing on it she wanted was a cup of black coffee. Her wish of the day would be for the coffee not to be cold. She lost that one but drank the coffee anyway while sitting on the steel bunk. Her stomach tightened, along with the muscles across her forehead. She craved the liquor Ted had been trying his best to get her to ease off of. The breakfast tray still sat on the edge of the steel bunk. She had touched only a portion of the cup of coffee. Cramps bent her over, and she sat with her arms pulling against the pain in her stomach. She needed liquor now, to bring relief. The pile of white half cooked potatoes with gobs of scrambled egg sticking to them would have to stay there and rot. She bit off a bite of the toast edge without the black cinders. The bite didn't make it down. Whatever had been left from the last two days, whiskey, a hot dog, and remains of food she couldn't remember, came up. The rim of the metal commode gave her a cold barren place to rest her arms as she cramped kneeling on the floor. She didn't look up when the shout from the cell door tried to interrupt.

"Randolph, you have someone to see you," the woman guard said, standing with the cell door unlocked and open.

"Go away. I just want to fucking die." She struggled to get the sleeve of the orange jump suit across her slobber covered mouth. "Shit. Who is it?" Her knees buckled from being in a cramped-up position for too long and left her falling toward the metal bunk.

"Easy, girl. You're going to need some deep rehab, it looks like." The guard took Sara's arm and lifted to get her off the bunk and onto her feet.

"I don't want to see anybody like this."

"Come on, stand up, Randolph. Some friends are here to pick you up." The guard dropped a travel bag beside Sara. "They brought you some clothes."

The casual green outfit had come directly from the Arkansas

Game Commission's wardrobe stock. Putting it on bothered her. So many times, she had greeted her lover and had the fun of undoing button after button on the shirt and pants of the commission's outfits. And then there were the weeks of wearing them herself at Morris; the green was too much to bear right now. The orange of her prison coveralls suited her better.

"Are you dressed yet?" came the call from just outside the open cell door.

Finally, she slipped on the green slacks, pulled them up, and finished with the zipper and the button.

"I'm coming."

The corrections officer led her through a mammoth gate with steel bars. The crash of the gate slamming shut behind them hurt her ears. She shook her head. It bothered her to be trapped in a narrow space between the gate and a solid steel door blocking their way now. A cloudy window along the side of the door, just inches from the pushbutton coded lock, showed a man standing outside. The doors would be forever frozen into a memory. Somethings she would never want to be captured by again. The deputy stood blocking her view and pushing in the unlock code for the door. A clicking sound, like pulling the launch trigger on a rocket propelled grenade, made Sara flinch and freeze. The deputy stepped out the door. Turning, she stood, waiting for Sara.

"Are you coming out?"

Sara didn't know what had happened. She retreated from the door to a bench along a narrow stretch of wall. A woman, wearing a black shirt and slacks with a loose black jacket on, slid down on the bench beside her.

"We came to pick you up. You're free not to go with us, but, judging from your condition, we offer the best outcome for you. I think you will find yourself back in a cell somewhere if you don't come with me."

For Sara, the woman's voice came with a reverb sound that made it not sound real. Whatever the woman had said, the result would be better than going back through the doors to a metal bunk. She nodded her approval. The woman offered a lift to get her up off the seat.

On the way to their car, Sara saw the large yellow letters on the back of the woman's jacket, along with the jacket of their driver.

The DEA had her and she had little choice in the coming car ride. The man driving the SUV pulled out of the jail parking lot. The two people that had scooped her up still hadn't offered her their names.

The woman laid it out. "We are working with the Arkansas Game Commission to offer you a stay at a drug and alcohol rehab facility. A stay there, and the commission and the DEA will reconsider the offer made to you before the tragedy of losing your fiancé happened. You have friends with us—and the commission—that want you back on duty."

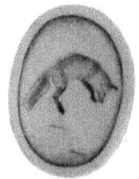

EIGHTEEN

MORE THAN A MONTH PASSED before Sara walked out the front door of The Evergreen Life Facility for Drugs and Alcohol. She paused in the open air and took a deep breath of the morning's clear, cool, welcoming air. No one had gotten out of the SUV sitting waiting for her in the driveway. The front seats were occupied, so she got into the back without a word or question. The passenger turned to her to offer an explanation of where they were taking her.

"Some of the people you know will be waiting for us at what we call a safehouse. In reality, it's a communications center for both the Game Commission and our branch of the Drug Enforcement Agency here in Arkansas. We assumed you would want to go there. Correct?"

"You're correct," Sara said, a determination in her voice that had been lost for months since Luke's death. She needed alignment and structure to fit in to her new slot of wildlife agent and DEA operative once again. "Please, hurry."

When the SUV pulled into the driveway of a two-story home, the garage door opened for them to drive in. The door shut behind them. They got out of the vehicle and the agents guided her into the house.

"You can take a seat in the living room. Your friends from the commission will be joining you shortly."

She followed the agents through the furnished kitchen and into a living room full of communication and video monitoring equipment. A wall of more than twenty monitors flashed scenes of roadways and the fronts of buildings. She was shown a couch seat back away from the monitors and an empty controller's desk. She scanned the monitors, trying to place the scenes they were filming. One showed a truck stop she remembered in Hope, Arkansas. It looked empty and deserted. Another of the active monitors showed an empty liquor bar. She jumped from the couch and went to stand closer to the monitor. She remembered each one of the bottles standing on display on the shelves behind the bar's counter. She had seen them dozens of times when Ted had poured from them.

To herself, "What the hell. My name is still on the barstool."

A woman had entered the room and walked up behind Sara.

"We're not sure what guided you into Ted's domain. Hope, Arkansas, is a small town, so who knows?" she said. "By the way, my name is Carlota. I'm a DEA agent assigned to work with the commission here in Arkansas." She turned to go greet someone coming in a back door and then left. Sara sat back on the couch, watching the monitor's screen and the bar where she had spent so much time weeks ago. She turned to see a welcome sight. Luke's friend, and her study mate at Morris, Patrick Reid. He took a seat on the couch beside her.

"I guess you can tell we kept our eyes on you during some of your low moments."

"Why? Why did the commission even bother with me?"

"Everyone got a lot of encouragement to do that from the top man at Commission Headquarters."

Sara didn't have to be told. Her quick thinking on the White River had saved the lives of the wife and daughter of the man sitting at the head of the commission.

"Just so you know, Sara, the encouragement came from a lot more folks than Brad Johnson. All the training cadre at Morris were pulling for you and hoping we would find you."

She didn't answer. Her disgust at what she had let herself sink into had now been tempered by the weeks of top-notch rehabilitation. Much of it was directed toward building self-worth and trusting one's own judgment again.

"Our liaison DEA agent Carlota DeAvila will spell out the program we have planned for you. It will be up to you to decide to enter it. Otherwise, a position in the field as the sworn agent you achieved is open for you. Should I send Miss DeAvila in?"

"Wait. Can we talk for a few minutes?"

"What DeAvila is going to tell you will explain a lot about what happened at the compound and then what the DEA has planned for you. I'll call you later and we can talk."

She nodded her head yes. Even a mention of where Luke had died, and she had frozen at talking about the men in the compound who had killed him. The only part of it was she enjoyed the fact the Oxford brothers were dead and buried.

"I'll send her in."

Sara paid a lot more attention to the woman Reid had sent into the room this time. She didn't wear the familiar black jacket Sara was familiar with from watching movies of DEA action. Carlota came dressed in casual looking black slacks and a white blouse with a wavy button line of pattern cut overlaps. Her dark complexion went well with her beautiful name. Only her green eyes seemed out of place. Sara aged Carlota at around forty and never married, since she wore no wedding ring. A professional DEA agent whether she worked in the field or office.

Working at reading people had become a habit while doing the circle conferences in rehabilitation with the other patients.

Carlota asked her to join her at the conference table in the room's rear. A clipboard with a lined tablet and a couple pens waited for Sara.

"I have the papers for you to sign if you want to go back on the path of working with the DEA on the drug problems in Arkansas. You also have a choice to return to your duty as an Arkansas wildlife agent. Your choice to make," Carlota said, sitting back in her seat, appearing relaxed.

Sara longed for the feelings she remembered from her days piloting a boat along a familiar Arkansas river. Some of the river time would still be there even if she took the DEA option. Luke had chosen to work with the DEA. She owed him her allegiance to do the same. Her answer came quickly.

"Yes. I want the path Luke had been on, working with the commission and the DEA."

"All right, then. The DEA will take you directly to their training program in Washington DC to complete the training a full agent in our organization receives. When you return, Reid will be your handler and has been given connections to move you into the investigation of the drug and human smuggling going on up through Arkansas from Texas."

She couldn't speak for more than a minute. It all was coming so quickly. Then she said, "Will my dad know what I'm doing?"

"Your dad will be the only person knowing what you are assigned to or doing. There's something else about your past you need to know. The two Oxford brothers Luke and the sheriff were after to arrest at the compound escaped."

"They escaped? How?"

"You will be able to read the report on what happened for them to get away."

"Luke was killed at the raid to capture them. Fuck!"

"I know. Going after those two men will be all on you, and not on the DEA as part of your job and position. They both need to be burned in hell as far as I'm concerned."

"I was there shooting at the men coming out of those trailers. I saw men die on their feet. They're still alive? No." Sara stood and slammed the clipboard against the conference table. "What the fucking hell happened? How did they get away?"

"According to the report, the Oxfords got to the filling station garage during the fight and just drove away."

Sara spun around and walked to the wall. She wanted badly to just stand there and bang her head against it. She paused, knowing it would cost her the DEA training and more.

"Sara, your job when you return from training puts you right in the crosshairs of where you need to be to find those sons of bitches. They did more than get Luke killed. They killed a grandmother to try and find some lost drug money. Luke said one of them tried to rape you. I know this history. I don't need to know what you are planning. You do what you have to do. I'll turn a blind eye to it."

"I'm going to write some of their last history when I find them." She returned to the desk and sat down with the clipboard in her hands.

"Your work when you return from the DEA training will take you and Reid both into drug smuggling and meth dealing interdiction."

She didn't need to hear more and asked, "When do I start?"

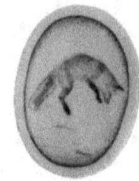

NINETEEN

THE DRONING SOUND GOT SOFTER and then almost quiet. Sara sat up, taking her ear away from the window of the DEA's Gulfstream Jet. The plane banked sharply, and she tightened her seat belt against the slick, sliding descent of their approach. She had picked a seat near the back of the cabin to be alone and have time to think. Only Carlota DeAvila and a man she guessed was also with the DEA were the other passengers. Early flight time to think had dwindled when her tiredness swept her away into a nightmare of RPGs coming at her from the adobe walls around her Humvee crew. The restless sleep had brought a burning in her throat for a drink. Turning on her cabin light, she tripped the latch on the small side cabinet hoping there would be liquor. She ran her hand along the several small bottles before taking one and shutting the door. Without drinking it, she dropped the bottle in her travel bag and sat up, turning off the light.

Bracing for a rough touchdown like the military transports she remembered, she tightened her seat belt for the landing. The sudden engine reversal told her they were already down. Sliding the window cover open, she studied the airport terminal on the far side of the runways. More than one time she had seen this terminal. The jet's taxi went on forever. The terminal lights across the way were lost in the turns the jet made on the taxiways. Finally, the jet stopped and the engines coasted down to quiet. The two agents at the front of the cabin stood, reaching to gather up their briefcases and small travel bags. When the cabin lights came on, Carlota walked back to where she was seated.

"Is there anything I can help you with, Sara?" Carlota asked.

Sara smiled. "I'm fine. Thanks."

In the days before leaving Little Rock, she had spent evenings over dinner with Carlota sharing stories of DEA raids and telling Carlota about fights with the male guides on the White River. Sara learned Carlota had been assigned to ensure the training coming her way would be a deep dive into how to break up the world of drug and human trafficking.

Sara lifted her bag and walked forward to deplane behind them. The cockpit curtains were pushed open and one of the flight crew stood smiling in the doorway to the cockpit.

"Welcome to Washington. I trust this isn't your first trip here," he said, locking the open lever on the cabin door. Both agents had gone down the steps of the plane. Sara paused in the plane's doorway. The smell of burnt jet fuel had smacked her hard. For a moment, her duffel bag swung over her back and an AR rifle sling draped over her shoulder. She started to take a step forward into Iraq.

"Easy, miss. That first step out is a little tricky. I hope we gave you a pleasant flight. I'm Captain Nelson," he said, reaching to take her arm to steady her. "Would you like to sit a moment before you deplane?"

"No. Some old memories of getting off a plane never seem to go away," she said, reaching for the cabin edge of the doorway.

"So, you're a veteran. Of Iraq, I would guess," Captain Nelson said.

"Yes. You too?"

"I get the feeling sometimes I have to climb out of the cockpit of my F-15 after we land. The bird is still sitting here under me with hot engines and empty bomb racks."

"Thank you for telling me that. It makes me feel I'm not alone with this."

"You're not alone. There are many of us feel as you do."

"Thank you."

"Your friends are waiting at an SUV for you. Can I help you down?"

"I'm fine now." Being fine for Sara had become a moment-to-moment thing for her. She still needed to measure her thinking and take stock of her surroundings to really know.

She took a breath of the still hanging jet fuel, mostly to prove she could get past it. She carefully eased her way down the short set of steps to the tarmac of the Washington airport. Carlota had the back door of the SUV open and waiting. Sara took a seat and Carlota followed. Carlota offered no conversation until they cleared the airport traffic.

"We're taking you first to the DEA's training center. I have a special program set up for you. It will depend on how you do, but for now there will be several weeks of hell in physical fitness and psychological work. Our training for this is the best in the world. So, know it's based on your coming out as tough as nails."

"And after that?"

"The drug command is setting up what will come next. You are a special asset like none they have had in years. So, it's going to be seat of the pants to measure you and what level you can be trained to."

"It sounds like I'm a prisoner here."

"No. You'll be free to leave at any time. Time out of here on weekends is fine. Just no trips to Arkansas, and no contact with anyone there but your father. Here's a fresh cellphone for you. Always treat it like someone is listening."

"Are they?"

"You can count on it, honey," Carlota said, sitting back in the seat with a short laugh.

When the SUV pulled up to the three-story building, Carlota was the first out. "I'll take you in and get you settled for the night."

The locked doors at the entrance soon clicked unlocked when the agent spoke to a call box on the wall. She led the way to a counter manned by two male guards.

Sara showed the guards her fresh ID with DEA Agent Trainee embossed across the top and a cold, drab picture of her she couldn't like no matter how hard she tried. The guard handed Sara a room key. "Welcome to the DEA training facility, Agent Randolph. Your room is on the second floor."

She followed Carlota into the elevator at the end of the hall. Following someone had never been something Sara liked to do, but she didn't mind her new teammate leading the way. Carlota unlocked her room door and stepped in, dropping the key on the room desk. The call won't be early tomorrow. You'll have the day to rest. Snacks and soft drinks are in the fridge under the desk. I'll see you in the morning and each and every day. "Welcome to the DEA," Carlota said, offering Sara a warm handshake. "Good night."

The door shut, and Sara was alone. Not sure what she had gotten herself into, she sat on the edge of the bed and reached into her travel bag for the small liquor bottle she had taken from the plane. She stood and took it to the desk. In the clear light of the lamp, she set it standing by itself. It reminded her of herself, alone and about to be emptied of so many of the emotions that needed to come out. The liquor bottle would survive the night, but she wasn't sure she would. It all came out in her muffled screams into a pillow. She saw it all again and had him die in her arms. She tore at her very being, trying to rip out the guilt of knowing she had caused his death. If she had trusted her gut instead of taking Jimmy back to that godforsaken place, if the Oxfords hadn't gotten their greedy eyes on Jimmy's money, Luke might still be alive. The facts causing her to hate them had come hard. Watching both of them die would not be hard. Her eyes, dry from the pain, finally filled with the much-needed tears the darkness and night brought.

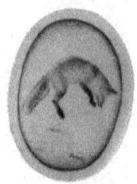

TWENTY

THE FIRST TWO WEEKS OF promised hell went slowly at first. Then, as her strength and resilience built, she began to enjoy the days full of physical workouts. At the end of five weeks, the trainers told her she had completed the last phases of her initial physical training and would be moving on to classwork on federal law and drug enforcement.

When the day ended, she sprinted up the steps to her room rather than taking the elevator. On other days, she climbed the steps past her floor, going all the way to the top of the staircase before turning and going back down, taking the steps two at a time. She couldn't remember ever feeling more physically in shape. When she went into her room, the unopened liquor bottle was still sitting on the desk. She had been keeping the pledge she made to herself, it would stay there for the duration of her stay. She laid the new camo clothes the DEA had issued out on the bed. She would be ready for the next phase of her training.

The evening was young when she went to the outside yard and found a bench where she could be alone and call John and Jimmy. She had charged the cellphone they had given her all day, and this would be the first time she had turned it on. Watching the screen flash its turn on logo, she thought of the number to dial in Cotter for home. With the phone clearly on, she punched in the numbers. Like so many times before when she had been at Morris, she knew hearing John and Jimmy's voices would bring a happy ending to the day.

The voice on the phone, "Hello, this is Luke. I'm not at home right now. Leave—."

Stunned at her mistake, she hit the cancel button. Just as fast, she dialed the number again. She got a busy signal. It was too soon. Luke's phone still hadn't hung up. Three more times she dialed his phone number. His voice seemed so fresh and real. Could he really be gone? The fourth time a different voice answered her call.

"Hello. It's Reid."

It hit her. Luke had told her Reid had been sharing the apartment with him. She ended the call without speaking. All the physical strength she had gained in the past weeks seemed to leave her, and she slumped on the bench from the surprise of hearing Luke's voice. The voice from the recording echoed again and again in her mind. If only she could hear it again. She punched in the number to hear Luke's voice again.

"Whoever you are, this is Reid."

Disappointed she didn't hear Luke's voice again, she hung up. What she needed to say to Reid would need to be on a private phone line and not on a cellphone monitored by the DEA.

She voiced a request for the Uber number. After calling, she raced to her room and got her billfold and the few hundred dollars she carried in it. The Uber ride only needed to be a couple miles.

Unpacking her new burner phone purchase on return, she called Luke's number again.

"Is this you, Sara?"

"Listen, Reid. I'm on a burner and I don't know how much of a charge comes on a new one. Why didn't you tell me the Oxfords escaped from the compound raid?"

"I planned to tell you when we could sit and talk about it."

"I want your help when I get back," Sara said. She didn't feel satisfied with what he had just told her. She wanted Reid to be on the same page as her. It would take time.

"Anything. You know I'll help."

"This isn't going to be part of our job description."

"Go ahead. I'm listening."

"I've got a whole list of scores to settle with the Oxford brothers. I think you've probably kept a list of them too. For my own sanity, and the safety of Dad and Jimmy, I need these two men in jail or dead."

"Sara, the pain of what they tried to do to you and what they caused is still going to be there, even with them lying dead on a coroner's table."

"You're not going to help me?" She held back from saying even more, not sure where he stood in her battle.

"I have my own score to settle with those two. What they did killing an old woman and attacking you helped to draw my best friend into a fight that got him killed. Yes, I'm going to help you put them on that coroner's table."

She breathed a sigh of relief before replying. "Okay."

"I have to say this. Our assigned work will not be to bring in those two killers. Arresting the men running the drug and smuggling traffic has to be at the top of our list."

"And that is exactly what we will do." She hung up. He was coming around. The sidekick she needed would be there for her.

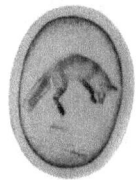

TWENTY-ONE

WITH HER BEDROOM DOOR AT the DEA Training Center locked, Sara stripped and put on her most comfortable gym pants and top. She ran for the bed and turned to do a back flop onto the middle of the hard military bed and mattress. Staring at the ceiling, she ran all the pictures of what her life had been like in the past weeks through her mind. A look at the time showed it was still early in Arkansas. She needed the refreshment of talking to her river folks from her home. She put John's number in the phone and touched the dial button. She hoped Jimmy would answer. She missed him the most.

"Hello, John Randolph here. If you're selling something go the hell away," he said.

"Dad, it's me!"

"Minnow! Jimmy has really been stewing to talk to you."

"We can do that. I'm here now, old man. You can talk to me first."

"I knew the things that happened threw you for a loop. Are you on your feet?"

She really didn't want to go there, but perhaps there would be no way to avoid it.

"I'm more than on my feet. I'm in training for a special assignment. It will be a while before I'm back in Arkansas and can come see both of you. Tell me, how is our boy?"

"He heard the phone and is hanging over my shoulder to talk to you. Here, Jimmy, talk."

"Where are you, Aunt Sara? Miss Marty is asking me all the time if I've seen you."

"I'm in school, Jimmy. I'm training for a new job."

"We miss you. Come back so I can show you some places I found to catch some really big ones."

"I will. I have a while to go yet. Is Marty still having you ride her horses?"

"Yes. She has one she says is going to be mine."

"She does? Is it a paint?"

"It's a buckskin. She has a trainer coming and working with him."

"Oh, boy, I want to see your horse."

"John has a picture of it on his phone with me riding it. I'll send it to you when we finish."

"Thank you. Can I talk to my father for a minute or two?"

"Can you tell me if they caught them men that came after me and the money?"

"They're looking for them. Some think they might have gone south to Texas."

"I worry they might come back. John still keeps his rifle sitting by his chair and he carries it to the boat when we're on the river."

"I'll find them, Jimmy." It just slipped out. The thought of her finding and killing them both still sat there as the top priority in her mind. She trained for it every day in every class they gave.

"Okay. Here's John."

"Jimmy, would you take the dogs outside for a last time?" He waiting a couple seconds then said, "Handling horses is really helping Jimmy."

"I'm so glad, dad."

"Tell me, are you on a special team to find those killers?"

"I'm training, Dad. That's all I can tell you. I'm fine and have both of my feet on the ground. Take care of our boy. I love you both." She clicked off the call before she said too much.

Tossing the phone to the edge of the bed, she got up and undressed and ran a bathtub full of hot water. A look through the bathroom cabinet again found not a single female pleasure like bubble bath. Next time out on a weekend, she vowed to fix that. Oh well, the hot water would feel good on the sore spots from the martial arts training. With a chuckle, she knew the student she had trained with would have a lot more soreness than she had.

***

Her military training in the MPs gave her a leg up on much of the weapon and hand-to-hand techniques they taught for arresting and detaining suspects. The cadre at the DEA Training Academy placed her into a group of trainees more than a quarter way through the course. They promised to call her out into breakout sessions to give her the special training undercover agents would need in the field. Having to live with a new identity would be hard. With a little laugh, she thought, *"Who knows the type of person I could be undercover? I'll get to choose."*

There was no DEA training on killing meth dealers and burying their bodies so they would never be found. Still, the thought raked her mind with each subject and class. Never criticized or graded on her performance there, she began to wonder why they did so much to push her ahead of the other trainees. After seventeen weeks in, she found out. Called to the chief trainer's office, she went there afraid she must be failing. Sara paused outside the door to adjust her black training outfit and knocked on his door.

"Come in, Randolph." The loud voice echoed in her ears, and she opened the door and went in to stand at attention before the chief's desk.

"Have a seat, Sara."

She moved a chair a little closer to the center of the man's desk and sat down as rigid as a fence post in Marty's horse pasture. "Yes, sir."

"You have been outstanding here. Rarely have we had a woman with your prison guard and military background. It's clear Morris gave you a rounded education on wearing a badge and working in the crazy world out there. We think we gave you the training you will need to sort out the drug and meth dealers raging in Arkansas and throughout the country. Congratulations, DEA Agent Randolph." He stood and walked around the desk handing her a gold badge and an identification billfold. "Store these somewhere back home. If someone finds them on you, it will probably get you killed in the field if you are alone."

She stood, taking the items and shaking his outreached hand.

"I'm going home?"

"We had a special request to expedite your graduation. Our Arkansas contingent asked for you. Tomorrow, we have a flight arranged for you. Our field office there will meet you and arrange for the weapons and items you will need."

"Yes, sir."

"You have tonight in the town here. So, go enjoy. We will want you back yearly for a few weeks."

Back in her room, she tossed the badge on the middle of the bed along with her DEA identification. She dropped alongside them, running her finger along the edges of the badge. Her fingers kissed the star points and then rubbed the embossed center emblem of the agency. It was really hers. She had to tell someone. There was no one she could tell. Sleep tonight would be out of the question.

***

There were still some things she needed to do in Washington. She thought for a moment and then put in the phone number for O'Dell, her Army first sergeant when she had been on duty. Her conversation with him needed to be a thank you for all the support he had given in getting her back into PTSD therapy months before, when he got her into the VA's program in Washington. O'Dell had been her only lifeline and friend to keep her sane while in Iraq and having to deal with a superior officer who wouldn't keep his hands off her.

***

"Sergeant O'Dell here," the phone spoke to her.

"Sarge, It's Corporal Rand. . . It's Sara," she said, almost sorry she had opened her Army can of worms again.

"Corporal, my God, where have you been these past months?"

"I know you don't know, but I've had some things to get past. I lost the man I loved, and was going to marry, in a drug shootout with a hoard of meth heads. It's taken a toll on me."

"Where are you? Are you close? I would like to see you."

"I am. Can't say where, but we can meet. Tell me where, I'll get a cab."

With plans to meet in an hour, she dressed in the same clothes she had worn on a short weekend trip to New York. There were

118

several cabs dropping off trainees at the front of the headquarters. She hailed one and sat back for the short ride to the restaurant bar O'Dell had suggested. She tipped the driver with a twenty and slid out, wanting to do nothing but hug the man that had been her savior in Iraq.

She found a welcoming maître d' who led her to a table booth. She tipped him and slid into the booth's seat. One diet soda finished, and now a second started, and her friend still hadn't arrived. Maybe she had messed up on the place he said to meet. She flipped her phone open and dialed O'Dell. The phone kept ringing. Closing her phone, she lifted her coke and took a heavy sip. The familiar profile of someone she didn't want to see led to her spitting coke out of her mouth. She needed to get some words out quickly.

"Why the hell are you here, Captain?" She came close to choking on the word 'Captain'.

Bartlett took a seat on the opposite side of the table from her.

"Hello, Sara. I'm no longer a Captain." He still wore his Army work uniform, only a single silver bar set on each side of his collar. "I'm glad you came. I'm in trouble. I need your help."

She continued to stare at him as she wiped up the diet coke on the table. Things got quiet at the table for a few minutes and then.

"What help? Are you wearing the first lieutenant bar because of me?"

"Word did get out we were having an affair. Someone in the company let my wife know about us. She divorced me."

"It wasn't 'us.' It was you abusing a female soldier in your company."

"Word got up the chain of command. I was called on the carpet two days before I sent you away. They wanted it all to be covered up and then hell happened having our prisoner escape and your crew getting killed. It went to hell for me."

"For you? It went to hell for you. Really? What the fuck, Bartlett? It went to hell for your men that died, riding in the Humvee with me. It was all about you, wasn't it? Shipping me out of Bucca Prison escorting a high value prisoner like Aziz. Did you know the attack on the convoy could happen?" The new glass of coke the waiter had just sat in front of her flashed through the air into her ex-commander's face. "I would fucking kill you right now if I had a weapon."

Bartlett wiped the soda from his eyes. "I didn't know the attack would happen. The order to move Aziz came from my command. Sending you to escort him to a different post where I had you assigned, well I thought it would be an easy way for us to end our relationship."

"Relationship? Do you remember how our 'relationship' started? I do. You pushed a backwoods recruit onto a desktop in your office. You were panting like a runout coon hound when you stripped my pants off and screwed me. Do you remember now, Captain?"

"You were attracted to me from the day we met."

"I was scared as hell of you. I didn't tell anyone, and I let you do it over and over again."

"You were meeting me at night in the compound trailer. Why?"

"Damn you. I don't know why. Maybe it became a game for me. Watching a man with the power to command you in the daytime plead and beg for more and more of what the sex with me meant in the dark of the Iraqi night. The horror of the war must have made it easy for me to fall in love with you. Goddamn it."

Bartlett stood and attempted to sit down by her.

"Oh, hell no, mister. Stay away." She shoved past him to leave.

"Please, sit back down. I'm in trouble over what went on at Bucca Prison with the prisoner Aziz. You were involved with his torture," Bartlett said.

"You must have forgotten. You assigned me to work with CIA agent Jason Myers to get information from the prisoner about an attack planned here in the U.S."

"The CIA believes Aziz was able to buy Myers's help. Myers gave up on torturing Aziz too early, and then Aziz must have realized Myers was weak. Myers left the prison several times. I had no idea where he went, but I think it was to get money from Iraqis helping plan Aziz's escape. In the end, he sold out to Aziz. All the recordings of the interrogations of Aziz went missing. Jason Myers disappeared right after your Humvee was attacked. He still hasn't shown up, and the CIA thinks he is back in this country. The CIA scared the hell out of me saying Myers is going to clean up any trace of what went on in that prison with Aziz. I know enough to put him in front of a firing squad. So do you. That puts us both at risk," Bartlett said.

For the two tours of duty under Bartlett she had never noticed a single trace of him being afraid of anything. Being afraid now was so out of character for him.

"What do you think I can do to help you?"

"Talk to the CIA and tell them I had nothing to do with Aziz's escape."

"They would already know that Bartlett. You're being paranoid."

"You're not going to help?"

"I'm not. Maybe you can live believing someone is coming to clean up his past and kill you. I can't. If Myers is in this country, the CIA will find the traitorous son of a bitch and hang him. You need to backbone up, Bartlett. I'm going to. If he comes for me, it will be in my territory and deep woods. I'll make him one sorry ass ex-CIA agent." She had heard enough from Bartlett to last a lifetime. Without a goodbye, she left him in the booth downing his third drink.

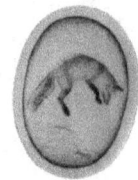

TWENTY-TWO

FEELING OUT OF PLACE IN Washington had become a daily reminder she really longed for the forests and rivers of her home state. Waking up in a Little Rock, Arkansas motel gave her a feeling of at least being closer to home. With phone call orders to meet at the commission's safehouse, she skipped breakfast and only had a cup of motel coffee. She had overslept and needed to rush. The commission had a taxi waiting to take her.

The door to the safehouse opened as she took the last step up the stoop. She didn't see who opened it until she took the first steps inside.

"Oh my God," she said, "Patrick, you're here too?" She didn't hesitate pulling him into a warm embrace. He held her through the first of her tears and then pushed her back just a little.

"We all miss him," he said, still holding her.

"I'm sorry," she said, clearing her throat and lowering her face to wipe away the tears.

"I know," he said, "Come sit down. There are some important things to go on in just a few minutes. It involves both of us."

He had her attention. Within minutes, Sara's friend, the head of the Arkansas Conservation Commission, arrived. After both of them greeted Brad Johnson, he asked them to stand at attention. "Both of you are to be congratulated for the extended training you have been through." Sara's army training wouldn't let her glance at Reid. It was a surprise he had also been in training.

"Both of you will now carry dual credentials that will include those of an Arkansas Game Officer," Brad Johnson said. He handed each of them the badges and identification credentials they would need.

"At this time there will be no record or announcement of your achievement. We are placing both of you in the field with weapons and no identification other than a driver license with a new last name. Miss Oliver, shake your brother Patrick Oliver's hand."

With her first assignment, Sara Oliver would head to her foggy memory stomping grounds of Hope, Arkansas. For now, Patrick Oliver will be assigned to the safehouse communication system. They learned the safehouse was ground zero for all the DEA commission drug work in Arkansas and northern Texas.

All calls from other agents working in the Arkansas, Texas corridor would be routed to the safehouse's communication systems. Agent Carlota DeAvila had been assigned to be Sara's contact within the DEA.

***

The two women left the taxi and walked through the dozen tables with diners talking and sharing drinks under a façade of old wooden beams over the street. Overhead lights dimly lit the intimate dining area. DeAvila went through the propped open door and stopped at the maître d's small counter.

"Carlota DeAvila, I called."

"Oh, yes, Miss DeAvila. We have your normal private dining ready. Follow me, please."

"It's all right. I know the way," DeAvila said, stepping past the maître d' and leading Sara down a long hallway to a door marked 'private'.

"We'll be in here."

She pulled back a chair for Sara to sit, then took a four-inch square plastic box from her purse before she sat down. Two small red lights flashed once and then didn't come on again as she walked the box around the walls of the room. Turning the box off, she sat down.

"The room is all right. I've found several places bugged when I've stayed out of the country."

"Who would be trying to bug us?" Sara asked.

DeAvila didn't get a chance to answer. A knock on the door

and DeAvila got up and slowly opened it, looking at who wanted to come in. The waitress was invited in by DeAvila for drink orders. Sara ordered a diet. DeAvila went for a Bloody Mary.

After the drinks came, DeAvila said, "I may need more than one of these. I had an informant in Texas taken by the cartel today. He had been my source for big shipments of cocaine coming up the Rogue Semi Trail through Texas. The cartel will cut his head off when they've got him across the border. I feel awful about it, but there isn't anything I can do."

"That's horrible," Sara said, wishing she had a stiff drink to wash the thought of the cartel cutting heads off away.

"I've been a thorn in their side for some time now."

"Rogue Semi Trail?" Sara asked.

"We had to call it something. It's there and being driven every day by the cartel's trucks."

"I thought we had some good equipment to x-ray the trucks coming in."

"We do. They come in full, carrying produce, and have meeting places with the coyote's backpackers. Then they load the backpacks for the rest of the trip north."

"In which area of the drug transportation do you see me fitting in?"

"Undercover and surveillance are the two areas we need the most help in."

Sara heard the knob on the door turn. DeAvila shoved her chair back, getting up and reaching for her pistol. "Get on the floor."

Sara slid out of the chair and pulled her side bag to her. Her hand went inside it for her pistol.

DeAvila slipped quietly to the side of the door and reached across to the knob. When the knob turned, Sara heard the soft puff of a weapon with a silencer firing outside the door. Pieces of wood blew out of the door's surface, hitting DeAvila's arm and chest. Her legs collapsed. She went straight down on her knees. The doorknob turned again. A pistol with a long silencer barrel loomed just past the crack in the opening door. Someone was coming in. Sara's hand had been resting on the Glock issued earlier in the day. Her years of practice with Glocks let her rack the slide to chamber a round. Not pausing to aim, her arm with the little minnow tattoo held the Glock and pumped four shots into the side frame of the door. She heard a bullet bite into the metal of the silencer and then another shot hitting bone. The attacker's weapon fell from their hand and into the room on the floor. She heard the man stumble against the half open door. Certain she had hit the man and disarmed him, she rushed to DeAvila.

DeAvila's shoulder wound pulsed short blood spurts. "Go after him, Sara."

Carlota tried to cover the bullet hole with her hand. Sara took her blouse off and pushed a wad of cloth into the hole. Carlota sagged as Sara eased her down to the floor.

"Who did this?" Sara asked, trying to keep the woman alert.

The door opened and the head of a man in a dress suit stood, staring at the blood and the wounded woman. Sara's pistol had his head in her sights ready to kill.

"Don't just stand there. Call an ambulance now!" She wanted DeAvila to herself for the question she asked again. "Who is behind this? Tell me, Carlota."

"Look inside."

"Inside what?"

"My informants file. On my comp—."

Sara sat flat on the floor with DeAvila's head across her leg. She held her in place with one hand. Her other hand held the still smoking Glock ready if the battle returned.

***

Her phone call went to Reid and the communications center. The police stormed the restaurant before the DEA's response to Sara's call could be answered. A half dozen pistols were pointed at her before she could get a word out of her mouth.

"Put your weapons down. I'm a DEA special operations agent. I'm laying my weapon on the floor and reaching for my badge and identification."

At the sight of her badge the officers lowered their weapons.

"Who's been shot here?" the officer with two stars on his collar demanded.

"A man in the doorway tried to kill us both. The weapon with the silencer is his." She didn't offer any explanation or information about DeAvila. She would leave it to Reid and his response team.

Barely a half day on the job and the danger of working undercover had already searched her out. All her training as a military police officer, wildlife officer, and a DEA agent came to bare in the moment a man had tried to kill them both. The horrors of being in a shooting war were not over for her.

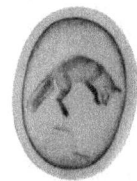

TWENTY-THREE

Her bright new F-250 Ford 4x4 looked expensive. It set her up just where she wanted to be on the drug totem pole. Her truck's GPS told her to turn into the next driveway at a two-story home like many others on the streets she had just traveled in Hope, Arkansas.

Sara parked her truck in the driveway of the house and climbed the five steps to the porch. She opened the envelope again and took out the door key tagged with the seventh street address. 1422 matched the faded numbers above the door. Turning the key, she unlocked the door and entered a house they said was hers.

A quick tour downstairs showed the house had been furnished with very nice used furniture. In spite of that, a brand new sixty-inch curved screen TV graced the wall opposite the large double windows facing the street. Upstairs she found the bedroom outfitted with a new queen-size bed and another slightly smaller flat screen TV. The only thing she had noticed to be unusual was the large screen TV in the living room, until she opened the basement door and went down the steps into a jungle of marijuana. A bright grow light hung over the rows of well-maintained plants.

"Jesus, what have I gotten myself into?" she whispered.

She reached into her back pocket and took out her cellphone and pushed the speed dial number for Patrick Reid. The phone was dead. She remembered they had removed the SIM card when she left the commission office. She would need to get another card quickly. She turned to go back up the steps. A dark shadow framed the door at the top of the stairs. Her hand drew the weapon in her shoulder holster.

"Sara, it's Reid. I didn't mean to frighten you."

"I wouldn't have meant to shoot you either, but I came close."

"I couldn't call."

"It's all right. Hang on, I'll come up there." They gave each other a warm hug on the landing, and she led the way into the kitchen. "Can we sit down? I need some answers about what went on at the restaurant. We were faced by a man that shot DeAvila and then tried to kill me. Who was the man that I wounded?"

"The man had a car waiting in front of the restaurant. A half dozen people saw him, and we have at least three different descriptions of the man. No one thought he had any Hispanic characteristics. So, we don't know if it rules out the cartel or not. They could have hired a hitman, which would be unusual."

Sara's head was spinning. Bartlett's warning of a rogue CIA agent cleaning up after himself may have come home to roost in Arkansas.

"I know the cartel would probably have a hit list out on DeAvila, but she has been very careful about being seen in public. She may have been to that restaurant too many times."

What he said didn't lessen her fears about her own past. She knew enough about CIA agent Myers to get him locked up for the rest of his life. But would Myers kill to keep it from coming out? Hell yes, he would. Now deep in Arkansas, and with an assumed name, there would be no chance he could find her.

"Sara, did I lose you?"

"Sorry. I was just thinking about an old enemy." She would make it a point to call O'Dell every few weeks to keep up with the status of the missing CIA agent.

"Where in the heck do I dive into this job, boss?"

"Don't go there with the 'boss' thing. You and I need to work out getting inside the trafficking going on up this corridor. Some things we need have already been set up for us." He laid out a manila folder on the kitchen counter. "Three months ago, the DEA bought the truck stop on the south end of Hope. If you're game for it, we can set you up to work there. The plan will be to lean toward a loose operation with some low-level drug sales under the counter."

"With that kind of truck stop, we should be inviting the north bound drug trade to stop right in. Is the truck stop open now?"

"Yes. It has locals hired and a DEA manager running it. He'll get you trained and then move on. Reports have been coming in of a lot of human smuggling and worse. Trafficking of young women and children from Mexico."

"The truck stop should be right at the heart of all that," Sara said, almost ready to tell Reid again she had a primary search and kill operation of her own. She knew the Oxfords were still out there dealing, stealing, and willing to kill to keep from getting caught. She wanted them dead.

"Is anyone still looking for the Oxford brothers?" she asked.

"I'm afraid they have disappeared off of the radar. I had a conversation with the sheriff who conducted the raid, and he said they have two detectives working the case to find them. I have his assurance he will let me know if they come up with any leads on where they are hiding."

"If there are leads to follow, I want to know," Sara said. She made sure the harsh tone of her voice conveyed her determination to be there when they were captured. "Oh, yes, Reid. I want the damn pot growing operation out of this basement if I'm going to stay here."

"It had been used to open several doors for the agents staying here. They worked finding street dealers with the pot being raised here. I'll get it gone for you."

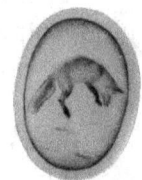

TWENTY-FOUR

RUNNING A BUSINESS AND STANDING for days selling soda and candy bars somehow just didn't fit Sara's profile. A quick social media ad for station help went out the day after she got there. She wanted a person she could find who would steal from the truck stop and work the counter. The hidden cameras the agents had placed would pick up the underhanded stealing when it went on. With a record of the stealing, she would have just the person she needed to run the station and be bound to her by chains.

The two-dozen people showing up gave her little to judge their character. She went by talking to them and asking basic questions about their education. Late in the day a girl showed up. Twenty-five years old, with long black hair like Sara's, only pulled back and draped behind her back. Far from being dressed for a job interview, she wore blue jeans with worn open windows showing a lot of the girl's tanned thighs and legs. Her blouse draped open more than enough to see the girl's endowments. Seeing the girl would have been enough for Sara to hire her. She asked the girl to join her in the truck stop's office.

"We need to talk some. Do you have time?" Sara asked.

"Me? Sure."

The girl followed her down the narrow hallway toward the office. When Sara stepped aside for the girl to enter the office, the pot smell of the woman's clothing almost choked her.

"Have a seat," Sara said, sitting down and kicking back in her chair with her feet on the desk. "You don't happen to have another one of those joints, do you? I'm tired as hell after today and really need a hit."

The woman didn't waver; she brought out a rolled one from her shirt pocket. "This is all I got left. Is two dollars okay for it? I can get you a bag later. It'll be eighty bucks."

"It's all right. I won't need the bag. Let's start with your name," Sara said. "Then you're hired."

"My name is JoAnn."

***

JoAnn took to the front counter and cash registers like a pro. Sara kept watch at a distance to see the extent the girl would go to give hints of places the locals could get fixed up with drugs besides pot. Each of the cameras in the different areas of the truck stop fed into a laptop of Sara's she kept private. She kept the camera recording under wraps from JoAnn and the other help. Sara went to lengths to hide the cameras out front on the truck ports, so they were not noticed. The goals set down by the DEA were mainly directed toward trucks and cross-country traffic using the truck stop. Cameras recorded each of the semi-trucks making a stop at the station. A new identification system has been installed with the cameras. Head shots of drivers and passengers were automatically compared with known or wanted people under investigation. Information was relayed north to provide data for state patrol and the DEA to make stops miles away from the detection center Sara and Reid now controlled.

During the past weeks, Sara's behind the scenes personal hunt for the Oxford brothers had taken her away from the truck traffic and onto the deals for drugs JoAnn would mention and talk about on the counter camera Sara had recording. Reid must have noticed on the camera feed he got from the truck stop. She got a call.

"I've got a rig and some camera dates for you to check. A stop for speeding and a K-9 search found a thousand pounds of coke. I want to see if anything might have shown up in your neck of the woods on this."

"Do you think we might have missed something?" She knew darn well where this was coming from. Her attention hadn't been on the trucking. She had been looking for leads for the men she wanted to find. The leads she wanted would come from the local meth and pot dealers.

"I just want to check to see that we had no evidence of anything when they passed through Hope."

With the dates and truck pictures captured from her cameras transferred to Reid, she had to tell him what was bothering her.

"Reid, I'm having trouble sitting tight on this truck stop operation. I guess my man hunter gene is trying to get loose."

"We can schedule you some time out. It's the Oxford hunt that bothers you, right?"

"It is, Patrick."

"I knew it would. Stick it out a while until the truck stop is fully operational with other agents. They have someone trained in diesel mechanics they want to bring on board. He will be able to deal closely with truckers. Are you getting any information that could lead to the Oxfords?"

"Not much. A couple came through here and were talking about heading for the Buffalo River with their kids this next week. They were trying to sell pot to my cashier. She told me later they could also supply meth."

"Did the cameras get a license plate picture?"

"Yes. I have the names and address on my desk. I'll send it to you."

"Could you please report things like this without me asking? Anything else?"

"There is something. A customer. A Hispanic woman came in for just a look around the counters and food area. I passed her coming out of the john. It's been a while, but she reminded me of someone I met on the river. She had offered me a job working for Ruiz, a human trafficker, a long time back. Does the name Ruiz still ring any bells?"

"I'm not sure. Get back to you with what I find. Keep the place together. I miss seeing you."

His comment went over her head at the time, but it hit a warm spot later in the day. She missed him, too.

***

Sara often took walks along the back edge of the truck stop property. Arkansas's forests graced the edge of the concrete parking area with a short grass area and then a stand of chestnut oak trees supplying the squirrels. They raced about carrying the acorns in their mouths. She knew they were building winter stores for their families. She sat on the three-foot-tall brick wall marking the boundary where the squirrels would allow her to go and still get to see them. She liked how so many of the squirrels could disappear into the trees if she went past the wall.

The afternoon had slipped away, and the sun had dropped deep into the tree line in front of her. From in the woods near her, she heard a sharp snap. She had heard the sound before, and welcomed the coming it would bring. His antlers broke out of the brush first as they rose and then dipped as the buck dined on the acorns the squirrels had left. She froze in place. Seeing the buck again would fulfill her almost constant dream of being back out, scouting the wilderness. Back there in the woods, finding tracks, stooping to run a finger along their edge, and then lying out her hand to measure the breadth of the animal's hoof. She missed tracking them to only experience their beauty. It had been a while since she had realized how much she missed the clean air and freshness of the Arkansas wilderness. A trip home and time on the river needed to come soon.

What came was not what she had been thinking about. Her cellphone broke the silence of her sneak away place. She heard the buck pick up on the sound and break away for quieter places.

She answered, "Yes?"

"I need you up here," JoAnn said. "I have a problem, needs fixin' bad."

"On the way."

JoAnn had sounded desperate. Sara ran for the back door of the building. JoAnn met her as she opened the door and started down the hall. JoAnn hung to her side all the way down the hall.

"Three shabby girls came in and went into the restroom. I noticed it was taking a long time for them to come out. Then a man from the truck came in. He looked around and went straight for the women's john. I thought he was going in. I stood my ground watching and said, 'what the hell you doing?' to him. He said he needed to get going and his kids were in the restroom. That's when I called you and met you in the hall."

"All right." Sara went to the restroom door and went in. The large, five stall area looked empty. JoAnn stood at her heels.

"I think they're gone," JoAnn said.

"Check the stalls." Sara went down the line pushing the doors open. The fifth one didn't budge. It was locked. "You can come out." Sara knocked on the stall door.

They both heard the sliding click of the door lock and then it opened. Three girls Sara guessed to be under fifteen came sheepishly out of the stall. Certain the girls were Hispanic; she offered a hello in Spanish. No one offered a reply.

JoAnn took the hand of one of the girls, "Come on, let's get you something to eat out front." The girl yanked her hand away. The three backed up against the wall. Sara knew they were looking behind her. She turned and saw the man standing in the doorway. A black baseball bat hung from his right hand.

"Them girls my kids. Hard to make 'em do what they told."

Everything about the man reeked of coyote. Sara's DNA demanded she make a stand against the human trafficker. Her training and planning with Reid said no. Let this fight walk out of the truck stop without giving away the truck stop's agenda. Fifty miles north of the truck stop this coyote will have State Troopers and DEA special operations officers swarming him and freeing the girls.

"It's all right, mister. The girls looked like they were hungry. Sorry we got in your way," Sara said. JoAnn pushed by her.

"No way in hell is this fuckin' coyote going to walk out of here with these kids. Piss off, dude," JoAnn said. She had grabbed a mop handle from the bucket standing near a closet and had taken a stance a few feet in front of the man. Sara's moment of realizing JoAnn had no idea what the true purpose of their operation was had put them in danger. The mop handle would not be a good match for the man's bat. The bat rattled off the tile floor of the restroom. He had dropped it.

"This crazy bitch really don't want no fight now, does she?" He held a big revolver pointing at them with a barrel longer than any Sara had ever seen. He cocked it. Sara took JoAnn's arm and pulled her back behind her. "Stay there."

"Put the pistol down and take your kids. We're sorry we got in your way."

JoAnn had a grip on Sara's arm she knew would leave a bruise. A steady stream of cuss words were spewing out of JoAnn's mouth in a whisper so tough it could kill. The near fight ended with the man only making a motion for the girls to come. They rushed past him as he turned and headed out of the truck stop.

"What are you doing?" JoAnn demanded, trying to rush past Sara.

The brick wall of secrecy blocked her from having the conversation with JoAnn she needed to have right then. Uncertain of there being any foundation of stableness in JoAnn, she still needed to have a talk to bring the woman emotionally down from what had just happened.

"Come on. My office, now." She led the way down the hall. "Sit and listen."

Sara lifted her cellphone and pushed the panic button for Reid.

"JoAnn, listen. I'm placing a call to the State Patrol."

Reid answered quickly.

"Hello? Yes officer, I'd like to report a human trafficking case."

Reid replied, "I got it. Someone is listening. Go ahead with the information."

Sara reversed the video file on her recorder to the time the girls got in the truck and froze it to not erase. She reported to Reid the truck type and the license number. "There are at least three girls in the truck, maybe more, headed north from Hope. I have video and can provide it." She gave the truck stop information and the call ended.

"JoAnn, relax. That truck will be pulled to the side of the road within an hour."

"I'm sorry," JoAnn said. "I've been in that same spot as those girls. A damn pimp ran me all over Little Rock, until I had the courage to beat the hell out of him with a baseball bat like the one, you know."

Sara went to her and took the girl's hand. She wondered, when she touched the strong grip of the calloused hand, where all the courage the girl had shown came from. It wasn't the first time Sara had seen courage. Iraq brought out courage in both women and men. Back then she had tried to analyze why they could push past fright and face danger and death one-on-one with both.

JoAnn spent the rest of the afternoon sulking and staying mostly to herself. Sara now understood what had triggered her reaction while trying to protect the girls being trafficked. More than two hours had passed since the truck had left headed north. Reid and his team should have made the stop when it got to the edges of Little Rock. He had always been prompt when letting her know the status of stops triggered at the Hope truck stop. JoAnn's thinking of rescuing the girls at the truck stop may have been the best thing to do. Stepping outside the box when it came to plans laid down had never been a problem for Sara. Why now?

Reid's call came at the three-hour mark of the truck leaving.

"Listen, Sara. The girls were not in the truck when we stopped it. In fact, only the driver. The man you must have faced was gone. So far, the driver isn't giving us anything to go on."

"Can you get a readout on the road cameras between there and Hope? See where it might have stopped?"

"We're running a quick data load on them now. I'll let you know."

"This is crap. I let those girls get taken out of here instead of fighting the son of a bitch. I should have been able to help those girls."

"I've no doubt the trafficker would have shot you. He had nothing to lose at that point."

"We talked about our mechanic placing GPS tracking on trucks like this. We need to step this up, Reid."

"It will be done. Gotta go. Back to you soon."

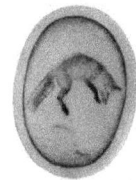

TWENTY-FIVE

SARA JUGGLED HIS NAME IN her mind throughout the next day. Ruiz, Ruiz—and then his first name came to her Hector. Her run-in with him and his family came at a time long before she entered law enforcement. Ruiz had her marked as a perfect driver to ferry the girls he had been trafficking up the corridor through Texas and Arkansas. Ruiz's effort to hire her had ended when she sent his car into the White River for following her. Ruiz had never retaliated. The girls she had seen at the truck stop had been a reminder of the day she met Ruiz's sister at the river. Her resemblance to his sister she had met led her to think the woman was family. There could be a connection to what had happened in the truck stop restroom. Reid had promised to get back to her with any information in the system on Ruiz. She still waited.

Reid's call came the next day.

"Sit down, Sara. There isn't anything good about what I have to tell you."

"What the hell, Reid?"

"The three girls have been found. Their bodies were dumped in a travel stop's lagoon outside of Little Rock. From the coroner's analysis, they have been dead since the day we were to stop the truck."

Sara threw the phone across the room into a mirror. She had fucked up. The DEA and best laid plans had fucked up. The whole damn job was just so damn fucked up. The DEA had put her in a position unarmed, where there had been nothing, she could have done at the truck stop to save the girls she knew were being trafficked. To only observe illegal action didn't sit well with her soldier training to react. She went out the back door of the building, pushing JoAnn, who had just been coming in, aside.

"Jesus! What's with you?"

Sara didn't answer, she just went to the wall marking the end of the parking lot and climbed over. She crossed the grass divide leading to the woods and pushed aside blackberry vines to get into the timber. JoAnn stood at the wall, shouting, "You coming back? We'll have to cash out soon." Sara didn't answer, and only went deeper into the oak trees, out of the girl's sight and voice. She stumbled and tripped on the rolling carpet of acorns and went down onto her knees. She stayed down. Crying could not explain the emotion Sara was going through. Throwing up and puking would better define her condition. Shouldering the blame on herself for everything that had happened in her life came front and center again. It took her more than a few minutes to recover, but when she did it became oh so clear what she had to do on this one. She had to talk to Reid about what she had asked him to get information on.

Embarrassment reigned over their DEA crew for losing the three girls because of weak and late tracking of the truck carrying them when it left Hope, Arkansas. Sara's request to jump into the middle of the Arkansas human trafficking got top approval. Now it fell in her lap to make the assignment work. She liked working the murder case alone.

Hector Ruiz had left no clue to where he would pop up next when he left Cotter, Arkansas. Sara verified again with the local sheriff; Ruiz had not been seen in the county. Finding Ruiz would be her inroad to learning the leaders of what she had just gone through.

Reid came up with very little on Ruiz's whereabouts. Only a report his family could be found in the Mexican population of southern Little Rock. Sara bailed on her house in Hope and bid goodbye to the truck stop and the manager Reid had brought for her temporary replacement. Really, temporary? She would be fine to never go back to the truck stop and how the DEA wanted it to operate.

She hadn't forgotten Ruiz and their first meeting at the bar in Cotter, Arkansas. It hadn't been a hangout of Hispanics. He just happened to be there, and she just happened to beat the hell out of him over his attack on her dad.

She needed clothes to fit in at the bars where she would be looking for him. She wanted to bring up the job he had offered her after their run in. The excuse would work to help find him. Driving his car to shuttle the girls being trafficked would be where she could nail the bastard and the others running this shit.

Trying on black slacks, she finally found just the right fit. Her long slim legs were outlined by the tight pants. She turned in front of the dressing room mirror and lifted her leg diagonally in a flash across the flamenco dancer who wasn't there yet. She scored a point for herself and the good fit of the black slacks. She bought three more pairs of them. Next, the blouse. It had to be white and sheer. Just the blouse that brought Ruiz off his chair at the bar when they first met. Finally, she found just what she wanted. Putting the blouse on over her black bra gave her just the attraction she wanted to offer. Three-inch ruffles graced the blouse's buttons. Buying the three on the rack gave her a start. A pair of long black heels lifted her almost six-foot frame too much. She settled for a two-inch lift and a rich looking shoe like a dancer would wear.

Someone would pay for what had happened to the girls. She paused for a moment. The momentum of the killing of the girls had drug her away. Away from the men that had been responsible for so much more destruction and death around her. She needed to keep the pledge she had made. She would find the Oxfords and kill them both, but it had to wait for now.

A stop at a Staples store got her one hundred business cards. She thought of them like the bait she tossed to the trout when fishing the White River. One of them would hook Hector Ruiz and she would reel him in. She took the card on top of the package and read it.

WANTED: Hector Ruiz

This Señorita has a pregnancy test result.

Just for you. Love, Sara R.

501 528 7546

She wrote on the back with her pen. *Stand by, Reid, I'm going to raise some hell out here.*

With a cellphone picture of both sides, she sent them by Facebook Messenger to Reid.

Her phone rang within seconds. She didn't answer. Then a text message.

This is going to get you killed. Stop it. You don't know what the hell you are doing. Come in, Sara.

Reid.

He was wrong about part of what he had written. She knew exactly what she was doing. How she would do it became complicated quickly. Her first visit to a Little Rock bar in her new outfit brought a lot more attention from drunk truckers and redneck pickup drivers than she could handle. She pushed her way past the two Caucasian men harassing her and left the place. It reminded her she was treading on having her picture on a missing poster in every police station in Arkansas. She decided to break down Little Rock into sections. She needed to visit every Mexican restaurant in the city.

She knew only enough Spanish to help get a conversation started. With her dinner almost finished, she took the last bite of her tamale. A man that looked like he could be the manager stood at the side of her table.

"I hope you enjoyed the meal."

She barely got the tamale bite down before she spoke. "Yes. Very good, señor."

"My wife waited on you. She said you're looking for a Hispanic man."

"Yes. His name is Ruiz. Do you know him?"

"No, I'm sorry. I do not know him. My wife wanted me to tell you a lot of the locals find their Mexican food in the markets and small Mexican restaurants in the south part of our town. Sometimes my food is prepared with flavors and different ingredients. Should I say, more gringo-style. I don't want to offend you. I'm just trying to help."

"No, you didn't. Sometimes I feel lost out here looking for a Mexican man." She reached for cash to leave with the bill the waitress had slipped around the manager onto the table.

"Leave a few more cards and I'll pass them on to my cooks. Would you like the names of places like I mentioned?"

"Yes, I would. Thank you."

She had written down the names of six places he gave her to start really digging to find Ruiz. With a map in hand, she drove past two of the authentic Mexican restaurants. Both of the buildings were small, almost what she thought would be holes in the wall. Sara needed a different approach. The tight black slacks and flamboyant white blouse would not fit the small places with less than eight tables she now needed to visit.

Wearing her black hair streaming down both sides of her face had become her habit since being in the service. Her hair now draped across the edges of her shoulders and down across the middle of her breasts. She brushed it all off the scar on the left side of her face, pushing it completely to the other side. She wanted to let the scar tell her story and show the tough side of this gringa woman. Ruiz had a close-up look at it the night she took him down to the floor of Bear's Bar and Grill. She had ended Ruiz's fight with her dad and probably would have killed him without someone pulling her off and stopping her from choking him. He had seen the scar up close. It was right there above his bleeding face. His pursuit to hire her stemmed from the fight. He wanted her, the tough gringa that could transport his illicit cargo without attracting attention.

The clothes to wear here were a different matter for the section of town and the small Hispanic bars and restaurants she needed to visit. It took a dozen visits to local shops carrying jeans and shirts like she wanted. Her long legs needed jeans with legs to fit tight with just a couple of worn through holes showing the tan skin of her legs. She skipped the shirts and instead selected light weight pullovers. The tight-fitting pullover showed more of her than she wanted, but with the game she was playing, what the hell.

With new business cards printed in Spanish, she knew passing them out would eventually get Ruiz's attention. He would control the day and find her when it came time. The next restaurant on her list had been built at least a thousand years ago. Its adobe look blended in with the street where she found it. Two blocks away a flashing fifteen-foot-tall sign tried to draw cars and men passing on a main through street, away from the quiet of the old buildings down to assurances of FULL NUDES for their enjoyment.

Earlier, she had made a quick stop to get a post office box in a little mail center. She turned her cellphone off and left it in the mailbox. Too many of the text messages on it could get her killed. She pushed her hair back clear of her left side battle scar and reached for the first of two entrances into the restaurant. The metal rails of the tall gate squeaked as she turned the knob and pulled the gate open. Inside the gate, she stood in a porch area lighted by shaded red lanterns hanging from the ceiling. Another metal rail gate seemed to be part of the wooden door she needed to open to get in. Someone was just coming out and met her in the doorway. The two Hispanic men stepped back to let her pass. The man closest to her in the doorway continued to hold the door open and backed away as far as his arm would allow. The other man stood around the corner taking his cap off in a polite manner. Sara didn't try her Spanish. It would not even come close.

"Thank you, gentlemen." She walked by the men and knew both of them had just taken a deep breath of the strong perfume she wore. Both men graced her with a light bow of their heads as she went past. She chose the center table in the room and dropped her cheap imitation purse in the middle. No one rushed to take her order. It would be okay. It gave her eyes time to adjust to the dim multicolored lights coming from all directions in the dining area. Several four-foot-tall vases as wide as whiskey barrels but narrowing to little more than a half a foot graced corners of the room. She thought the vases contained fake palm branches. As her eyes became more accustomed to the light, clearly the branches were fake blue agave. *Fitting*, she thought. She really needed a double large margarita right now.

The waiter came to the opposite side of her table. He held a napkin she guessed wrapped around a spoon and fork. When the man dropped the napkin on the table it turned out to be only a napkin. He clearly did not want her here.

"I'm sorry. No menus. All the people come here know what we serve. But maybe not you?"

"It's okay. I know. Thank you. A diet coke and a burrito with rice and beans, please," she said. She laid one of the cards with the message for Ruiz on the table in front of her. She lifted it and gave it to the waiter. He looked at the card and shook his head no. He didn't question what it said, only a no was all she got. He laid the card back on the table. By now, and by the look of his apron, she knew this man did it all, including the cooking. He went on his way to the kitchen.

The neon sign in the center of the window above the booths flashed red, telling the mostly not interested the place was open, open, open. The waiter had set a coke can and a glass of ice in front of her. She filled the glass of ice with coke as she watched the three new customers coming in. They sat along the windows in the booth. Between the flashes of the neon, she could tell the men had a natural curiosity about the woman at a table in the center of the small restaurant. She bit the bullet, stood, and went to the side of the booth where the men were sitting. Both of the men slid to the side to allow room for her to sit. She picked the seat closest to her and slid in. She could feel her eardrums pounding from what she knew Reid would be saying if he watched what she just did.

A flurry of Spanish hit her eardrums instead. Fast and sexy from what she could understand, except for the word 'puta' but it didn't surprise her in the least. Maybe the word fit what she had been trying to pull off here. Instead, she laid two cards in front of the men. With each one she recited his name, "Hector Ruiz," She patted her stomach and added, "Mucho baby." The man next to her scooted up against the wall away from her. He lifted one of the cards to read it.

"This Ruiz fellow, you look for him? Sí?"

She patted her stomach again, "Ruiz's baby. Sí, Señor. Yes, I know him."

The man shook his head 'no' even before she got the question out of her mouth. He knows Ruiz. What came next was another burst of Spanish and her food.

"The men are saying you are bothering them, señorita. Your food is there," the waiter said, pointing at her table and walking to hold a chair for her. She left the booth and settled into her chair and table alone. The large burrito in front of her lay surrounded by orange and brown sauce and was pushed to the side of her plate by the rice and beans. With a bite of rice bordered by some of the thick bean paste in her mouth, she swallowed and then cut a large bite of the burrito. She waited a second for the last of the rice to clear her mouth. She took a drink of her coke and then went for a big bite of the burrito hunk. It was only a second before she realized the restaurant's level of spicy hot fell way off the warning charts for eatable. She spit the large bite into a napkin before nearly finishing off the rest of her coke to stop the burning. She turned to see the cook, headed around the corner for the kitchen. The two men were nearly doubled over with their hands covering their laughter. It wasn't funny to her. She knew it had been a setup to get her out of his restaurant and the neighborhood. The cook had filled the burrito with bright red cayenne pepper. It left her with the question in mind as to why the hell she was doing this. A much scarier one arose. Why were three young girls murdered and their bodies dumped into a fucking lagoon?

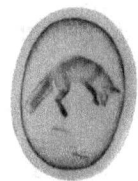

TWENTY-SIX

THE ONE-BEDROOM APARTMENT SHE had rented for working on the trafficking assignment was right in the middle of what could be called the southwest edges of Little Rock. It suited her undercover identification. The apartment did little else. She had looked for ways to defend herself if Ruiz came for her in the night. The best she could do was a table against the bedroom door. She needed time to talk to Ruiz about the job he had offered when she had been on the river. He would have no idea about the woman he would face now and the training she had put herself through. Reid had expressed doubts about Ruiz being in Little Rock. The population of Hispanics stood around fourteen thousand, and most were spread over the city. He tried to get her to go to Fort Smith instead. A memory came back from the day on the river when she went to Ruiz's sister's car and slammed it with a baseball bat to break out a side window. There, neatly tucked in the corner of the front window, was a Little Rock city sticker. She would keep looking here in this city. The sheriff in Cotter had told her Ruiz had a way of keeping his family in the same area where he conducted his business.

Without any change to her modus operandi, she visited two more Mexican restaurants in the next two days. With little to report to Reid, she sent a 'no luck yet' text. More than a dozen men and women now had her card with a message for Ruiz and her phone number. It hadn't surprised her when her phone had rang twice in the last day. No one responded when she said, "This is Sara. Hello?" Ever since she had lost Luke, any incoming phone buzz or ring would key an extra heartbeat. She had no way to stop or control the tightness across her chest. Maybe she only imagined it happening. Still, stopping and trying to disregard it never occurred to her. Luke was still there, a part of her she would never lose.

She had second thoughts about her own safety and picked up a burner phone to keep with her at all times.

She chose the middle of the afternoon for getting a drink. Her mouth had been sore for two days after she got scalded by the cayenne pepper. She wore her tight legged blue jeans with a couple more tears providing viewing spots of her legs. A low-cut pullover tee topped the outfit off.

She paused at the outer door of the building and pushed her hair away from the scar on the side of her face. She had done nothing with makeup to hide it in any way. It was a part of her Ruiz would remember.

A few faces turned from the two filled booths along the street side window. She had gotten used to being stared at for being so far out of bounds for a Caucasian. The nearly six feet of slim woman with long hair draped over her right shoulder could be the bait that would reel in Ruiz.

No one was sitting at the back along a long bar graced with upside down glasses with red rims hanging from the ceiling. They seemed out of place. She would expect to find the red rims in other parts of town catering to mainstream traffic. She slid onto a stool made to just the right height for her long legs. Her gaudy purse and billfold with keyrings holding circular charms rang as she dropped it on the surface of the bar. No one came at first, only the face of a man with a goatee peering through a six-foot wide counter window for setting out food. Today wouldn't be about food. She would let her non-alcohol self-down for one of the rimmed glasses, the red edges bristling with salt and surrounding what she guessed would be a fine margarita. With a shallow greeting from the man behind the bar, she watched as he filled the glass with small ice cubes and then poured the drink from a pitcher in an undercounter refrigerator. He smiled as he wiped the handle of the glass. Sound in the room echoed in the emptiness from side to side. She turned to find no one else was there. Nothing registered about her situation until she realized the men in the booths had left right after she had sat down. The bartender sat the margarita in front of her and offered a single page menu.

"Would you like to order something to eat?"

Then her weeks of training at the DEA struck her across the back of the head. The men in the bar clearing out—she had struck pay dirt here.

"I'm sorry, sir. Why did they all leave?"

"Get back to work. It was siesta time for them."

A strong urge hit her to get out. Still, the red rim with the salt. She wanted a taste of the salt first. She ran her tongue along the edge of the frosty drink. The taste matched her mood, and she needed to sit for a few minutes to see if the men had been ordered to leave. After another taste of the salt, she reached for the straw but couldn't find it. The red rimmed glasses above her head were going in circles around her. Someone had her around the waist and she could do nothing but collapse against the person. In a moment of awareness, she felt the sting of a needle going into her arm, and then nothing.

***

She watched the streetlights and neon signs flash by the window. Reading them became a challenge because only a few were in English. Some read pharmacy and doctor's offices, others were in Spanish, and she couldn't read them. The signs frightened her, and the rush of adrenaline shocked her awake. They were in Mexico. She tried to sit up in the back seat of the car. Having her wrists in handcuffs behind her back made it hard to do. Clearly Hector Ruiz had found her.

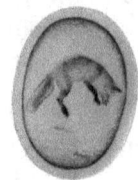

TWENTY-SEVEN

THE MAN DRIVING THE CAR had nothing to say to her. His companion in the front seat had started reaching and touching her legs. She understood enough Spanish to know he was laughing and calling her a whore. She asked to see Hector Ruiz. The man knew what she wanted, and her request brought only laughs and the words 'sure, pronto, puta'. The outside got dark. When her eyes adjusted, they were in a large warehouse. Someone held her arm and pulled her out of the car. She tried to sit on the edge of the seat to get her bearings. The man pulled her upright and pushed her toward a wire cage. He unlocked the cage door and shoved her in. Four girls were in the cage. One sat with her back braced against a corner pole. The others sat on the edges of three of the four wooden homemade bed frames with stuffed mattresses on them. Clearly, she had gotten into the search for Ruiz a lot deeper than she had planned.

She awoke from a restless sleep on one of the mattresses. She rolled to the side and floor to escape the tentacles of the mattress's straw-ticking sticking through and trying to engulf her in its moldy stink. Only one of the four girls remained in the cage. The girl sat in the corner. Her whole tiny body seemed to fill nothing more than a bushel bucket. Sara offered several times to talk with the girl. She didn't respond, but it didn't surprise Sara, because she knew Spanish could be the only language the girl knew. When a man came and shoved two trays under the door, each with a tortilla and a glob of beans in the middle, the girl in the corner got up and pushed the tray away. Looking at Sara, she laid her head to the side on both her hands. Sara guessed the food had been spiked. She went to sit in the corner by the girl. When she got close the girl pulled her against her and whispered in perfect English.

"They have a camera watching us. Sometimes they speak in English because they don't think I understand. Why are you here? You're too old for them to sell for prostitution."

"I'm here because I made a stupid mistake."

The two of them sat together for the next several hours. Sara kept watch. The drugs they had pushed in her had worn off and she wasn't sure she could ever sleep again. Not in this cell. When two Mexican men came toward the wire cage, Sara almost prayed one of them would be Ruiz. Maybe she would have a chance and hopefully another offer to help him with his smuggling. When they said her name and motioned for her, she nearly froze in place. She had faced one of the men and the meeting had been with the three girls that had been murdered. This man had held a baseball bat and then a long-barreled revolver she would never forget. One of the men grabbed Sara's arm and pulled her upright.

"You, come."

Sara staggered from sitting so long. The man slapped her in the middle of the back.

"Now, Gringa. Come."

The man she had recognized led the way through a doorway into a smaller room of the warehouse. The men pushed her forward and stood behind her. She faced a table with a man on the other side of it with his feet up. She had found Ruiz! She felt almost like letting out a sigh of relief until he stood and gave a command. The man she knew was pushed past her and into a metal chair near the wall. A flurry of Spanish was coming from his lips and his hand was pointing directly at her. He remembered her from their run in at the truck stop. Ruiz pulled the man back in the chair and reached under the man's coat to get out his pistol. Sara remembered the long barrel and how it had scared the heck out of her when he pulled it on them in the girl's restroom in Hope. Sara could only listen to the Spanish Ruiz was throwing at the man in the chair. Then Ruiz broke into English.

"Miss Sara Randolph, is this the man you have been looking

for? Sanchez killed three of my girls not far from your truck stop. They ran away from him, and he wanted to make an example out of them. He caught up to them at the edge of the rest stop. I knew you weren't looking for me, little Chiquita."

"So, he shot them for running away?" The little bit of bravery she had gathered let her move closer to stand by Ruiz looking at the man in the chair. The man caught on to what Ruiz was saying in English.

"Ruiz! Bullshit on this," he said, starting to get up from the chair. Ruiz swung his pistol's butt hard. It struck the man solidly on the side of his head. He handed the man's long barrel pistol to Sara. She checked to see if the pistol was loaded. It was. Now she couldn't be sure which of the three men she would shoot first. One of Ruiz's other men swung a rope over Sanchez in the chair and tied him against it.

"Now you are going to make him pay, Chiquita."

"Stop calling me that," Sara said. She held the pistol pointed at the floor, not sure of why he gave it to her.

"I'm not sure who you work for, Chiquita. Right now, you work for me. Shoot this son of a bitch child killer!"

She looked at Ruiz like if she shot anybody right then it would be him. Shaking her head in about the strongest 'hell no' she could muster, she tried to hand the pistol back to Ruiz.

"You shoot him. No one knows where you are, they will never know, if you don't shoot this child killer." Ruiz had pulled a Glock from his belt, and it was pointed at her face. She doubted Ruiz would kill her. Still, she had not detected any uncertainty in his voice about what he would do to her.

"I'm taking him back. The state will burn his ass for you."

"Who the hell do you work for? You can do this?"

"Take your pick. Right now, I work for you, but I'm not going to be the one to shoot this Mexican national." She handed the pistol back to Ruiz.

A shot fired right next to her head was deafening. It had surprised her. She went to her knees with both hands over her ears. She saw her soldiers blown apart again and falling around her. She stayed on her knees when Ruiz's second shot blew the side of the man's head away. Ruiz looked at her. He held the smoking pistol and then forced it into her hand. She stood, holding the dead man's pistol with the long barrel.

"You keep the pistol, little Chiquita. It will remind you if you come looking for me again, I'm going to find you and kill you with it. Comprende? Her ears were still ringing, but she heard his warning. The man who killed the three girls on the outskirts of Little Rock lay dead. There would be no chance she could take Ruiz in for running the operation. Trying to fight her way out of the warehouse, let alone out of Mexico, would get her killed. She gave in, but not completely. She stuck the long barrel of the dead man's pistol under her belt and nodded her head yes. She turned and motioned for Ruiz to follow her back into the large room with the wire cage.

"Now open this cage door," she said, standing to the side ready to go in.

Ruiz hesitated and then motioned for his man.

"Unlock the door for her."

With the wire door open Sara went to the corner of the cage. The girl cowered with her shabby coat covering her arms. Sara reached under the coat and took the girl's arm.

"Come on, we're both getting out of here." She pulled the girl to her feet and urged her to follow out of the cage.

Ruiz stood blocking their way. "Your luck has run out here now, Sara Randolph. You take her. A car is waiting to get you both to the border. We didn't harm her. I found out she has American citizenship and planned to let her go. We don't traffic American girls or women."

The girl's courage had gotten a lot bolder. A string of English mixed with Spanish curse words blistered even Sara's ears. Sara got an arm around the girl's neck and a hand across her mouth. "Shut up."

Sara didn't mind the black hoods Ruiz's men placed on their heads for the drive to the U.S. border. They let them out of the car a block away from it. It was a long way to Arkansas.

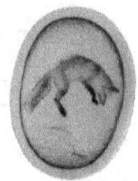

TWENTY-EIGHT

SHE KNEW THE COVER FOR the truck stop had been blown. All the trafficking operations heading north would never use it again. For the cartel and the drug traffic, Reid and the DEA oversight thought it still had value even after being debriefed. Sara's victory in finding the murderer of the trafficked girls gave her leeway in where her dual life of the DEA and the Arkansas Game Commission would take her next. Her self-prescribed mission to find the men most responsible for her lover's death had to come front and center for her. At her request to spend some time in the wilds of Arkansas, the Game Commission assigned her a truck and an ATV. She would patrol an area of the Buffalo River Basin short of agent coverage. It could be a good place for her to start her search for the two Oxford killers.

Scouting the basin road, she watched buzzards circling a section of the river off the road by a half mile. To her, the circling birds represented a tell on a dead animal she hoped could have died of old age or the ravages of unforgiving gray wolves. It had become a goal of hers to check out the death scenes. Rarely did she report the time away from her commission vehicle. It was easy to strap on a two-way radio on the short treks she would go on to stay in touch. Backing her truck into a ditch, she drove her ATV off the back. The National Forest area she needed to enter offered no fences to block her way. She checked the loading of her Glock and then slid it back into the holster. The small spider pistol she always carried rested just inside the top of her right boot. It wasn't commission authorized. It didn't matter. It would always be there ready, as a last-ditch resort to save her life. She slid her AR into the scabbard in front of the ATV. She looked again for the circling buzzards and using them for her direction of travel, she picked a spot to enter the timber.

She could never be sure why she loved the tall pine trees and heavy stands of oak and hickory she often found herself in while on commission assignments. A heavy branch slapped her face, then out of nowhere a vision of a thousand yards of sand in front of her. Dust blowing sideways made driving ahead to the base difficult and dangerous. Always going on knowing the compass would guide her and often be her only way out of the Iraqi desert. The smell of the pine branches brushing her arms was enough to bring her current reality back. She had been home from the deserts of Iraq for more than five years.

She wound her way through the timber toward the circling cleanup squad. The timber opened ahead onto a long sandbar along the river. A hundred yards ahead, she could see the turkey vultures landing on a carcass. The birds were fighting with each other, often driving a weaker bird away and back into flight. Parking the ATV, a short distance away, she lifted her camera from its case and slipped the rifle's sling over her shoulder. The vultures could be possessive of their find, so she might need to make some noise. She could tell from her distance the carcass was large. It could be someone's bull or cow that had gotten out and followed the river to die. As she got closer, her heart sank. The carcass the vultures had been feeding on was a bull elk. One side of its heavy rack of antlers lay pressed deep into the sandbar. The sand around the animal for yards showed tracks where the dying animal had struggled to its end. She fired two shots in the air to get the buzzards backed off the carcass. Most of them took flight, rising to circle above her. Two of the biggest birds stood back a few dozen feet. They stared at the intruder after their meal. She walked to the dead animal and rubbed the tall rack of antlers reaching more than three feet above the bull's head.

"Sorry, old boy. I guess it was just your time to die." She

rubbed again and turned on her camera to get some feedback for the elk project team from the commission. Taking pictures from both sides of the dead animal, she realized most of the bull elk's right front leg was gone. She knew in an instant it had been blown away. More than once she had witnessed the results of hidden Iraqi IEDs. She struggled to think where the same thing could happen in the deep woods of Arkansas. Sitting back on the ATV, she recorded the GPS location of the carcass and looked at the pictures on her camera's viewfinder. Jumping off the vehicle, she went back with her camera in hand to get more pictures. This explosion had been meant to wound and to cause a slow, lingering death as the animal ran.

A game warden's position required an agent to keep their emotions in check. She didn't remember which lecture had told her this, but right now she didn't give a crap. She had gone off scale. What low-life son of a bitch blew up this beautiful animal purely for the need to inflict pain and death? Or was it to protect a hidden field of drugs? Her weeks of training at the Morris Training Center and the DEA kicked in full throttle. Finding some leads to this killer became overpowering.

The animal's time of death became important. She went to her ATV and opened a small case all the agents carried. With a long, slim thermometer, she went back to the carcass and inserted the instrument into the animal's rectum. After five minutes, she took the thermometer out and read it. Flipping open a small reference book from the case, she read the animal still hadn't cooled to the ambient temperature of the woods. It wasn't much to go on. The animal had possibly been wounded in the evening before or after dark. She cleaned and stored the instrument back on the ATV and stood looking at the dead elk. The vultures had landed in the trees around it and were perched ready to feast. Not bothering to scare them off, she started walking a pattern around the animal's body. A weak blood trail and the elk's laboring prints led from out of the woods. The animal had nearly made it to the river to die. It didn't surprise her. She had seen it many times before. With her rifle slung over one shoulder and the camera on the other, she started following the tracks, not pausing for a second to consider what she might be walking into.

Twice in the next hour, she lost the trail when the elk had crossed rocky ridges. And then on the other side of the rock, she found spots of blood and the deep three-legged tracks of an animal dragging a destroyed front leg. The tracks led straight away from what she knew would be the boundary of the National Forest area. With no fences to block her path, she followed the blood spot trail. She guessed it had now been over a mile, and the blood spots were bigger. It would mean she could be close to where the animal had been wounded. A look at her GPS tracker map showed only a narrow winding road leading into the valley just ahead. She didn't see a house anywhere on the map, only a barn. For a protected animal to be blown up shocked her. The caution flag for what she might find ahead came up. The guilt for getting the Humvee crew she was responsible for blown to hell haunted her, and kept pressing her to go into dangerous situations with no one else with her to be hurt or killed. Going ahead alone suited her best.

The deep woods opened onto a plowed field just ahead. A wall of six-foot-tall corn stalks marked a farmer's acres. An open path of broken corn stalks showed her where the bull elk had plunged out of the field running for its life. She followed the path through the cornfield at what she guessed to be around a hundred yards. She came out the other side where the deep tracks left by the bolting elk showed her where the explosion had been set. The elk had started to enter a cleared path leading up the hill. Walking out of the cornfield a dozen feet, she photographed the tracks and the north side of the field. The woods to the left of the elk's tracks had been left standing. It bothered her. The heavy thicket of trees could be cover for the person that set a death trap for a human or an animal. Still, she saw no cabin or signs of someone living in the area, only trails made by four-wheelers led along the ridge and then looked like they headed toward the hilltop. Turning the camera toward the woods, she clicked off two shots and then froze at what the telephoto lens showed her. The circular camouflaged tent sat nearly hidden in the trees and brush.

After taking a deep breath she walked toward the trees and the blind. A path presented a way through the brush growing on the edge of the woods. She stopped halfway up the path, and there in all its shining glory just off the path's edge, she saw the brass from someone's shooting. Again, she photographed and then lifted the brass with a small writing pen she always carried. With a guess she put the brass to be from a 30-30 round from a lever action rifle. Without an evidence bag, she carefully slipped the brass into her shirt pocket. Then taking two more steps forward, she froze. It was more than difficult to see. It shocked her when she realized the trap she could have tripped. Iraq had been a great teacher for finding tripwires. Backing away, she saw the pile of leaves covering what she knew could spell the end of life for an intruder. Turning, she hurried down the path toward the cover of the tall corn.

The bullet zinged by her head and snapped corn tassels before ripping on through the corn field. Someone must not have seen the green of her uniform and the gold of her badge, let alone the AR-15 dangling around to her back.

"Fuck!" she yelled, running for the cover of the corn to hide from another shot. The rumble of the four-wheeler coming down the hill in a rush let her know someone didn't give a damn about the uniform, badge, or gun. Never the best at running a hundred-yard dash, this time she knew her own best record had been bested. The forest surrounded her, and a fallen tree ahead gave her the fort she needed now. Jumping over it, she dropped to the ground with her rifle pointed at the place where she had run out of, and the four-wheeler stopped. The fight had just arrived.

Reaching around her belt, she pulled out her Hail Mary alarm. All field operations now require this device. Snapping the top off, she set it off. The red light on the transmitter showed the little device was sending her SOS and GPS coordinates out once every minute. The satellite signal could not be blocked and would now be reaching the Arkansas Game Commission's communication center and at the same time the DEA agent center working the central Arkansas area. The device had come to her attention only a month ago, so just how long it would take to get an in-person war party to her wasn't clear.

"It needs to be quick, goddamn it," she said to herself. She tried her best to work off the sounds coming from the cornfield and find a target. The next sound from somewhere on the hillside came as a first from there. The buzz and constant hum of the drone's electric motors filled the valley. She saw it rise straight up from the trees. The camera on the bottom turned as it pointed the lens, searching for her. It flew a few feet above the corn stalk, scanning the area ahead before the lens fixed on the log in front of her. They had found her. The camera on the drone fit nicely in her rifle's scope. She paused a second to make sure someone knew what was coming and then placed her first shot in the middle of the camera's lens, the second in the middle of the drone. Pieces flew for yards away from the pile of junk falling out of the air.

"Next?" she yelled.

"You're going to be next, bitch," came the answer, this time over a loudspeaker mounted above the camo tent.

Standing to run brought more gunfire. After being pinned down for more than an hour, she heard only the crack of a bullet when she tried to move or change position. When two more four-wheelers came down the hill, it became time to really worry.

The loudspeaker blared again, "The last person who found this field is buried under it. You are going under there next."

She didn't answer, but checked her rifle and took out the second magazine from her belt in case she needed it.

Again, the speaker continued. "We found your truck where you came in. It's been moved and sits at the bottom of a lake. Guess you know your two way or phone ain't working in here. We got blockers on twenty-four seven in this valley."

She had found out an hour ago.

"Walk out now and your good-looking body won't be all shot to hell."

"Iraq took care of that a long time ago," she yelled back. "Come on, damn it. Not so much talk."

She tried her best to piss the men off and get someone to try to advance on her. It would be her best chance to fight here and not get shot trying to run. She turned toward the right side of the cornfield. Someone had just crossed into the woods. Two shots came and flung wood chips out of the log and onto her legs. They were coming for her now. She raked the cornfield with five shots and then added another at the brush area she had seen the shadow of a man run into. At least three weapons opened up on her position. This time it was Army-grade rifles, firing fast. She slipped lower behind the log. Several bullets came under the log to her left. She had moved now, and they must not have known where she hid. Ready to empty her magazine on the corn, she paused at the sound of the thump, thump she knew so well from her helicopter support in Iraq. The calvary had arrived. The bird made one turn over the field, searching out her trouble, and a side gunner waved when Sara stood and pointed at the wooded hillside behind the camo tent and the ATVs sitting there. He nodded a understanding, and when the bird turned again, the ATV became scrap metal.

A different voice screamed into the loud speaker, "Stop shooting, we're coming out." She saw two men standing near the edge of the woods with their hands up. She saw two other men were in the woods running up the hill.

She waved to get the pilot's attention and pointed to the two men giving up. The chopper circled again and landed off to the side of the cornfield. Four men wearing DEA agent jackets came out of the bird when the blades stopped, and the engine wound down. Taking her eyes off the two men that had given up for a second, she saw a DEA agent walking toward her and then realized it was Reid.

He took her in his arms. "Your alarm woke up the whole DEA team. I had been helping them get on board here in Central Arkansas and saw it come in. Why are you fighting this battle alone?"

"I saw two of the men head up the hill. Can we talk about it when we put an end to this fight?"

"There's an old barn at the top of the hill. Let's get up there,"

Reid said. He started walking up the path.

"Stop! There's a tripwire across the path. It's just ahead."

Reid keyed his communications unit, "Heads up. Tripwire." He pointed to the place.

"Bob can strip it out." He looked at Sara. She had questions.

"Bob is a bomb guy, and he served in Iraq."

She nodded and led the way to the path the ATV made coming down the hill. It would be a safe way to the top. Both Sara and Reid went the last fifty yards going off the path and into the woods to approach the barn. They carried their AR-15s pointing directly ahead. As they got closer, the old barn idea evaporated. This building had been camouflaged as a barn. The short crack of an aircraft engine starting and then a burst of power as an airplane started its takeoff roll.

Reid pointed ahead as he ran. "There's no airfield here."

"Well, I think there is one now." They both broke around the building running down a grass pasture strip toward the airplane. "The airplane had been hidden under a lean-to hanger. That's one hell of a short takeoff aircraft. They're out of here."

"Let's get in the building. I want to see what else is going on here. This isn't just a small pot-growing operation," Reid said, turning toward the building.

She saw the flash of an igniter through a window. "Stop, Reid. Get down."

The explosion ripped the air. Sara dropped almost before the sound hit her; she had seen bomb igniters before. The shockwave tore at her clothing, blowing her rifle out of her hand and into the dirt cloud. "Reid. Where are you?" Dust and dirt filled her eyes. She reached for the canteen of water she had on her belt. She uncapped it and poured the whole thing across her face and eyes. Reid had been blown flat on his back. She crawled to him.

"Reid! Talk to me." She felt for his carotid pulse. It wasn't the first time she had witnessed a man down from a blast. She guessed the wind had been knocked out of him and he had to get a breath. She sat him upright and got behind him to pull on his stomach.

"Breathe, Reid. Deep breath."

The next pull, she made Reid cough and spit dirt. It took her minutes to start to make sense of what he was saying.

"You knew the building was going to blow," he said, trying to get on his feet.

She helped him. "We need to get away from here. That building is probably full of meth chemicals and we're way too close."

The DEA chopper brushed the tree tops going over them. It set down on the short runway. One of the DEA agents came and got an arm under Reid.

"Do you have suits and air packs on board the chopper?" Sara demanded.

"We do have. The chopper needs to be moved away as fast as we can."

The blast had only taken the top and a side of the building off. There had been no fire. What she wanted to find would be in the rubble. A drug operation as big as this one could have tentacles in all directions, even to the small operators she knew about and wanted to find and take down.

"I'm going to suit up. It's critical we see what's left in there of any kind of product," she said, and then ran for the chopper's open door. Reid had been helped inside the cargo area of the chopper. She didn't tell him she was going into the exploded building. With two suitcases lying on the dirt, the chopper took off and moved to the far end of the dirt runway. Robert picked up one of the suitcases.

"I'm going in with you, Randolph. I've neutralized the tripwire trap down the hill."

"Get suited up, then," she said.

Sara dressed carefully in white coveralls and slipped the hooded air supply on. The backpack running the air supply hummed, pushing out the clean breathable air. She finished getting ready by using duct tape around the suit's sleeves on her wrists.

It took both of them to push the bent door to the building open. The inside of the building looked like a high school chem laboratory where all the students had gone crazy and busted it to pieces. The granite tops of the sinks across the room had glass beakers broken with pieces covering their tops.

It wasn't the broken meth-making equipment she wanted to see. Sara veered off from Robert and went into an area that looked like an office. Four large drones had fallen off shelves that had been turned over. Each of them had a cargo carrier attached. The men had a modern delivery system going. A single computer console lay on its side under a desk. The sides were bent but still on the computer. Sara pulled the plugs out of the back and set them on the desk. A dime coin in the desk served to take out the screws holding the side on. The hard drive slipped out just as quickly. It could be what she needed to get leads to where the product had been going. She especially wanted to find the name Oxford there. With them being pushed out of their home territory, she guessed they would be buying from a wholesale operation like they had just found. Their name raised her blood pressure every time she played a game with it in her mind. Both of the men were tied against a shooting gallery's target post, and she made them flinch each time her pistol shots got closer and closer. A disk recorder sat nearby on a small floor cabinet. They had attempted to smash the case in their hurry to leave. On a chance the disks inside the case could still be okay, she unplugged the recorder and, with it under her arm, went to join Robert. He looked up from a metal case. He showed a package to her and shook his head.

"I believe it contains cocaine. They may have changed over to a cocaine operation. There're so many little meth operations, the money is on cocaine for the future." He spooned a sample of the powder into a glass bottle.

"I'm ready. Need help carrying anything?"

"I've got them. Let's get out of here."

Once loaded in the chopper, they lifted off. The pilot told her over her headphones a call to air traffic control to look for the small plane had gone out minutes before. Sara knew there would be no way to spot the aircraft on radar. It would be at treetop level, headed for Texas and Mexico. She needed a DEA electronic laboratory to get the data and disassemble the disk drive. She hated to give up either of the devices to a team effort. Reid wouldn't want her to do it alone. Still, she wanted to see the data first. She leaned against Reid, hugging him and then keeping a soft grip on the man's arm she thought so much of.

TWENTY-NINE

WITH A ONE-DAY TURNAROUND from the DEA's electronics technicians, she left the safehouse with a two-terabyte drive filled with bookkeeping data from the hidden labs computer and hundreds of pictures saved from three of the unbroken CDs in the six security camera recorders. She needed time to study the data taken off the hard drive. She checked in with Reid to be sure he was okay and then headed her Ford F-250 north toward her family and home on the river.

Jimmy and the two dogs were the first to greet her when she pulled into the cabin's yard. The hound her dad had named Blue lost interest even before she climbed out of the truck. He went around the cabin, headed for a cool place under the deck. Jimmy climbed up on the side mounted bar step and peered into the passenger side of the new truck.

"I hope you're going to let me drive this."

"Drive? You've got a ways to go before you have a license, young man."

"John lets me drive just over to Marty's barn once in a while. I'll be really careful and all if you let me drive it."

"I'm going to have to talk to John about letting you drive anywhere at all."

He jumped down and came around to meet her as she got out of the truck. Tank had hung back at the sight of the new truck and smells he didn't recognize. When her feet touched the ground, he stood and came to her. After a half dozen tail wags, he assumed a sitting position with his nose nearly touching her leg.

"This old boy is really starting to show his age, Jimmy," she said, kneeling with both her hands scratching the dog's head and neck. "I love you, buddy."

"I have to feed him special now. Blue can sometimes get to his bowl first."

"Thank you, Jimmy. He's like our veterans that came out of the war. They got old fast."

"Are you talking about your dad?" John said. He had just come out of the cabin. He offered an arm to Sara for a hug.

"Hello, Dad. I guess I was talking about both of us, and Tank." She turned and headed for the cabin door.

"There's a surprise for you on the other side of the cabin."

"A surprise?"

"They were here for more than two weeks building an extra bedroom for you."

"You're kidding. I can't wait to see it." Then after giving her dad a hug, she hurried to get into the cabin.

She found the bedroom perfect. It had already been outfitted with a double bed and a desk and chair. The men had obviously forgotten about storing things like bras and underwear. There would be plenty of space for a chest of drawers. She headed for the truck to get her laptop and briefcase with the downloaded information the DEA technician had obtained for her.

Jimmy walked alongside her. "Can you go over to Marty's barn with me? I've been training a horse we want you to see."

"We? You and Marty?"

"Both of us."

"I'd love to go. It's late, so will tomorrow be, okay?"

"Sure. I'll wake you up early."

"Maybe not so early. I haven't slept in for quite a while, young man."

Back in her room, she laid the briefcase on the desk. Standing and looking at it, she realized the huge amount of work needed to study the hundreds of words of data she would have to go through. She got no takers when she offered to share the mountain of data with the DEA crews assigned to work the drug traffic moving up from Texas on the highways. Keeping alive the hunt for the

Oxfords now rested with local sheriffs and their individual county-by-county assigned areas. With no overlapping search underway, she knew the best chance to find them now rested in her hands and the data she had found in their raid on the drug barn.

Finding a clue to the men she searched for would at least give her a starting point or an idea. After scanning the first of the data on her laptop, it became clear the drug dealers dealt in numbers instead of names. Each of the entries included latitude and longitude and what she guessed was a customer or dealer number. With a search program pulled up, she transferred several latitude and longitudes to check the locations on a map. She had to take a deep breath. The locations were all over the map. None of the hits were in towns. Most of the locations fell in forests or fields. All were fairly near roads. With a Google search, she found a couple of locations near where she and Luke had first met the meth-dealing Oxford brothers. The drop site for the drug carrying drones lay less than a hundred yards from a popular sandy beach on the Buffalo River. It would at least be a place to start her search. She folded the laptop.

***

Morning found her walking with Jimmy to the horse barn at Marty's. It seemed to her he had grown more than a foot taller since she had started her training. He was tall for his age; she didn't have to look down now to speak to his five-foot six-inch frame of a man. Jimmy had her promise to dig out her cowboy boots and wear them this morning. She couldn't remember a time seeing Jimmy not wearing his. This morning he wore them with a pair of blunt spurs. He told her the rounded ends encouraged the horse without inflicting pain. By the time they reached Marty's barn, Sara was giving a little to the stiff, hard soles of her boots. It took her back to the time she wore the combat boots of Iraq. As they searched the streets of Bucca, she wished the boots had steel for soles instead of leather. Small noises of tiny pieces of glass breaking beneath their feet on the Bucca streets could send shudders up the best soldier's back.

A white truck sat parked half through the door of the barn. The words "Cotter Equine Veterinarian" lettered on the door told them why it was there.

"Doc Bryant is here. I may have to help," Jimmy said, as he ran

165

ahead into the barn.

She picked up her pace to follow. Running seemed out of the question. The boots hurt too much. It surprised her when she recognized the veterinarian. She had met and helped Doctor Ralph Bryant while in training to be a Wildlife Officer at the Morris center.

Doctor Bryant was working on a horse with its head in the stall doorway. A metal apparatus surrounded its mouth, holding it open. Jimmy came toward her.

"You gotta see this. Doc is floating the horse's teeth. It don't hurt the horse none, 'cause he's partly asleep."

Sara moved a little closer, watching the veterinarian working with long, heavy rasps in the horse's mouth. Floating teeth didn't ring any bells with her. It seemed Jimmy knew and wanted to fill her in on it all.

"Their teeth get sharp edges and it's hard for them to chew. He has to file them down smooth. I helped him do one horse the last time he was here."

Sara had gotten close alongside the doctor and his filing on the horse's teeth. He handed her a heavy rasp without even looking back.

"My arm is getting tired. Just work a little on the left side of her mouth. The mare still has a sharp spot there."

Sara didn't hesitate. She took the next step up and laid the file in the horse's mouth based on her left hand holding the file.

"Horses left, not yours," Doctor Bryant said, finally looking around at her. "Randolph, darn. I thought it was Mrs. Johnson behind me. It's been a while, Sara."

"I know, Doctor." Sara didn't slow down with the file. She had it on the right side of the horse's mouth and had given a couple pushes against the sharp-edged tooth.

"There, I think that experience is all I need of floating teeth."

She handed the file back to the doctor. She heard Jimmy and the doctor give a little chuckle from what she did and said. The doctor stepped back up and looked at the teeth on both sides of the horse's jaw. With two more file pushes, he dropped the file in a bucket of water and declared the floating done. With the floating harness off the horse's mouth, he gently walked the mare back into the stall.

"Give her a couple hours to wake up fully before letting her out," he said, closing the stall door and picking up his bucket of horse dental tools.

"Sara Randolph, you helped me out at Morris with the animals they kept. I lost track of you before graduation."

"This graduation?" Sara gave him a glimpse of the gold badge she kept on her belt. "I've had a couple special assignments that took me away for a while. I'm back now to stay. I hope."

"If you ever have a day or two off and would like to ride along on my calls, I would love to have the company. Oh, and the help."

"I would like that. I believe Marty is going to help me become a horse owner soon. So, a little education can't hurt."

"I have to keep a private cell number because I like a day off now and then. I work with two other vets to make that happen." He turned his business card over and wrote the number on the back.

Her first meeting with the doctor had been at her Morris training over a baby raccoon. She had found the little raccoon on an evening walk around the dorms. It had scampered up to her on the pathway and stood on its hind legs, reaching toward her. The baby made a chuckling noise that almost got her to pick it up. The doctor must have been following the raccoon.

The doctor's friendly hello went on to tell her the raccoon had escaped from its cage, and he had been looking for it. She learned Dr. Bryant was the veterinarian for the Morris Training Center and he came often to care for the animals that were kept for study purposes. By now the baby raccoon had gripped her leg and tried to climb up to her hands. She offered a hand, and the baby reached and took hold of her fingers. With her arms wrapped around the little guy, she softly cooed to it. A love of wild animals had been deeply ingrained in her very being from childhood. Over the next months of her training, she spent a number of evenings helping the doctor care for the animals at Morris. She enjoyed helping him.

Seeing him at the barn had been a surprise. He hadn't asked for her phone number, but she wanted him to have it.

After thanking him for his card, she dialed his cell number while he watched and saw it ring.

"Now you have my number, too. I promise I won't use this number to call for a sick horse."

"Are you keeping a horse here?"

"Not yet. All my roads seem to be leading that way, however. It would be fine and something Jimmy and I can do together."

"You have my number regardless. Do call." He offered a warm handshake and then closed up the back of his truck. "Take care of Jimmy. He's going to be a fine horseman."

"Will do. Bye." Being so forward with the doctor surprised her. She hadn't forgotten turning him down for an evening away from Morris and a dinner out. She hoped he would still like to spend an evening with her.

***

Back in the horse barn arena, Jimmy had saddled a paint horse. He covered the ground around the big circle with a slow, easy trot. When he saw Sara returning, she saw him urge the horse into a lope. Jimmy offered a bit of information about the horse as he passed her.

"Watch her front legs as I go by."

She looked but didn't know what she was looking for. Next time around, Jimmy added more.

"Her right leg is going out first," he said. He pulled up and trotted back to her.

"I was going clockwise. So, the right leg is reaching out first."

Marty came up by her side. "It's what horse people call the horse's lead. When you turn the horse counterclockwise the horse should be on the left lead. It takes a bit of training for the rider and the horse."

"I'm proud of Jimmy and his learning so much," Sara said.

"You got your boots on, why don't you ride the mare around a few times and see what you think."

Jimmy pulled the horse up in front of the gate and dismounted. He held the reins as Sara reached for the saddle horn and stretched to get her foot up to the stirrup.

"Boy, do I need to do more walking and jogging. I'm way too stiff for this."

Jimmy offered his hand. "Step on my hand, I'll toss you up there."

His strength surprised her. She had to grab onto the saddle as she was pushed up.

"Just walk her around. Lope a little when you're comfortable.

It just takes a little urge with your knees," Marty said.

Sara gathered the reins on the mare.

"Let the reins have a little sag. She's not going to run away with you," Jimmy said. "That's better. Now take her around."

The feeling of the horse's movement carrying her around the arena gave a feeling of freedom she loved. She looked to see if the horse had taken the right 'lead', as Jimmy called it. The horse's travel felt correct, and no one was yelling, 'wrong lead!'. She continued.

"Try her trot!" Jimmy yelled.

Sara tightened up on the reins, and the mare responded by slowing and falling into its trot. Getting to like the trot didn't seem to be something that would happen for Sara. The jarring on her butt never seemed to match her place and position in the saddle. She slowed the mare to a walk and took one more turn around the arena. She pulled up by Jimmy, and he slid over the wall and held the mare's reins as she slipped her leg over the saddle and let herself down.

"Thanks, guys, for the help and ride. She's a nice mare."

Sara didn't offer any encouragement to Jimmy that she would want the mare for her horse. She still needed to settle some old history and maybe find a small ranch of their own where her dad, Jimmy, and she could be together and have more than one horse. She could tell, as Jimmy walked to the cabin with her, he was disappointed that she didn't take a big liking to the mare. She didn't try to explain to the boy.

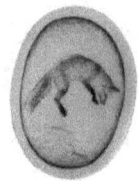

THIRTY

WITH A RUBBER RAFT IN the bed of her truck, Sara crossed the Buffalo River on a high concrete bridge. The sandy beach location near a drone drop off spot lay ahead. A sign marked "Pruitt's Landing", a state access area, sat just to the right of the highway. She turned off and down a dirt road to a sand and gravel bar. A pickup truck sat on the edge of the woods with both of its doors open and the tailgate down. The truck showed a lot of its rusted bare underbelly and wheel wells. The rust hadn't been kind to it. Sara took measure of it and the older minivan nearby. She snapped cellphone pictures of both vehicles as she passed them. She hoped going through the dozens of pictures she had been taking on drives away from the cabin would later key a thought or a chance memory if she saw them again.

Two kids ran across the gravel bar and into the shallow waters of the river. She pulled up, feeling her new truck didn't fit the place where she had picked to start her search. She needed her own older truck with its work history showing all over the dented bed and tailgate. Today was all about rooting and turning over the dirt until the murdering meth dealers were uncovered.

"Hey, can we get your raft out for you?" The two boys at the truck window swept her thinking back to the river's gravel bar.

"Why don't you give me a minute? I need to get down to my swimming suit," she said, rolling up the truck window. She dropped off her shoulder holster and slid the Glock into a sack with her lunch. She watched the boys run down the sand and stop by a table filled with empty beer cans and two men and two women with their heads down, talking. They gave no notice to the boys, only motioned and yelled for them to get the hell away. Sara buckled her belt and left her jeans on. With her shirt off, the modest bikini top would be enough to get some sun.

She rubbed the springing fox tattoo on her wrist, and it brought the memory of leaving Luke's burial site and the soaring eagle along the bluff. The eagle had saved her life. Someday an eagle would join the fox and little minnow tattoos on her wrists.

She had the truck's tailgate open, and the rubber raft untied, when the boys slid under the raft and started helping her with it on their shoulders. She carried the paddle and held on to just the front rope of the raft. They carried it down the sandbank and then across the gravel bar. The barefoot boys waded out up to their waists and set the raft in the water.

"Can we take a float with you? We got two more paddles."

This was not what she had planned—however, maybe it would work. "Go ask your mom and dad if it's okay."

Sand flew into the air off the boys' feet as they ran to the table where the adults were sitting. One boy touched the back of one of the women. She barely looked around, only spit out, "Go, damn it."

The boys returned with two paddles they got out of the back of the white pickup. They took places in front and back of the raft, leaving the center seat to her. She had pushed her lunch sack and her weapon under the boat's seat.

She stepped in as the raft caught the slow current of the Buffalo and started them downstream. The fresh smelling waters of the river swept her back to her second home, the rivers of Arkansas. The last months of being away had taken a toll on her spirit.

"Come on, you lazy boys. Let's paddle this ship upstream a ways so we can sit back and just drift."

Both of the boy's paddles hit the water. They weren't new to rafts and boats. They pulled together to turn the rubber raft and head it upstream.

"My brother wants me to ask you, how come you got that scar on your side?"

Being dragged back when she had just escaped thinking about

her scars surprised her. She needed to have fun with the question. "A bad dude came at me with a big knife," she said, turning so the boy could see the long cut in her side.

"I bet you got him good for that."

She guessed his young life may have already been filled with too many knives, guns, and fights. All were distractions from things like fishing and hunting she knew her dad had given her and now Jimmy. She let his statement drop.

The boys' determination to paddle had taken them just under the high bridge she had crossed earlier. Both boys used the bridge to bounce echoes off. Mostly hellos and 'hey, you's.

She yelled, "hooah!" The echo never had a chance. The rumble of a vehicle crossing the bridge followed right behind by a second vehicle stole her hooah away. She got a glance at the two black pickups coming off the bridge apron and turning into the access area.

"Dang, slow down, pickups," she said to no one. The speed the trucks came into the area keyed an alarm. An alarm she had learned to watch for in Iraq. A speeding truck coming toward the prison compound could mean death had arrived. Both boys took on a look she had seen on men going into battle.

"What's wrong?"

The boys jumped out of the raft and into the shallow water, heading for the bank. She heard the screech of the trucks' tires stopping in the parking area of the turnout. Slamming truck doors were shortly followed by the loud voices bracing both sides of an argument that gave her a good idea why the boys were running away from their kin.

The terrible reality of a pistol blasting, followed by the screams of the women, made her adrenal gland empty into her heart. She tossed the lunch onto the bottom of the raft as she pulled out the holster and pistol. She didn't mess with putting the holster on; the Glock was in her hand as she jumped into the waist-deep water and pushed hard to wade to the shore. She ran across the gravel and sand toward the trouble. The boys were running and almost out of sight upstream. They were headed away from the hell happening back at the table.

Her truck sat between her and the picnic table ahead. She ran against the truck's door, backed off enough to open it, and reached under the seat for the DEA beacon she carried. She pulled the top off and pushed the button. The newly acquired satellite device keyed an emergency signal with its GPS location. Certain Reid was reading her code and location, she stooped and went to the back of her truck's bed. Her search had landed her right in the middle of a drug killing. She wanted to get into the fight in front of her and stop it. Not sure who to shoot at, she leaned around the truck. One of the men kicked at the slumping body of a wounded or dead man that had been sitting at the table. The other man and the two women had run to their van and were burning rubber up the slope to get away. She took aim at one of the four men and fired.

"Some bitch has got a gun over there," one of the men yelled, ducking from her fire.

The bullets spewing out of an AR-15 racked the side of her truck. She backed up behind the truck's cab and leaned around, leveling her Glock on the AR's shooter. She fired three rounds into him before he realized he was dead. The man fell forward on his face. She had made a dent in the carnage in front of her. She fired again at the man reaching for the AR. He must have had second thoughts. Backing off, the three ran for their trucks, turning to shoot at her with every few steps. She saved her rounds. Her second magazine still lay in the back seat of her truck. The two trucks left one hell of dust cloud in the loose gravel as they turned and drove out of the site parking. They didn't cross the bridge. She knew if they had, she would have been a sitting duck if they stopped and had another AR in their trucks. Her firing on them stopped them from taking the man she had shot. He still hadn't moved, she assumed he was dead. She advanced on the table where the women and men had been sitting. The pulse of the man that had been sitting at the table they had shot was flat. He was dead. Checking the man, she had shot, she got a surprise. He was still alive. The man had no signs of a breath. Two of her shots had entered his right chest. She had witnessed soldiers walking and holding their chests with similar wounds. She pulled him over and started CPR. In half a minute the man coughed up blood, and she could feel his heartbeat.

With little choice, she knew getting the man to medical care quickly would be the only way to save him. With only a tiny cellphone bar for a signal, she tried anyway. 911 didn't respond. With her shirt from the truck belted against his wounds, she used her war carry from Iraq and loaded him into the passenger seat of her truck. Belting him into the seat, she turned out of the sandbar area and headed for Harrison, the closest town with a hospital. As she gained the top of a ridge, her cellphone rang. She didn't wait to hear who was calling.

"I have a man shot in the chest twice."

"We have a team on the way, Sara," Reid said. "They are helicopter mounted and would be about twenty miles from the cellphone GPS I'm reading from you. Find a flat spot and pull over. They will fly right to you."

"I'm doing that now."

"Did you shoot him?"

"Yes. It's a long story. I've got photos on the cars and plates of the truck the shot guy had been in. I'm sending them to you now."

She pulled over to wait. Checking the wounded man's pulse, it had gotten weaker. Like her, the man had tattoos on each of his arms. She had looked through hundreds of drug gang tats while in the DEA training program. Too many to remember. She photographed both of the man's arms and the single tattoo on the side of the man's forehead. They could tell a lot as to where the man was from. She marked him as Hispanic but didn't know for sure.

The unmarked helicopter circled her truck and then set down in the middle of the blacktop highway. With the blades still turning and set to flat pitch, two men jumped out and pulled a transfer board from the open door of the bird.

She offered her badge and identification to the two men as they approached her truck.

"Never mind, Sara, we know who you are. Who's the patient?"

"I've no idea. He had no billfold when I hoisted him off the ground. The men with him probably had it in their truck. I heard an argument before I shot him. He had killed a man at the table. I'm headed back there now. The women and another man who were there hightailed it as I got to the scene and started firing. Two boys belonging to the woman at the beach were with me paddling on a rubber boat. They were the first to know what was going on and hit the woods, running away before it happened. It wasn't the first time for these kids."

The medics had the wounded guy loaded onto the transportation board and were starting for the helicopter.

"I don't know what you did to keep him alive this long. I can hardly feel a pulse. Reid will let you know how this goes," the men said as they ran under the rotating blades carrying the nearly dead guy.

She turned her truck and sped back the three miles to the river sandbar. At the picnic area, she yelled for the boys before starting a search around the table where she had wounded the man. Lying under the table, she found a round golf ball-sized roll of aluminum. Certain there would be remnants of meth inside, she bagged the roll. Finding the meth gave her confidence she might be on the right track for her prey.

She needed more from this. The dead man's shirt pocket gave up two packets of white powder. Testing would be out of the question. She had no kit and no way in hell would she smell or touch the powder. Her guess would be cocaine and fentanyl mix. She kept the packs and went for an evidence bag and handcuffs from the truck. Getting in so deep on other drugs put a damper on the methamphetamine trafficking she so wanted to find to help her search for the two killers named Oxfords. The four sitting at the picnic table when she pulled in didn't give her the impression of cocaine dealers. The rusty pickup and old van didn't fit in the picture of carrying around a wad of cash from dealing cocaine. They fit nicely into the low life profile of meth dealing. Maybe she had a connection and a trail for her hunt after all. She had pictures of the van, and the license plate would give her a path forward.

The search for the two shell cases that killed the man at the table would take longer. The two hits to the man's chest showed powder burns. He had been shot from just across the table. The two thuds she had heard were too loud to come from a rifle. Certain he had been shot with a pistol, she spent her time looking for the two brass casings at the distance and area she had been trained on by the DEA.

It took her only minutes to find them. Carefully placing them in an envelope, she sealed it. A fingerprint here could be a big lead in finding the shooter.

She stood and heard the boys. They were on the water in her

boat and headed downstream from the bridge. She ran to the water's edge to block them. The boys paddled to her and jumped out of the boat, pulling it up on the sandbar.

"My brother was scared and made me run away when we heard the shootin'."

"It's good you did. A man got shot here. Was he your dad?" she asked, not sure the boy knew who got shot.

"We ain't got no dad. He might have been our mom's boyfriend. Are you going to take us home?"

"Help me get the boat in the truck and I'll drive you both home."

The boys loaded the boat in the truck and Sara tied it down to the bed rings she had installed.

"Okay, boys, where are we going?"

She slowed and stopped alongside the county sheriff's car coming into the beach area.

"Go ahead, miss. We were notified of your DEA connection. We'll tie down the scene and take care of the body."

She nodded a thank you and left the area.

It was nearly dark when she drove into Jasper, Arkansas. The boys had been begging her to stop at every gas station they had passed. They claimed to be both near home and starvation. She was not far behind them in that situation. Letting them both out of the truck at one time was not going to happen this close to where they lived. She could lose any chance of finding where their family lived. She knew the boys had a slick side and would ditch her in a heartbeat if she relaxed. Together they would leave her in their nighttime dust. With a ten-dollar bill in the hands of the older boy, she waited for hot dogs and sodas. She needed to know where the boys were taking her and what she might be getting into.

"Does your mother live here? In Jasper?" she asked the younger boy. He had been the quiet one of the two and now looked like his mouth had been sealed shut. Meth user parent training for sure.

She gave him a stern look and tried again, "You live here, right?"

He pointed toward the service station and his brother coming with his hands full of drinks and a sack that must contain hotdogs.

"No hotdogs unless you tell me."

"Grandma lives here," he said, reaching to open the door for his brother.

Finished with her own hotdog, not wanting to think about how it got put together, she tried again to learn where they were going.

"Where is your grandmother's house, boys?"

With a last bite of the hotdog in his mouth the older boy pointed down the street.

"Okay, tell me where to turn," she said, starting down the highway.

The edge of town came quickly, and the boy pointed down the last street before the upcoming open highway. Turning in the street, the boys guided her to a trailer home sitting on a town lot. The boys jumped out of the truck seat and ran to knock on the trailer door. She shut the truck down and followed. A gray-haired woman in her sixties opened the door.

"You boys get in here," the woman said, acting like she was about to close the door behind them. Instead, she stepped out onto a small wooden platform with steps leading up to the door.

"It's so dark I thought you were their mother," she said, opening the door a little behind her to put some light on Sara. "Who are you?"

Sara realized she was treading on some unfamiliar ground but needed to know more about the women and the dead man at the river access.

"I'm Sara, ma'am. Something happened out on the river with their mother and her friend. She left in a hurry with a man and a woman in a minivan. I'm sure she is okay."

"You brought the boys all the way here for her?"

"No, not for her. She ran off and left them alone. I just happened to be there."

"I'm not surprised about that. She's been running with some trash lately."

"Some of the trash got shot up pretty bad today," Sara said, hoping to get in the trailer to talk. "I think the boys were shook up at what happened."

"Why don't you come in? I have our last coffee for today just finishing up. We can talk some."

After a half hour of drinking coffee and hearing how her thirty-year old daughter had slipped into doing pot, and now doing anything else she can get her hands on, Sara led the conversation by telling her how frightened the boys were when the shooting started.

"Honey, those boys and their drug using mother were shot at in the big meth raid on the compound."

"I didn't know. They weren't hurt, were they?" she asked, knowing full well the boys had to be traumatized. She had found a link to the Oxford brothers she searched for.

"I know it scared them up some. They both wake up screaming sometimes," the grandmother said, pouring Sara a cup of the fresh pot of coffee.

"Does their mom live here with you?"

"She did for a couple weeks after the raid."

"Do I need to take the boys to her?"

"No."

Pushing to get information on the mother had reached an end. Asking the grandmother where to find the mother wasn't going to work. Sara finished half the cup of coffee and stood to leave.

"I'll tell the boys you said goodbye," the grandmother said.

"Maybe I'll get back over here again," Sara said.

She left knowing the story at the trailer in Jasper still could help find the Oxfords, but not tonight. She ran her hand along the bullet holes in the truck's bed as she opened the door to get in.

The sound of the truck's engine starting took her back to that night at the compound raid. Flashes of gunfire with echoes bouncing in her mind locked her down, unable to move. Yet she saw herself running. Running from medic to medic to get him help, and to save the man she loved. Her hand pressed the shoulder of the medic working on Luke. Luke had left the battles she was still fighting as he lay in her arms. The PTSD memories of her terror were finding a way to fill the screen of her mind. The night was late, and she still had a long drive.

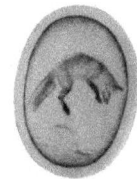

THIRTY-ONE

AWAKE FOR JUST A FEW minutes, Sara glanced at her cellphone to get the time. She had only slept four and a half hours. A couple messages were sitting in voicemail. Both were from Reid. He had been trying to get in touch with her. She hit his phone number button.

He answered almost immediately.

"Got something for me?" she asked, still sleepy and only half awake. "Did the shot-up fellow make it?"

"He did. We're going to question him."

"Who is he, Reid? Is there any history of him in the system?"

"He's in there several times, an up-and-coming cartel killer. There was a BOLO out for him."

"I'd like to know why he was intent on killing a man that looks way out of place from trafficking cocaine."

"I think making and selling meth has made some of the small-timers look up the food chain at selling cocaine and other hard drugs. Dealing in the cartel's area can get them killed. We can talk later."

"Wait. I've got to tell you this."

"Go ahead."

"The woman with him on the sandbar and her kids were in the compound when the raid took place. I took the kids to their grandmother in Jasper. She gave no hint where the woman from the shooting scene is living. The woman left the sandbar in a big hurry with the other couple. The folded-up tinfoil ball I found under the table was a good sign they had been using meth at the picnic table. This could be a strong link to the Oxfords. I'll push on it."

"Send me the grandmother's name and address and we'll run it and see what we know about the woman."

"Will do."

"Yes. Later. Check your computer. I sent some info on the vehicles from the pictures you took at the sandbar."

Her computer screen flashed with a coded email from the FBI. The names and addresses of the truck and minivan at the river were now in her hands.

With two days of clothes packed, she was ready to stay in the field. This time she included her Arkansas Wildlife Officer outfits. Her old truck had been sitting behind the cabin for more than a week. She hoped it would still start on the first crank. She needed the old girl on this journey. The new white F-250, still with bullet holes, was going to get a rest.

Two hours later, she drove through the small town where the report said the minivan and truck were registered. Her phone GPS showed one of the houses just ahead. There was no truck or van in the driveway. She drove on a few blocks and found the old white truck. The minivan was parked across the yard on what had been grass years ago. Parking on the street one house beyond the vehicles, she walked back and onto the driveway. She leaned over as she passed the white truck and attached a magnetic GPS tracker under the rear wheel fender and then adjusted her Glock to a very visible position at her side. She wore no other identification badges or clothing.

She approached and knocked once on the thin veneer of the front door. She hated being afraid, and it almost made her leave before anyone answered her knock. She carried two hundred dollars in twenties in her front pocket with a plan on how to use the money.

It took a second knock to get someone to the door. Her knock had been a lot lighter than the first and she knew why. She could be making a deadly mistake being here alone. The door opened a few inches, pausing, she guessed with someone's foot against it. The face of a meth user stared at her through the narrow opening.

The woman's hair looked as if it had given up life and retreated to somewhere near the woman's scalp to die.

Sara knew the slightly open door would not last long. She needed to speak first.

"I found a billfold at the river when you folks left without the kids."

"Give it to me," the woman in the house said.

"I ain't got it," Sara slanged. "The sheriff's office took it. I got the money out before they came."

"Those men that shot Bill got the money," the woman said, the door opened several inches more.

"Bill must have hid the billfold under the bench. That's where I found it."

"How much money?" she asked, the door opened halfway.

The woman was wearing a man's t-shirt. The neck stretched far enough to see she was wearing no bra. Her camo pants hung low, with a rope tied in front to hold them up. Her hand came out, reaching for another fix.

"The money?"

"Can I say hello to the boys? We had a good time on our little float trip."

The woman seemed to relax a bit and backed up some to give Sara room to step inside. She knew the woman had seen the Glock at her side. It hadn't bothered her, which frightened Sara even more. Weapons strapped on visitors didn't cause the woman a lick of worry.

"I ain't seen them boys since we were at the river. Their grandmother got them?"

"That's where I took them."

The woman backed up and stood aside for Sara to walk in. A feeling of doing something totally stupid flashed across her mind. She remembered an adobe building and a woman in a black robe and headcover letting her in the door. Luckily, she had been backed by six rifle men pushing in behind her. She wished for any one of them now. The woman didn't offer a seat. She stood. Sara knew she was waiting for an answer about the boys.

"The young one was scared really 'bad by the shooting," Sara said, getting the money out of her pocket. "Was that his dad that got shot?" She had just made conversation. She knew the answer.

"They killed him, didn't they?" the woman asked.

"He was your husband?"

"Boyfriend. That's all."

She could hear men laughing and bottles bumping in the back of the house. A man called out for the woman. She knew her time to get out of there had come. Only a short additional question to learn more.

"The boys said they were caught up with you in the damn raid at the compound. The young one is still afraid. Lucky some of the men got out of there. I bet they ain't never going to stop running after that," Sara said, afraid she had said way too much.

"They ain't running nowhere. Got too much business going on all around here. They just headed for some deep Arkansas woods for a while. I was in there getting shot at. Damn sons of bitches. We killed two of them fuckers."

Her hand had gone instinctively to the Glock and her finger went to the trigger. Blistering hate raged inside her at the woman's disregard for the senseless deaths. Luke's senseless death. Sara swallowed hard to press down the hate. This wasn't the place to shoot a woman. She doubted the woman had fired the shots that had killed Luke. The woman's words had just caught Sara off guard.

Sara shoved the two hundred dollars at the woman and turned to go. The woman didn't offer her a thanks.

"With Bill gone, it's going to take us a while to get our dealings back up. Got a cell number, and I'll call you when we got stuff again."

"Sure." Not certain why the woman offered her this, she wrote the cell number on the back of her old truck stop card and handed it to the woman. "Thanks." She got the heck out of the meth-cooking den.

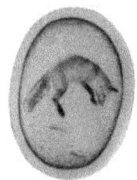

THIRTY-TWO

SHE HAD PARKED JUST OFF the grass ramp of the Cotter private airstrip to wait. Reid had given her an ETA of around twenty minutes, and so far, he hadn't been late. She had a few more minutes to wait. The airstrip thing was something new with Reid. She guessed someone would be flying him in. She heard the way too familiar sound of a chopper clearing the hill to the north as it approached. The sounds told her the bird was small but very fast. The helicopter crossed over the airfield and turned on a dime, letting down as it headed back. It touched down on the grass in front of her car. She saw Reid at the controls and alone in the bird. It shocked her seeing Reid as the pilot. As soon as the blades stopped rotating, Reid eased down from the cockpit of the chopper. She met him in the middle of the grass, off-ramp.

"I suppose there is a long story about how you learned to fly choppers?" she said, giving her friend a light hug. He returned it with a bit more. It pleased her.

"The flying lessons all came with the dual career I've been leading. With the team efforts by the DEA, FBI, and the Game Commission, they want me a dozen places at once. I only wanted this one place today. I've missed seeing you."

"Me, too," she said, turning to lead him to her car. "We have a great little restaurant in Cotter where we can eat and talk. It's quiet."

He grabbed her hand. "Not today. Come on. This lunch is on

me and the FBI." He led her to the passenger side of the helicopter and opened the door. "Get in and belt up. We're going to take a ride."

"How long have you been flying choppers?" The surprise still hadn't worn off and she had gotten a bit uneasy flying with such a new pilot.

"I soloed a month ago. So, long enough to know how to fly safely." He pulled her belt and harness up tight around her and handed her a communications headset to put on. He helped her adjust the headset fit and then shut the passenger door. He walked boldly around the front of the bird. She would have to see more before she believed this guy was about to fly her.

She relaxed a little about the ride when he got in and belted up and picked up a takeoff checklist from the side pocket. He went through the list as he checked the instruments and controls for flight.

With the rotor spinning, she figured he was aching to lift her off the ground in grand fashion. The lift came quick and straight up about thirty feet before he turned in an easy bank and climbed, headed west from the airport and Cotter.

"Okay, flyboy. You've kidnapped me. Where are we going?"

"In less than twenty minutes, you'll see."

She sat forward on the seat looking at one heck of a lot of lake just north of their flight path.

"Bull Shoals Lake is beautiful. It looks like it goes on forever," she said. "Dad and I fished some of those coves a while back."

"Do you want to go lower? So you can get a better look?"

"No. This is fine. I had enough low helicopter flying in Iraq."

"This lake has been a favorite of mine for catching smallmouth bass," he said, reaching and adjusting the rotor rpm. "Branson is just on the horizon. Are you getting hungry?"

"Starved. You do know how to get us down from here?" she said, grabbing his arm in faked apprehension.

"I don't think anyone has ever had to stay up here," he said. "Except my flight instructor. I got him caught at two thousand feet and we couldn't get down." He reached and gave her a warm grasp on her arm. It came as the first sign he thought they were on a date.

"Fly the damn bird. Fool!" she said and then laughed. Fun for Sara had not come easy for a long time. The seriousness of the things that had happened had driven her far away from what others around her called their fun. "Are we landing in Branson?"

"No, just outside of Branson, in Hollister, at the School of the Ozarks. It sits up on the high ridge just ahead. The runway is just past the college and their cattle ranch."

With a call to the air traffic in the area, Reid flew over the airport and made a left-hand turn into the pattern for the runway. Easing the bird down gently he turned and sat down on the grass alongside the runway. A four-wheeler with a young man and woman pulled near after the blades stopped rotating.

"Are you going to need fuel, sir?"

"We won't need fuel, but how about a ride up to the restaurant?

"When you're ready, hop on the back and we'll take you to the airport office. They have a golf cart you can take."

Their drive to the restaurant took them through the center of the beautiful campus. Reid pointed out the buildings like he knew them by heart. She didn't know he had been a student there.

"Why didn't you tell me you went to college here?"

"Maybe because I didn't quite finish my degree. Long story for some other time, okay?"

"Sure."

"If we don't run out of time, I want to show you the inside of the church we just passed. It's beautiful. Food is next."

"Can't wait."

With a booth selected for a little privacy, they settled in with iced tea for Reid and a diet coke for Sara. The student waiter had been quick to take their food order and promised it wouldn't be a very long wait.

They looked at each other with questions. She didn't want to break up the magical chopper ride with a man she liked by going where the conversation would take them into her search for the Oxfords.

"I think you have some private things to talk about," Reid said. "Let's eat, I'm starving. Then we can take a walk down by the lake. It's a good place to sit and talk."

Reid's insight surprised her and warmed her feelings for the man who had been so close to Luke. Reid really had never had a chance to get anywhere close to her emotionally. She wanted to let this man in.

"Reid, you surp. . ." The waitress and a helper stood at the side of their table with some beautiful lunches.

What she wanted to say about how much she liked being with him needed to be said in whispers. She would have to wait.

Both of their meals disappeared quickly. She had hurried her meal to get it down. She needed and wanted his take on what she had learned in her investigation of where the Oxfords were hiding. Reid had gotten up and offered a hand for her to slide out of the booth.

"Let's take a walk, and I'll show you the lake. I think you'll like it."

"I'm sure."

The walk down the small hill to the lake seemed different for the chemistry of their relationship. Reid walked close, taking a hitch around her arm and pulling her to him a couple of times. Was it just an effort for comfort in walking?

A bench near a small lake he had mentioned seemed a good place to get out their information and questions about where to hunt next. A dozen geese voiced their disagreement with them being there. They waddled and plopped into the water's edge. Reid waited for her to sit before following and leaving only a little room between them. His closeness on the walk had given her the closeness she wanted from him.

"Tell me, what you've been learning?" Reid asked.

"The license plates you ran for me took me to a crack house in Jasper. Before you say it, I know I should have had someone along to back me up. I made up a story about having found money at the river where the man had been killed. Fortunately for me, a woman answered the door. On a scale for taking meth, she had passed eight. She said she and the boys I picked up at the river had been in the compound when the raid happened. The man shot at the river was a boyfriend, not the boys' father. When we got around to the fight at the compound it all went to hell for me. She bragged the raid failed and they had killed some damn law officers."

"You wanted to kill her, didn't you?"

"Oh, so badly. I could have knocked her off her feet."

"Did she give you any ideas on finding the men you're looking for?"

"Without naming them, I got her to say they had headed for the wilds of Arkansas. That only gives us a million acres to search, right? I got out of there when the men partying in the back of the house got louder and I thought one was headed for the woman and the door."

"Maybe she didn't tell you where to look, but men raised in one area generally find someplace to hide nearby. It could be someplace they know and feel safe to hide from their crimes. It could be close to where you first met them."

It had become hard for Sara to sort out their many crimes. There would be no way she could kill each of them three times.

"I can start tomorrow with you if you feel ready. We can start on the roads around where you and Luke first saw the Oxfords at Jimmy's burned-out trailer."

"I'm so ready," Sara said. "I need to know about the man I shot at the river. What's his connection to the man he killed?"

"He still isn't talking. From the wanted stuff they have on him, he's a low-level enforcer for the drug cartel. The man he killed is part of a white supremacist group starting to sell cocaine in the cartel's territory."

"Who's supplying the group?"

"We don't know yet."

"Does it have anything to do with the barn we found and the drone delivery system that was set up?"

"It could. Did you learn more from the data you got from the barn?"

"Maybe. I'll have to rethink some of the GPS drop zones they used for the drones to deliver drugs."

"Take me through it when we have a chance."

With a promise to drop the shop talk, they headed for the airport. With them both seated and belted in the chopper, Reid went through the bird's flight check list and then started the engine. The blades on the helicopter were turning in a steady, slow rhythm when Reid leaned toward her. She had been so ready for whatever came since she got his hint on their walk this was a date. Then again maybe long before that. They kissed.

"Ready?" Reid asked. She nodded a yes. Her nod had a lot more meaning behind it than "ready for takeoff, sir."

Crossing Bull Shoals Lake, he flew lower. She watched a boat speeding up on its keel and creating a beautiful wake as it headed down a channel. The man and woman on the boat waved as they flew over. It seemed to be almost a dream she might never get to have. Two people in love, just going nowhere on the water, and all for pleasure. She couldn't remember ever being there on a lake like the two people below them. Their airship and his kiss was enough for her tonight. She wanted the flight to go on forever.

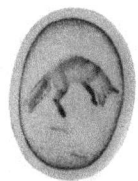

THIRTY-THREE

HE SHOWED UP AT SIX in the morning at the cabin in Ponca where she was staying. She liked that he kept his word, and his promptness to go after the men she hunted. They headed south toward Jimmy's dad's meth making past.

Reid turned off the blacktop onto the gravel road. She led him to the burned-out site where Jimmy's father and mother had died when his father's meth making mistake killed them both. In the back of her mind, she thought the men that had tried to rape her and then killed Jimmy's grandmother would not be far from the backwoods area they had once lived in. The old white truck she had tagged with a GPS tracker at the river shootout had been through this area twice in the last two weeks.

Reid slowed at the site of the burned woods where the trailer had exploded. The area was taped off and the wreckage of the poisonous trailer remains had been removed.

"I'm glad that mess is gone," she said. "I don't want to even stop near where it burned again."

"The county must have cleaned this up," he said, driving on by.

"I think the state had to get involved because of the high hazmat conditions," she said.

As they passed the few run-down houses and barns along the miles of ridgetop road, she asked him to drive slowly so she could study the barns and shed. She wasn't sure what she was looking for, but it made her feel good to be finally into the search for the two Oxfords. She had Reid pull over at a house and garage sitting back from the road a hundred feet or more.

"It's too run-down. No one could be living in that shack," he said, pulling just off the road. The ditch alongside the road pitched down quickly. She slid out the door and down the steep incline. Turning, she climbed back and leaned in to reach behind the seat for the AR-15 they both now carried with them. They also wore shoulder holsters with Glocks. Camo shirts and pants made them look like just another pair of hunters looking for game. DEA badges of authority in hidden pockets were their authorization to make arrests.

"Are you sure you want to do this?" he asked, coming around the truck to join her.

"The driveway looks like someone has been using it to get into the garage. We should check."

"You realize if we stir someone up, there could be a lot of trouble," he said, "Even someone running a little liquor still is not going to welcome our presence."

"So, we can at least have a quick look around the place," Sara said,

The garage sides leaned almost to the point she thought they would fall. It sat open and empty. The weather worn boards had never welcomed even a splash of paint.

They both walked to the front of the shack and then around the side to the back. Weeds two feet tall filled what at one time had been a backyard for the house. A kid's swing surrounded and hidden by five-foot-tall tree starts she recognized as walnuts were evidence of squirrels burying past winter food around the swing. The poles struggling to support the chains of the swing sagged and showed rust and broken open cracks letting in the killer rains that would someday bring the poles to the ground.

"Thank goodness there aren't kids living here," she said, walking past the swing to a shed with a door hanging limp on one hinge. She stuck her head inside and then backed away quickly.

"Shit fire! There's a nest of copperheads in there."

"Ready to go now?" Reid asked.

She heard the truck coming even before it pulled in the driveway. It stopped just outside the garage. Reid led the way back around the house.

He turned and looked at her. "Let me handle this."

An old man got out of the truck and stood just out from the truck's side looking hard at them. He cradled a rusty double barrel shotgun in his arms pointed in their direction.

"Howdy, sir. We don't mean any harm. Could you please point that at the ground?" Reid said.

"What's the hell you two doing coming around my house?" the man asked, his long beard lifting and flexing with each word he spoke. He had eased the barrel of the double barrel down.

"Do you and your wife still live here?" Sara asked, not sure how anyone could possibly live in the house she was witnessing.

"My woman died five years ago. I'm the only one lives here now."

"We didn't want to bother anyone. There's some bad dudes that could be out here somewhere, and we want to see them caught."

"You talking about them meth head boys we had running around here a while back. Me and my wife always knew they would end up no damn good even back then."

"How long ago has it been since you saw them here?" Sara asked.

"They had a place a couple miles down this here road a couple years ago. They moved in there 'cause the old man owned it died. I seen them once in a while speeding down this here road. Ain't seen them since the big meth raid up west of Cotter. The place on down yonder, they were staying, had yellow tape all around the house and barn until the wind took it."

"We'll check on down the road, mister. Thanks for your help."

"Them boys need catching real bad, so get on with it, then."

"You might want to stay out of the garage. There's a nest of copperheads in there," Sara said.

"Them copperheads is the only way I can keep the rats and mice down around here."

It didn't surprise her, what the old man had said. She had heard it from farmers many times before. Only, then the snakes had been blue racers or kingsnakes, not copperheads.

***

A hint of yellow tape hung from a bush near the road. She slowed the truck.

"We need to find who hung the tape and how they knew the Oxfords had been staying here," Sara said. Pushing a little at Reid was becoming a little more commonplace for her to do.

"I'll check with the sheriff's office on it."

Sara turned off to the side and parked their truck. She wanted a look at what had been left by the Oxfords in the house and barn. The two cases Reid had loaded in the truck had the air packs and coveralls they needed to wear.

Dressed for the environment, they went up the three steps to the porch. Sara tested the boards of the porch by pressing against the ones that looked rotted. Satisfied with her footing, she stepped ahead, putting her weight down. She had been there many times before, only the footing then had been sand and stepping down on a landmine's trigger would mean the loss of a limb or your life. The minesweeper had been the lifesaver then. Her squad relied upon the man assigned to this job. Their lives depended upon him. Today it all came from the feel of the floor and the boards. The floors inside the house were just as bad as the porch. Dampness and mold showed on corners of the rooms. An old couch sprouted seedlings of weeds she didn't recognize. They had chosen the thickest parts of the couch to grow from. Those parts had been the wettest and kept the moisture for the plants.

"I'm buried in spiderwebs," Sara said, as she wiped the webs stuck to her face mask away, trying unsuccessfully to get them off her gloved hand.

Both of them wove their way through the webs. What had been the kitchen lay just through the door frame.

"Hold up a minute," Reid said, pointing into the room ahead. "The webs are all torn down in there. Someone has been coming in through the back door."

Sara went to the gas stove across the room. A lot of spillover of liquids had been burned onto the top. Turning one of the stove knobs brought a hiss. Gas was present. The floor around the stove showed clear signs of someone's footprints in the dirt that covered the kitchen floor.

"Someone has been using this. I'm going to guess for cooking meth," Reid said.

"Then they must be carrying away all the stuff they used each time."

"Maybe not. There's a ton of pans and crap stuffed under the shelves in the closet. I'll get a residue sample from a couple of the worst looking ones," Reid said, bending and scraping the edges of a pan. With the samples bagged, he offered, "Let's get out of here. I'm sweating up a storm in this suit."

Back on the road, Reid pulled over at a turnout a little over three miles from the man's place.

Two conservation area signs marked the turnoff parking with the words 'parking for hiking to the lookout point'.

"Can we take a little time off from this manhunt for a short hike?" Reid asked. "There's a view of the Buffalo River valley I want you to see. This valley could also be a good hiding place for wanted men."

She was already out of the truck and walking around to join him. She carried the two lunch sacks she had put together in one hand, and two pair of commission binoculars in the other. Reid reached back into the truck and opened the cooler. He came around carrying two bottles of water and their AR-15s.

"Might as well take the rifles with us. Out here breaking into a strange vehicle would be considered a fun day's work. We can head down the trail. It's about a half-mile walk and ends up with a high bluff view of a wide valley of nothing but heavy timber and no roads."

The narrow trail followed the ridge for a while, then dropped deep into a ravine before coming up on the far side. He led the way down the bank and turned to slow her descent as she followed. Without pausing at the bottom, Sara grabbed a branch from a small tree and pulled her way up the bank.

"We need to get out of this dark spot on the trail," she said. She paused a few seconds and then started up the steep side of the ravine. He followed close behind, using the scrub brush branches to help pull up the incline.

"The bluff overlook is just over the ridge. We'll be able to see miles of forest on the valley floor. No roads go through this part of the National Forest. There are only a few narrow trails some four-wheelers use to get into the backwoods this far," Reid said. He pushed a line of brush open and stepped out on the narrow path along the edge of the mountain.

She stopped beside him and turned her head, looking down the long valley lying far below them.

"There's not a road or cabin in sight anywhere. It would be a good place for the Oxfords to hide, wouldn't it?" she said.

"The place is totally isolated. They would have to come out somewhere and go for food unless someone was bringing it to them."

Sara took a seat on a fallen log on the cliff and uncased her binoculars. She made a sweep across the entire valley before pausing and lowering the glasses. "Where to start looking? It's nothing but heavy timber."

"Try looking for any breaks or open spaces in the woods," Reid said, using another set of binoculars to scan below.

"I'm seeing no movement except the buzzards flying way down there. The birds are scanning the valley for prey, just like we are."

Both took turns looking for any signs of humans in the valleys and the far cliffs leading down into the deep flats of timber. The flats turned with the cliff's guidance and seemed to go nowhere. She liked the lookout perch and could have stayed the rest of the day. Reid paced after two hours and then sat, resting and waiting. She knew he had given up on finding anyone in the valley.

"I hate to give up this vantage point, mister, but is it time to go?" she asked, starting to put her binoculars in their case, but taking one last scan of the valley.

"Wait!" she said, "There." She pointed to the midpoint of the valley below. Reid stood over her side. "What do you see?"

"It was there only for a second. A whiff of white. I think it was smoke," she said, pointing below. "There it is again."

"You're right. Someone is staked out deep in the valley."

"Could it be them? Hunters, maybe?"

"There are no seasons open now. So, I doubt if it's hunters," Reid said, looking carefully with his field glasses. "It's a hard spot to get to." He reached into his backpack and took out a topo map. Unfolding it, he pointed at the rising contour lines that marked where they were standing.

"We're right about here," he said.

Sara pointed at the map's flat contour that marked the valley where she had seen the smoke.

The walls of the Iraqi town came out of nowhere and

surrounded her. The pounding sounds of the city of Bucca filled her Humvee and made it hard for her to hear what her driver, Johnson, was trying to tell her. "We shouldn't be stopped here."

She shook the image and sounds away quickly. She needed to concentrate right now. Today!

"There. It should be about there," she said.

Reid drew a circle around the area she had indicated. "Getting there will be hell if we have to go in for them."

"We need to get in there and see where the smoke is coming from. But, not today," Sara said.

"If those crazies are there, it will take more than you and me to get them out," Reid said.

"Sorry, but this hunt is in my DNA now. We need to at least see if we can find the place they are going in at the head of this valley," she said, pointing again at a point about a mile or more west. Reid circled it with the marker.

"If you need to go back on an assignment, I'll stay," she said. She knew her truck sat parked at the Ponca cabin where she had stayed.

"You're sure you want to even wade in there a little?" Reid said, putting his binoculars back in their case.

"I sure as hell want to," she said. "I want those bastards dead. I'll only look for places they could be leaving the road to head into the valley."

"Not without me, you won't," he said, turning as he headed back into the woods and the trail off the cliff leading to the truck.

Oh, it would need to be so without him. Tomorrow she would be armed to the teeth with the AR-15 and her two pistols. This time, she planned to be alone and find the murdering sons of bitches that had caused the deaths of so many.

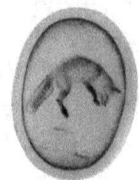

THIRTY-FOUR

THE MORNING SUN STILL LURKED somewhere behind the tall timber rising along the valley road she traveled. Her cellphone hadn't stopped ringing from Reid's calls until she turned it off and tossed it into the empty passenger seat of her truck. The phone landed right next to the rifle barrel pointing forward. There was no regret for taking it and leaving the cabins while Reid slept. She wore her army fatigues, the ones she came home from Iraq in. A camouflage shirt, pants, and jacket. Today she meant for it all to be on her. Anything she would do now could drag someone else deeper into the depth of her fight. Her only mission was to capture or kill the men she now hunted alone. She sucked her lips tight and blew a deep breath at the memory of the man with his pants around his ankles coming down at her. She had let her first attempt to kill him fall short with only shots around his feet. This time she would put an end to the hunt.

Now with enough sunlight to make out the turn-offs on the valley road, she passed a half dozen well-worn and traveled. The one she sought would be less used, maybe even closed off to hide any coming and going. Slowing the truck, she stopped and backed up to check something she had seen. One deep wheel mark in the dirt at the edge of the gravel road had been enough to catch her attention. Getting out of the truck, she walked back to the track. It seemed to lead nowhere except under a wall of brambles. Someone had thought their tracks were hidden. She had the urge to rush through the brush and follow the tracks to a battle she now needed. Training and experience from Iraq flashed through her memory. The Iraqis planted mines along the roads and would show themselves for seconds to draw out the soldiers from their vehicles for a chase. Stepping on their mines ended the chase even before they began. She needed caution here to not rush blindly into the traps that could be ahead. Hiding her truck would have to come first. Starting the truck, she drove a half mile before finding a well-used turnoff and parking area for hunters. Pulling in, she got out and slipped on a backpack. After checking the loading of her pistols and the AR-15, she slipped the rifle's sling over her shoulder and quietly eased the truck door closed. A few steps away, she turned and went back for her cell, but turning it on was not an option. Reid would rush to join her. This was on her; no one else needed to die helping.

She checked the direction she had come and went fifty yards directly in from the hunter's parking area. Turning in the woods, she made a beeline for the hidden truck entrance she had found. The tracks were clearly there. The truck had gone on into the woods.

Stopping, she looked back at the bramble dam the men had used to hide any trace of being there. Maybe going in here alone was too much for her to handle. She had been so certain of her ability to put an end to the Oxfords, but now the realization they could be yards or even feet in front of her hit home. It was unlike her to question herself. She never did it when in command of a squad in the Iraqi desert. It got men killed when they slowed an advance to question their motives and orders. She would not be able to face herself or Reid if she turned back now.

She went on deeper into the woods. Clearly, the truck followed an old logging trail. Brush pushed in from both sides now and driving through it would not have been fun. She couldn't think of a safer place to be hiding from the law. After thirty minutes of fighting back the brush, she left the tracks and found a spot to hide on the side of a hill. She pulled the brush together in front of her. After a drink and eating on a day-old donut, she settled back. Thoughts about what she was doing started rushing in. Now, she gripped the cramp in her stomach with her arm, unsure the donut would stay down. The enemy could be ahead. Pulling her knees up close to her chest, she rested the rifle across them. Going in here alone was part of her stupidity for the month. Going back now without knowing if the men were hiding deep in this valley would haunt her even more later. She stayed put for a little more than an hour, wanting something she would have control over to happen. The damn truck must be just ahead. Driving it any deeper into the valley would be impossible. The idea of finding the truck somewhere just ahead tore at her. No way could it have been driven deep into the valley where she saw the smoke the day before. Finding it would mean she had a fight coming.

Her nerves wouldn't let her sit any longer, so she left her hiding place. The tire marks went on deeper into the valley. She lost the tracks of the truck for a few yards, but going back a short way, she saw where the truck turned and drove across a low rock ledge. Then the tracks were gone, and the truck was nowhere in sight. She continued in the direction the truck had been going. A wall of brush with leaves turning brown from being cut a while back blocked the way. She slid through the wall. There it sat, totally covered, and hidden from view from above. The back window of the truck showing a 'Come take it' sign and a decal of an AR rifle. She had seen the truck before at Jimmy's burned-out trailer when she had been with Luke, and he had confronted the Oxfords. Her heart raced and the blood rushing to her head gave her a flush. She wanted to back down now and get out of the woods. The place she had seen the smoke still lay ahead. Now she was certain it would be where the Oxfords were camping. The change of heart came from remembering her levelheaded mother and how she would face a challenge. It for sure never came from John and his rush-ahead Marine Corps Semper Fi.

She froze and dropped alongside the truck at the sound of a daytime owl's call. She heard brush being pushed aside and saw a woman making the sounds of the owl as she came down the truck tracks. Likely the woman gave the call to keep from surprising the Oxfords and getting shot. The woman carried a large backpack, and it looked like a lever action rifle in her arm's cradle. Following the noise making woman would make it easy and safer. Letting her get a few yards ahead, Sara left the brush around the truck.

Years ago, John had taught her how to get close to deer in the woods without them knowing you were there. He told her to ease her heel down first and then the rest of the foot lightly to avoid breaking a branch or stick in the pathway. She advanced on the woman. Twice she stopped off to the side of the pathway to give the woman time to gain more ground in front of her. Still, the woman's owl call gave away her position. Time raced for Sara. How long had she been following the woman? Could she be getting close to the valley spot where they had seen the smoke rise from the valley the day before?

It became quiet. Not one owl call in over thirty minutes now. Once she thought she had heard a distant owl reply. She hadn't been sure it was there in front of her. What lay ahead worried her. She wouldn't let wanting to turn back rule her.

The snap of the hammer being cocked on the woman's lever action rifle surprised her. She dropped to her knees alongside a tree and scanned the woods in front of her. A rifle shot tore bark from the tree beside her face. She braced against the adrenaline rush she knew was happening. She had become the hunted. Killing a woman hunting her hadn't been an option she'd signed up for today. Getting shot by one hadn't registered itself either. She needed to get behind a barrier of rock for protection and to command the situation. Getting off the valley floor came first.

Standing and climbing to a cliff outcrop would only put a target in the middle of her back. She needed to crawl. She started up the steep incline on her knees. Her pants were torn, and both her knees were bruised and bleeding when a hundred feet up the cliff she found the rock fortress she needed and rolled over the edge. Laying the rifle across the rock ledge in front of her, she waited. She clicked on her cellphone and waited for the signal bar to light. It didn't. Cell towers were out of range on the valley floor. Twice she saw the woman change position in the valley floor cover. It would have been an easy shot through the AR's telescope to take her out. She knew it would go down as murder. She waited, ready to let the woman stalking her know, with a warning shot, she had better back off.

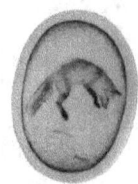

THIRTY-FIVE

THE THREAT FROM THE WOMAN increased tenfold when Sara caught a glimpse of two men coming from deeper in the valley. The men she hunted had to be either looking for the woman or now aware the woman had prey trapped on the cliff. She had last seen the woman move to her left. The woman now blocked her from going back the way she had come into the valley. Her military police background had taught her to always keep a way open to get out of a fight. At this she had failed. She studied the terrain around her. Climbing a steep cliff to get out of the valley would be her only escape. Or was it?

She waited and watched two people move around the trees where she had first seen them. She wanted them to come after her. Letting her stay hidden on the path to their camp would not be in the cards for the two Oxford meth heads. It was time to play chess, and it wasn't her move. She laid the AR and her pistol out in front of her, ready for them to come.

Minutes ticked by without anything from the three below on the valley floor. Then, one of the men started running and heading through the timber, going toward the road entrance and her escape route. The man was behind her and blocking her from getting out of the valley. She heard a rock roll down the hill. Someone running had knocked it loose. They had flanked her and were now headed to the high ground above her. The running stopped and it got quiet. Just across the valley floor, she saw the woman standing half-hidden alongside a tree, looking directly at her.

The woman yelled, "You, up there! This is private ground. What's you doing coming in here carrying that Army rifle? You hunting out of season? You should get on out of here now."

Stalling right now would be the only play Sara could come up with. After it got dark, she could probably get around anyone behind her. Getting either of the men she hunted now seemed out of reach.

"Why are you trying to keep me up here?" Sara asked, keeping watch now, off her front and back side. "I came in here looking for a coonhound. He ran away from us on a hunt two nights ago."

The stark whistle of a bullet passing near her head brought back way too many memories of Iraqi fights. Another bullet threw rock chips onto her back. She spun on the ground toward the fire coming from behind her. There the man was, hugging the back of a tree and leaning around it to shoot at her. He wasn't holding a long gun, so the shots came from a pistol.

She centered her rifle's telescope on the edge of the tree. She waited for him to come back around it to shoot again. She saw light reflect off the chrome pistol as he poked it around the tree. There in her rifle's scope were his hand and fingers. A clean shot for the AR she had sighted in weeks before. The ease of the trigger pull surprised her. Her single round hit. The pistol and the hand holding it were both separated from the man and strewn across the grass and brush behind the tree. Hearing a scream from the pain of having a limb blown off was not unfamiliar to her. She realized he would fall back on the ground holding an arm with a few remnants and sinews of what once was his right hand. She could feel nothing for the man's loss. It needed to be more. The woman left her hiding place and ran across the valley floor and then up the steep incline to where the wounded man lay screaming. Sara didn't waste a shot on her, instead waited until the woman dropped down by the man's side to yell.

"You had better get him to a hospital. He'll bleed to death."

The woman stood pointing a hand and finger at her, "You shot my husband, bitch. I'm going to come down there and fucking kill you myself," she said, stepping out and running downhill toward her waving a pistol. Again, killing a woman had no part in what she wanted to do. She would stop her cold in her tracks. Two close rounds on each side of the woman and another just in front of her froze her.

"Unless you plan on dying today, turn around and go help your husband. Tie a tourniquet on his arm to stop the bleeding."

"Tourniquet? I don't know. . . how," she said, backing up the incline.

"Use his belt, pull it around his arm tight," she said, watching the woman still holding the pistol.

Two rapid shots from the valley floor bounced off the rocks in front of her and then a yell.

"You done shot my brother. Ain't no way you ever going to get out of this valley," a man on the valley floor yelled up at her.

"He isn't dead yet. Why don't you go help him?" She ducked because a barrage would be coming. Certain he had emptied a magazine, she raised and fired a half dozen rounds into the trees where the shots had come from. The woods got quiet for a few minutes. Twice she heard the woman cry out or try to order her husband to lie quiet. Then the woman yelled again.

"You done shot him. Why don't you help me?"

"I've done some stupid things today. Coming up there exposed to his brother's fire ain't going to be the last one I do. These men murdered an old woman and tried to rape me."

"He says he knows you and he ain't the one tried to rape you back there by the spring pool. Your goddamn dog nearly tore his arm off."

About to do something really stupid, she hesitated and then. "Throw the pistol out way over the hill. Help your man up and walk him down here if you want help."

She watched the pistol fly out of the woman's hand, far out of her reach. The woman turned and stood with what was left of the man's arm around her shoulder. They struggled and slid down the slope toward her rock ledge fort.

"Stop there. Leave him sitting on the ground. You come in here." The woman let her husband down slowly and turned and walked directly to Sara.

"Raise your arms," Sara said, her rifle on the ground and her pistol in her hand. "Turn around slowly." There it was the memory of Iraqi women coming to visit their family members in prison. Touching them through their burka to search for a weapon had never been something she liked to do. This woman was different. She wore only a thin dress over a naked body. Sara's hand smoothed the dress and pressed tightly to feel under her sweat draped sagging breasts. She skipped the run up the woman's legs to check her crotch. It would be too much dirty flesh she didn't want to feel. The woman needed to be scrubbed with lye soap in the middle of a running stream.

"All right. Go get him and lay him along the rocks. If either of you so much as flinch, like going for a weapon, I'll kill you both," she said, moving back to wait for the woman to get her man. The woman dragged him back. When she let go of his good arm, the man seemed to black out. Sara pushed against him with her foot and then stepped hard down on his good hand. There was no response; the man was out cold.

"Get that rope off his arm. Take my belt and put it around his arm above the elbow." She stood behind the woman and watched her and also the floor of the valley below for his brother.

"Pull it tight. Now wait a few seconds to see if the bleeding stops. If it doesn't, pull the belt tighter," she said, afraid helping them would somehow backfire in her face. She had made a big mistake in helping in the middle of a fight that wasn't over yet. The sound of an airplane crossing the area high above the valley didn't register to help her current situation. When the sound of the plane returned, coming straight down the valley at low altitude, it got her attention. After a fast turnaround over the roadway, the plane returned and went back down the valley. They had to be searching for her. A few minutes later, she could hear the plane making large circles above the valley. Wishing she could signal did no good. She was trapped here by the man still below her in the valley. The brother she wanted to kill for so many reasons. Certain the plane belonged to the sheriff's department or highway patrol, she delayed trying to get the man below out in the open. Help for her would be on the way.

A half hour passed without any more flights over. She heard brush cracking in the valley. The other man she hunted was running away from her fight. She got halfway down the incline going after him before four ATV's roared out of the woods from back toward the road. Reid rode the first and didn't stop until he climbed the cliff to her side. She pointed down the valley trail. "He just went down there. He's carrying an automatic rifle and who knows what else. He's on foot and running up the valley," she said. "One of the brothers is up on the hill with a woman. He's shot and lost his hand."

"Stay here. I'll be back," he said.

"No! Hell no," Sara yelled and pushed her way onto a seat of the ATV behind Reid.

He motioned for a deputy on an ATV to climb the hill and the others to follow him.

"This is my damn fight," she said. He turned the ATV, and they sped up the valley in the direction she indicated. They traveled more than a mile before he pulled up and parked the ATV off the trail in the woods.

"From what we saw yesterday, their hidden camp must be just ahead," he said, and motioned for the sheriff's deputies to park. A man and a woman deputy joined them on the edge of the pathway leading down through the valley. Reid told them what they had seen the day before and riding any further could get them shot off the vehicles. The man they were after would be well armed.

The woman deputy took control. "Let's not let him get by us. I'll take the center path, you spread across the valley, and when I signal, we'll advance on him."

Sara wanted to resist when Reid motioned for her to go with him to the north side of the trail. This had been her fight, and she hadn't asked anyone to help. Sometimes people helping her were killed.

A whistle from the deputy signaled to start the push forward. Sara ran forward, taking cover behind trees and brush. She used the barrel of her rifle to push open the brush to look ahead. Reid advanced a dozen steps up the edge of the incline. The two deputies were doing the same on the other side of the path leading down the valley. A small stream ran along the valley. She crouched and advanced to the edge of the running water to stop. The man had slipped in the mud and fallen on his knees, going up the bank to escape. She motioned for Reid to join her.

"He's still armed. Nothing was left behind when he fell," she said.

"He left the creek bed and came up here. It looks like he's dragging one leg. He won't be traveling fast." She left the creek bed in the direction the man was going.

"Hang back. This is the sheriff's fight," Reid said.

She gave him a look that could kill and pushed ahead. The deputies had slowed down and were advancing.

She saw a tiny flash of light as it reflected off something the man was carrying.

"Get down!" she yelled. "He's over to the left behind that log."

Her call came too late. The hunted man opened up with a fully automatic rifle. The deputy sheriff on the edge of the woods went down, grabbing his chest and the bulletproof protection he wore. The man was shooting over the log and sending a river of bullets toward them. Both dropped down and became hidden targets. She heard the shooter's magazine empty, and nothing more came from his hiding place and weapon. A waving bandanna came around the tree.

"Don't shoot. I'm coming out!" he yelled. He stepped out from behind the log. He held his rifle in one hand over his head. He held it with his hand wrapped around the stock and a finger still on the trigger. She had seen insurgents ready to kill her have the same hold on their weapon.

"Don't shoot. I'm out of ammo," he shouted.

"Don't believe him. He's going to shoot," Sara said.

"Drop the damn rifle," Reid yelled the order.

She had her telescope crosshairs dead center of the man's chest. His next move would be to drop his weapon from over his head into a firing position. She wanted to kill him before his certain attack happened. She moved the crosshairs to his midface, exactly placed, to take out most of his spinal cord and brainstem. Something distracted her for only a second, off to his right. She hadn't managed to control her PTSD strikes that could come at dangerous times.

It was a mistake. The man hit the ground, firing the rifle on automatic. She stood in the hail of bullets around her and took careful aim again at the man's face. Her finger got tighter on the trigger. Three explosions echoed in her ear. Her finger went home on the trigger instinctively. Her shot would be too late. Reid had killed the man the instant before. The man's face was gone. Reid's rifle smoked as he stood holding it with his finger still inside the trigger guard ready to fire again.

Sara slumped to the ground, dropping her rifle in front of her. Her emotions raced toward the train wreck of a crash. Relief followed the things that had been driving her. Revenge! Not sure crying would help, tears flowed.

Reid knelt alongside her and put his hand on her shoulder. "Luke will know it's over now."

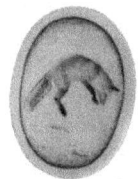

THIRTY-SIX

HAVING TWO WEEKS OFF TO spend with her family lulled Sara into sleeping late in the mornings. Jimmy became her saving grace to get out of bed early when he kept making plans for her to go for horseback rides with him. She liked the rides, as he planned them so they would trailer the horses and drive deep into the National Forest to visit the horse camping areas. She had needed the fifth wheel hitch addition to the bed of her new Ford 250 so she could pull Marty's three-horse trailer with a built-in camper. Sleeping in tents and on the ground was behind her now. The horse trailer had all the comforts of some of the best RV campers on the road.

Sara turned the truck and trailer into the gravel lane leading into the West Fork horse camping area of forest. Driving the rig along the lane gave her the feeling she was about to enter a land of magic and the mystery of some deep valleys with streams for the horses to cross and for she and Jimmy to explore. The trees had grown in gentle arches, covering the lane with complete shading from the hot sun of early fall. None of the trees came close to brushing the top of the camper trailer. Too many rigs had come this way before, clearing away the branches that would drag and rub protruding air conditioners and hay stacked on the tops of the trailers. She had eased the trailer along, not certain if there was enough clearance. At the end of the lane, she broke out of the trees into the campgrounds. Seeing the other campers with their horses standing tied to picket line ropes stretched between poles provided by the forestry service gave her the joy of others enjoying the same outdoors she loved.

She passed by two empty camping sites before she stopped to back into one. She had selected it for the two large oak trees bordering the trailer parking spot. Jimmy was out of the truck as soon as she stopped. Backing the long trailer into the gravel parking would be easy with him giving her arm signals on the side of the trailer she could see.

With the trailer parked, they led the horses out and secured them to a picket line. Getting the bucket of brushes from the trailer's tack room, she selected a stiff-bristled brush to use on the horse. The paint mare had joined Marty's small herd a month ago. With several days to ride the horse before their planned trail ride, she had made the purchase and bought the animal. Sara didn't rank herself anywhere near a horse expert to make the purchase. Marty's encouragement and time with the horse had convinced her this mare needed to be hers. The mare welcomed the brushing, and she leaned her head and neck against Sara as she started to brush alongside the horse's ears. Jimmy had been carrying wood to the metal ring firepit and stacked enough in the ring for a cooking fire. He joined her with a brush in hand.

"Why don't you let me do that?"

"Never. This is now part of my buying this horse. I need her to know me on the ground as well as in the saddle."

"Are we going to ride before night?" he asked. He started to brush the horse he would ride.

"Yes. Could we just ride around the roads here in the camping area?"

"So, you want to show off your new horse?"

"Well, maybe some of that. No, not really. It will give the mare time to adjust to being away from the stalls and arena at Marty's barn."

"Can we have some hotdogs before we ride? I'm starving," Jimmy said. They both finished brushing and gave both the horses a flake of hay.

The trailer's inside kitchen didn't interest her. She loved the smell of the outdoor fires and cooking. They both went to the firepit.

"That's enough wood to cook two dozen hotdogs and a couple of thick steaks, young man."

He stood by the fire pit with a can of charcoal starter and a box of matches.

"I'm real hungry. Maybe they'll cook fast." He left the fire pit and handed the can of starter and matches to her.

"You're going to have to light the fire," Jimmy said.

He didn't need to tell her. She had learned not to ask Jimmy to pour the starter on the wood and strike the match to light the fire. She knew the crack of the accelerant and the explosion of the flame at the first touch of a tossed match would set him off. It came across so much like her own PTSD when fireworks she didn't expect happened close by. A stoop to duck the incoming rocket fire was her escape from the past. She felt uncertain if the instant of fear would ever go away for either of them.

"Thank you for setting the wood up." She poured on a little starter and then lit the fire.

Jimmy opened two folding camping chairs and set them back away from the now burning firepit. Sara joined him and sat next to him in one of the chairs. She welcomed the invitation to take the chair offered. She noticed Jimmy watching the family camping next to them. She had an idea he had been looking at a fine-looking filly. The girl had saddled a black horse and ridden by a couple of times. It didn't surprise Sara when Jimmy had taken notice. The girl had certainly noticed Jimmy.

"It's going to take a while for the wood to burn down. I'm going to saddle up for a little ride," he said.

"I thought you were starving," Sara said, knowing full well where this was going.

"Quit. She's really cute."

"The girl or the horse?"

"Both of them," he said, taking off for his saddle and horse.

She didn't mind a little alone time. There would be lots of chances to get to know the boy—man—she now claimed as also being her son. John had told her Jimmy borrowed his truck and would drive it the short distance to Marty's barn to practice. The young boy she met on the mountain had grown a heck of a lot. It pleased her.

Jimmy was saddled and on the camp road riding in the

direction the girl was last seen. She was a little sorry to not be able to see the meetup when it happened down the trail a few hundred yards. Maybe he would tell her about it later.

Propping her feet up, she kicked back in her chair. Smells of the campfire cooking drifted in from the west side of the campgrounds. Someone had added a lot of barbecue sauce to their dinner, and it was making her hungry.

The coals from the burnt logs at her feet had started to show up and she had gotten way beyond just hungry. She had been watching the trail Jimmy had taken to follow the girl, and maybe it was time to worry. Darkness had crept up on the campgrounds without either the girl or Jimmy showing up. There had never been a lot of worry in her DNA but being responsible for Jimmy had capsized the worry boat.

Saddling up her horse to go check on him would not work. The darkness had closed in on the campground and riding in the heavy timber it would be even darker. She grabbed a flashlight from the trailer, checked on her horse, and found it standing quietly on the crosstie line. She started walking down the trail where she had last seen Jimmy. It would have been a much easier path to ride rather than walk. The trail dropped down a rise and crossed a narrow stream of flowing water. Not bothering to take her boots off, she waded across. On the other side of the stream, the trail climbed a short but steep bank. Almost at the top, the mud became slick from the horse hooves that had climbed it earlier in the day. She slid back down to the edge of the creek. She heard Jimmy's voice coming from the top of the bank. Lights from several flashlights were also coming from behind her. Someone was looking for the girl. She tried the bank again and managed to get to the top of it. Her flashlight illuminated Jimmy with the girl he had followed. His arm was under her shoulder and lifting her to one side. His other arm and hand led his buckskin horse. The girl's horse was nowhere in sight. Sara hurried to them.

"I found her. She got bucked off her horse and couldn't walk," Jimmy said.

"I was so worried for you guys. I think Jimmy wanted to meet you, young lady."

"I'm sure glad he did. He found me flat on the ground. A log or something rolled down a bank and hit my horse's back feet. I got dumped quick," the girl said, "My leg hurts bad."

"Here, let me check," Sara said, holding her flashlight to shine on the girl's blue-jeaned leg. "I'm going to feel for any breaks."

"Ouch! It hurts right there," the girl said.

"I don't think you broke your leg," Sara said, standing and offering to help carry the girl to keep the weight off the hurt leg. A man and woman had made their way up the slick bank and were headed their way.

"Mom, Dad, I'm okay. Jimmy found me and has been helping me walk. I don't know where my mare went after she threw me."

Her parents were quick to thank both Sara and Jimmy for their help. After checking on his daughter, the dad left to backtrack to find the animal. Jimmy left them to follow the girl's dad and look for the missing horse. With Sara helping with one arm and the mother on the other, they helped the girl down the steep banks and back to the campsites.

Sara and the mother let the girl down gently in a lounge chair.

"I think we should put some ice on her leg. It will help keep the swelling down," Sara said as she pulled a lawn chair up next to the girl. The girl's mother went into their trailer and returned with a bag of ice.

Sara spoke to the girl. "I'm Sara. I'm glad we got you back."

"Oh, I'm Laura," the girl said. "Is Jimmy going to stop back over here when he gets back?"

"I think he will. He'll want to know how you're doing."

The wait for Jimmy to show back up was short. He dropped into an empty chair near the girl without saying anything. He sat quietly, just staring ahead toward the campfire burning in a metal ring.

Sara knew the girl would probably have to speak first to get Jimmy to talk. She needed to get the conversation started if there was going to be one. But then Jimmy surprised her.

"We found your horse. Does the leg hurt bad?"

"I'm all right. It's just sore. Thanks for helping me."

Jimmy must have run out of things to say to his newfound friend.

"Well, see you guys tomorrow," Sara said, and stood to leave.

The mother and father were quick to offer a thank you to both her and Jimmy. It pleased her that Jimmy had followed the girl and had been there to help when she had gotten bucked off.

Back at their campsite, with Jimmy on his way to cook four hotdogs on their large fork, she eased back in her chair. Having time to finally relax outdoors pleased her. Starving and watching the hotdogs linger over a now-dwindled fire wasn't at all a pleasure. They needed to hurry and get done.

Jimmy had insisted on sleeping in the open air near the horses. She didn't mind having the trailer camper to herself. She was tired and hadn't realized Jimmy was also. He had slipped away from what was left of the campfire before ten. She joined his sleeping by pulling a light blanket over herself in her pj's.

A little after midnight, she awoke and heard the wolves calling their pack together for the hunt. She slipped out of the camper to stand facing the sounds they made running on the far side of the one-hundred-acre lake defining the horse camp. Her nights in the woods and on the river had taught her to sort out their vocal cries and commands.

Then, she heard a lone sorrowful howl from an old wolf. It had fallen yards behind the pack, now running and yelping on a new chase it could not keep up with. Was the old wolf calling for the pack to return and join it? She knew it would always be alone from now on. The pack would move without the old wolf. Somewhere out in front of the pack, she again heard the dominant female calling the pack to follow. Sara knew in the days ahead she needed less time chasing demons and more time listening to wolf packs running in the night. There would be much for her to learn there.

AUTHOR'S NOTE

Bob Hergert is a micro-scrimshaw artist.

Scrimshaw is the art of incising or cutting designs into bone and ivory. Early whalers used whales' teeth and bone to create their work of art. Eskimos used mammoth and walrus tusks. Today we scrimshanders use woolly mammoth tusk and ivory substitutes like micarta and Corian.

Bob's scrimshaw work on the mammoth bone now graces the cover of the novel 'Scrimshaw Foxes'. When he read the early release of the unedited novel, he graciously agreed to donate his work for the cover picture. He has my thanks for his beautiful work for my Scrimshaw Foxes novel.

Richard O. Snelson

Below scrimshaw artist Bob Hergert at work.
http://www.scrimshander.com

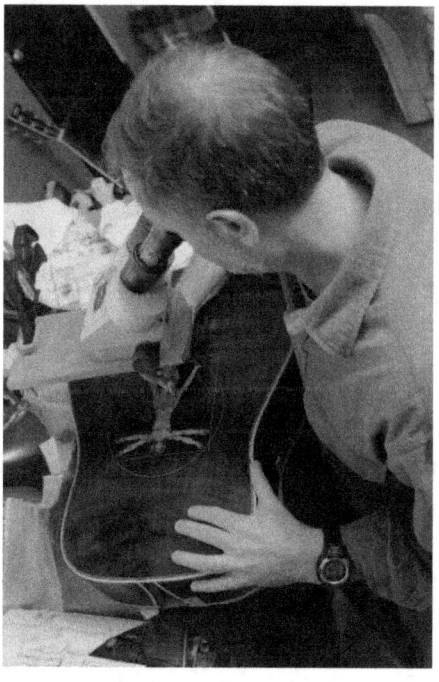

www.ingramcontent.com/pod-product-compliance
Lightning Source LLC
Chambersburg PA
CBHW060640260626
47161CB00008B/2939